PRAISE FOR
THE CHRISTMAS CLASH

"Take me to Riverwood Mall! In this rival families, enemies-to-sweethearts story, Peter and Chloe are the sparkling lights on a Christmas tree. It's the perfect book to read for the holidays, chock-full of humor, banter, food, mall shenanigans, and a side mission that brings these two opposites together."

—Tif Marcelo, *USA Today* bestselling author of *The Holiday Switch*

"Suzanne Park is a master of the enemies-to-lovers rom-com, and *The Christmas Clash* is a snowflake-dusted classic of the genre! Think of the perfect, coziest Hallmark movie but with way more edge, wit, and authentic representation. The ideal stocking-stuffer for anyone who loves the holidays, ridiculously adorable romance, delicious Asian food, and malls!"

—Stephan Lee, author of *K-Pop Confidential*

"*The Christmas Clash* is a delicious romp of a rom-com. It left me craving spicy pork and sesame balls and nostalgic for the feeling of the mall at Christmastime. Chloe and Peter are characters you'll root for, believe in, and miss when you close the back cover."

—Tiffany Schmidt, author of *I'm Dreaming of a Wyatt Christmas* and the Bookish Boyfriends series

PRAISE FOR
SUNNY SONG WILL NEVER BE FAMOUS

An NPR Best Book of the Year

"Sunny Song is one of the most hilarious, heart-warming, relatable teen characters I've had the pleasure of encountering. A must-have for any YA shelf."

—Sandhya Menon, *New York Times* bestselling
author of *When Dimple Met Rishi*

"A true delight!"

—Helen Hoang, *USA Today* bestselling
author of *The Kiss Quotient*

"Sunny will easily endear herself to many readers."

—*Booklist*

"Park smartly and honestly weaves Sunny's nuanced experience as a Korean American into a story that is ultimately about human identity in our advanced age of social networking."

—*Kirkus Reviews*

"Suzanne Park smartly explores identity, specifically when it is intertwined with social media...an insightful, pertinent and humorous novel."

—*Shelf Awareness*

PRAISE FOR
THE PERFECT ESCAPE

"Pure fun! A hilarious rom-com that head-fakes you into tumbling headlong into a techno-zombie survival thriller propelled by banter and plenty of heart."

—David Yoon, *New York Times* bestselling author of *Frankly in Love*

"*The Perfect Escape* is just that—perfect. Filled with humor and heart, it won't let you go until you're smiling."

—Danielle Paige, *New York Times* bestselling author of the Dorothy Must Die series and *Stealing Snow*

ALSO BY SUZANNE PARK

THE
CHRISTMAS
CLASH

THE CHRISTMAS CLASH

SUZANNE PARK

sourcebooks
fire

Copyright © 2022 by Suzanne Park
Cover and internal design © 2022 by Sourcebooks
Cover design by Liz Dresner
Cover art © Jin Kim

Published by Sourcebooks Fire, an imprint of Sourcebooks
P.O. Box 4410, Naperville, Illinois 60567-4410
(630) 961-3900
sourcebooks.com

Cataloging-in-Publication Data is on file with the Library of Congress.

Printed and bound in Canada.
MBP 10 9 8 7 6 5 4 3 2 1

For my nerdy family.

ONE

CHLOE

THE PROJECTILE PACIFIER GRAZED MY LEFT EAR.

"I'm so sorry, would you mind grabbing his binky off the floor? Little Timmy's got quite a temper when he's hungry."

Important note: Timmy was not in fact very little. I suspected he was five, maybe six. Way too old for a binky. He liked to bite them during our photo sessions, and they made a grating chewy noise as he gnawed against the wet, rubbery plastic with his teeth.

I handed the pacifier to his mom, and she scrubbed it down with an organic baby wipe.

"Mommy, I want a Corn-Dog-on-a-Stick and a slushie. I'm hunnnngryyyyy."

See? Not exactly baby or toddler food. Much too old for a binky.

I smiled at Timmy. "We're almost done, kid. Just one more picture! Smile at the camera. Say 'Orange Julius!'"

Timmy perked up, and his red sweater vest smoothed out as he sat up straight. "Orange Jule-yesss!"

CLICK. CLICK. CLICK.

"Mommy, can I have an Orange Jule-yesss?"

I stepped forward and showed his mom the last photo. Timmy had opted for a Santa-free picture, but one with a lit tree, a fireplace, and piles of presents. Meanwhile, Santa Dave took the opportunity to step out for a few minutes to go vape in the east wing loading zone. In the photo, not-so-little Timmy sat erect, looking at the camera, beaming from ear to ear. Perhaps visions of Orange Julius drinks danced in his head as the flashes went off.

Timmy's mom sighed with relief. "I swear, you're a miracle worker." She walked over to my "elf tips welcome!" jar and dropped in a ten-dollar bill. "You're the only one who can get him to smile like that. Thank you. No wonder they call you the baby whisperer photographer."

It was true. I had a reputation for being a baby whisperer of sorts. Also a corn-dog-eating kindergartner whisperer. It was the one of the few things I was good at.

"I'm so glad Santa's Village is open earlier this year. This gives me a head start on sending out holiday cards and buying gifts. You can't be too prepared, right?" She held out her hand toward her son. "Ready to go get a drink and snack?"

He pulled a pacifier from his pocket and popped it into his mouth. He scrambled off Santa's chair and waved at me while he exited with his mom.

Santa's Village opened earlier and earlier every year, and the day after Halloween was this holiday season's soft opening. It was the result of "Christmas creep," which was in turn related to the "pumpkin spice latte economic effect," when stores sneakily promoted the fall season earlier and earlier into the summer months. The fact that gigantic bags of fun-sized candy and novelty costumes were out for sale immediately after the Fourth of July was criminal. And now, in early November, Santa Dave had parked his ass at the end of Riverwood Mall's East Wing, ready for business.

As I turned to the laptop to upload the photos to the image portal, I heard Timmy cry out, "Mommy! Can we do that too? After Orange Julius? It looks so fun! I want *that*."

I didn't even bother to look up from the laptop because I knew what *that* was. Nearly every kid who exited our photo area beelined to the new attraction next door: the North Pole virtual reality experience. It had opened the same week as Santa's Village, and it included a bonus video of the customer's experience that patrons could download immediately. Who wouldn't want to be on Santa's 3D virtual sleigh, flying over any address they typed into Google Maps?

Santa Dave plopped down on his chair. "Ready for the next family, Chloe?"

I nodded as our frontline helper elf ushered in a young couple and their baby. "This is baby Caroline." Sweet Caroline wore a headband with a giant red bow the size of her head. She howled as her family entered Santa's cozy living room and none of her parents' bouncing and cooing helped.

The mom held out the baby in Santa's direction, which made her wail even more.

Caroline's mom let out a long breath. "We wanted to get holiday photos before she started teething, but I think it's too late," she said, her eyes watering as she pulled her baby closer to her chest.

I jumped into action. "Mom, while you're holding Caroline, can you please stand next to Santa, by the tree? Dad, I'll need you to sit on Santa's armrest."

They assembled per my instructions, and I looked at their positions in my camera. "Parents, if you could move in a little closer to Santa, that'd be great."

Caroline took another look at this jolly bearded white dude and burst into tears again. Santa Dave was great with the toddlers and older kids, but babies were not his favorite. He made all of them cry. Every. Single. One.

But that's where I came in—they didn't call me the baby whisperer for nothing. From my pocket, I pulled out my trusty pair of black, chunky glasses and perched them on my nose. "Caroliiiiiine!"

The infant tore her eyes away from Santa and looked at me. Her crying stopped for a brief moment as she stared at my new frames.

Now that I had her attention, it was time to go for my classic baby crowd-pleaser. From my other pocket, I pulled out a small yellow bird plushie.

I whistled one of my many rehearsed birdcalls and perched the bird on my head. "Hey baby! Look over here, kid!"

Caroline not only stopped crying, she pointed at the bird and grunted.

Now, for the winning move.

I said, "Mom, Dad, Caroline! Look at the camera! One. Two." I squeezed the bird and it let out a long squeak. "Three!"

Caroline squealed with delight and clapped. I took several photos, each one revealing different levels of contentment and relief from all three family members. Lots of options for the parents to choose from for their holiday portrait.

I pulled the bird off my head and displayed the images on the camera's screen for the parents to review. The dad nodded at the last photo. "This one. It's perfect."

I continued squeaking the toy, and Caroline tried so hard to say "ba-ba-ba," which we all agreed was her first word.

Bird.

Caroline's mom wiped the baby's drool from her mouth while chatting with Santa. The dad said to me, "Caroline loved that bird. Amazing how you were able to stop her crying."

I nodded. "They all love the bird. I have a whole arsenal of animals, but she looked like a bird lover."

"Can I buy it from you? Or could you let me know where I can get one? We're desperate," he chuckled.

I shrugged. "Petco."

He scratched his chin. "Pet...co?"

"It's a cat toy. The dog toys are louder if you don't mind the excessive squeaking."

Caroline's mom fluttered over to us, and the baby reached out for me. "Awww look, she likes you!"

I laughed. "She just wants these glasses. Isn't that right, Caroline?"

She gurgled and swiped at my face.

The mom dropped a twenty-dollar bill into the tip jar. "She's been crying all day. I'm so relieved she stopped." She turned to her husband as they exited. "Did she tell you where she bought the bird?"

I smiled while uploading the photos. The pictures of Caroline's family really turned out well. Photography was the only thing I could do right, and with enough family photos under my belt so far this season, it was becoming natural to me.

After I took a swig of water and a bite of granola bar, I called to the front, "I'm ready for the next family!"

The elf cashier popped her head in. "Um, there aren't any families in line. We're taking lunch now while we have downtime."

"W-What? The mall is full today." Our lines had dwindled with the passing of each day, but I never thought we'd get to the point of having no customers. This was a first.

She pointed past the exit.

My gaze followed her finger to the 3D North Pole exhibit. The line was wrapped around the corner, and Peter Li strutted around the perimeter, handing out flyers to passersby. "New fall and winter themes added! Choose from twenty different immersive rides! Hey, nice coat! Love your hat!" Timmy and his binky were near the front of the line, underneath the giant sign that read NEW! ULTIMATE VIRTUAL REALITY SLEIGH RIDE SPECTACULAR!

I narrowed my eyes.

Peter.

Of course.

Peter, the bane of my existence, as far back as I can remember.

Boys' varsity soccer Peter. Editor-in-chief Peter. Perfect PSAT score Peter. And now ruin-my-job Peter.

He was smirking right at me.

Time to wipe that smug smile off his face.

TWO

PETER

"VIRTUAL REALITY, TAKEN TO NEW HEIGHTS! LITERALLY! The downloadable videos are available in *seconds*, not *hours*!"

Chloe was staring at me. Actually, glaring at me. I'd mentioned the video download time just to get a reaction from her, like a nose scrunch or a frustrated sigh. I didn't expect her to stomp over and point her elfin finger all up in my face.

Chloe was cute, but also a little bit scary, like a feral kitten. I used to tease her a lot in middle school but pretty much never interacted with her in high school because we only had one class together. I forgot how easy it was to get a rise out of Chloe.

"Our photos are downloadable in seconds too. We just upgraded the software. So stop saying that."

I offered her a wide grin while adjusting my Cubs baseball

cap. It was the only thing I owned that was red. It was as "holiday" as I could get. "I didn't say yours weren't. I was simply remarking that our upload and download speeds were the best around."

She shook her head. "You're unbelievable, you know that?"

"I do. Nice glasses by the way." They were too large for her face, but sort of suited her, the way a toddler adorably tries on a pair of parents' shoes. "Wait, do those even have lenses? Are they a prop or something?"

Chloe scrunched her nose and snatched the frames off her face, then shoved them in her pocket.

"And nice Baby Yoda ears."

Her face turned beet red. She planted both hands on her hips. "They're elf ears, thank you very much."

Chloe was so much fun to pester. "Elf ears kind of fold down." She flinched as I leaned forward to examine hers. "Yours are green and stick straight out. They look more Mandalorian than North Pole to be honest. Can I call you Yoda? Or...the Child?"

She let out the exasperated sigh I'd been waiting for. Success!

Chewing her bottom lip, she looked over at the long line and muttered, "Huh."

I looked over my shoulder. "Huh what?"

"Timmy's made it to the front," she muttered, pressing her lips to prevent a smile from forming. "You shouldn't keep your customers waiting. That's bad business."

I rolled my eyes and walked over to the kiddo with the

pacifier and pointed at the available VR options on the pull-up banner by the entrance. "Number one is the lowest intensity, very kid-friendly. Lots of kids like the Turkey Tornado, it spins but not too fast. Overall it's a two, and the levels go up to ten, but I wouldn't recommend those higher ones unless you like hills and drops on rollercoasters."

Timmy's mom shrugged. "I don't know anything about this. Timmy wanted to come so badly so I promised him we could stop here on our way out."

The boy said, "Number five, because I'm five." Number five was a sleigh ride in a blizzard sequence. Not one of my favorites, but it was a popular one.

I heard a tinkle of laughter coming from Santa's Village. It was Chloe, but when I glanced over I couldn't tell if she was laughing at me or at something on her phone.

"Yes, sir. Number five coming right up." I put Timmy in one of the open vinyl chairs and mounted on a headset. "Are you sure about this, buddy?" I looked over at Chloe again, but she was already back inside, helping another family.

Timmy said, "Yeah! I have something like this at home. But Mommy only lets me do cooking and shopping games." I loaded his video and stood by his side just in case he regretted his decision. It was quite a leap from cooking and shopping to hilly sleigh riding.

"Whooooaaaa! So cool!" He swayed in his seat, ducking and dodging the virtual snowballs.

Timmy's hands flew up. "Wheeeee!"

Another happy customer. I chatted with his mom as I took the payment from her, but soon noticed Timmy had gotten quiet.

"Buddy, you okay?"

"I'm—" Timmy's voice hitched.

I knew this look. The deepening frown. The yellowish-green hue of the face. All warning signs of—

Timmy leaned forward and sprayed Orange Julius onto the tips of my shoes. My brand-new checkered Vans.

"A little sick," Timmy finished.

The janitorial staff shut down the exhibit for twenty minutes while they sanitized the area and gave me a few cleaning cloths for my footwear. Some of the patrons toward the end of the line walked over to Santa's Village to kill time, taking group photos as they waited for us to reopen. I looked for Chloe, who popped her head out of her photo area and smirked in my direction. She raised her right hand, like Baby Yoda trying to use the force.

Touché, Chloe. *Did you know about Timmy and his affinity for Orange Julius? I bet you did.*

I smiled back at her as I reopened the exhibit, letting in the next two tween customers: twin girls who wanted to try experience number ten.

Just because Chloe won this round didn't mean she'd won... whatever this was between us she had ignited. A challenge? A competition? A duel? My job suddenly became so much more interesting now that she was on my radar.

Okay, Chloe Kwon.

You're officially on my naughty list.

THREE

CHLOE

SOPHIA AND I WASHED OUR HANDS AT THE ART ROOM sink station. She took only a few seconds because she'd been working with no-mess air-dry clay, whereas I'd decided to use charcoal. Sophia was not only artistic, she also had the unique ability to not spill or smear stuff all over herself.

There was no easy way to do cleanup with charcoal. It was all over my fingertips and palms, under my nails, and judging by how Sophia stared at my face longer than usual, I probably had smudges above my eyebrows and cheeks too. "I like painting with acrylics better," she said. "Way less messy. Way less...you know—"

"Way less...soot-covered chimney sweeper look? But I love the starkness of the black and white. I don't mind charcoal, except for this." The charcoal on my hand mixed with the liquid soap to form a dark gray foam.

"Everything you create is like a masterpiece, even your smudges." She pointed her dripping finger at my chest. "I hope you have a jacket."

My formerly white tee also had charcoal smears on it, and the two biggest swaths of black were coincidentally located on each boob. It looked like they were crying, like the theater masks displayed in our drama department hallway.

Damn it, I should have worn a smock.

Sophia started to say, "Whatever you do, don't—"

But it was too late. I instinctively took my damp hands and tried to brush off the charcoal from my shirt. This not only made the unfortunately located smudges worse, but also darkened the spots from (aptly named) charcoal gray to jet black.

"Crap," I muttered, dabbing a paper towel with soap and water.

Sophia grabbed my arm. "I know what you're thinking, and it's definitely going to make it worse. Please...stop."

I sighed. "I don't have a jacket today, or anything extra in my locker to cover me up. This shirt is all I have." I looked down at my two damp, downturned stark black breast semicircles. "I think you're right about making it worse, though it's hard to imagine that even being possible."

My friend Elias scooched between us and reached around me

to grab a paper towel, bonking my head lightly with his elbow once he retrieved it. "Oops, super sorry!"

After taking one look at my shirt, he said, "Oh no, you can't leave here looking like that. Hold on." He walked back to his chair and pulled up a crumpled gray hoodie wedged in the back of the seat. Elias was the lead designer of the LGBTQIA organization at the school, and the hooded zip-up showcased the logo he designed and his custom artwork on the back. He held it up by the upper sleeves, shook it out, and handed it to me. "Here. Don't lose it, or I will murder you." He wasn't exaggerating. Elias would actually murder me if anything happened to it. It was his most prized possession. A perfectly worn, snuggly hoodie, and that art was something he'd worked on last summer at the prestigious Governor's School program. The sweatshirt was oversized, warm, and smelled like a container of Tide pods. It was perfect.

I gave him a hug. "Thank you. My boobs thank you too. I'll wash your zip-up and bring it back tomorrow."

"Delicate cycle, please. Use a dryer sheet. Don't you dare cause static cling."

I laughed. "If you stop by Riverwood I'll even give you a free photo with Santa for your generosity. I promise."

Elias clasped his hands together. "Ooooh, would you all come with me? Can you imagine us taking photos with Santa together?"

Sophia cackled. "We should make it look like a family portrait, with Santa being our dad. We can dress up!"

"Come by tonight." I texted them a coupon. "Just show this to the elf at the door. You'll get VIP treatment. I'm not working tonight, but you'll be in good elfin hands. You can also use it another time when I'm there."

"What does VIP treatment at Santa's Village look like?" Elias asked. "Like do we get special props and premium chimney backgrounds?"

I smiled. "You get to skip the line, and Santa gives you a small stocking full of dollar store candy, if you must know. Mmmm."

Elias clapped. "I'm in." He turned to Sophia. "Did you hear that tonight was senior night at that North Pole virtual reality place? Maybe we could get a quick glimpse of Cheremy Mills."

Cheremy was the hottest guy at Hillcrest, and maybe in the entire universe. He was the guy everyone admired from afar, especially Elias and Sophia. Both of them had had crushes on Cheremy since junior high. The big reason I wasn't in his fan club? His name was pronounced *Jeremy* but written as *Cheremy* with a "Ch." I couldn't get over this, ever.

Sophia shot Elias a look. "You know you're not allowed to mention *that business* at the mall. Or you-know-who's name that rhymes with 'Teeter.' Look, she's got steam coming out of her ears now."

I cocked an eyebrow. "C'mon, surely after all these years you know why I can't stand that guy. Why *we* can't stand him."

I said "we" because when one of us hated someone, we all did.

Elias sighed. "Yeah, yeah, we know. A tale as old as time. Your parents hate his parents, and the descendants of the Lis and Kwons keep the animosity going for generations to come."

My mom and dad thought the Lis were competitive, nosy, and braggy...those being their better traits. The Lis' kids went to the same school we did, and like my family, they had a restaurant in the Riverwood mall food court too. My sister was named valedictorian a few years ago, and Peter's older brother came in second. It was close, with Hannah beating Sam by only one-tenth of a point at the end. The Lis were the Kwons' top competition. And sworn enemy.

Elias added, "I remember that first time when Peter said you were being overly dramatic in elementary school after he drew a spider on your arm with a Sharpie and you cried. Which in retrospect is kind of funny now, isn't it?"

I narrowed my eyes at Elias.

"Okay, okay. Still not funny," he yelped. "You are the queen of grudges. But remember that time he ate string cheese and told you he'd eaten a candle and you thought you needed to give him mouth-to-mouth because you believed him? *That* was funny."

I raised my eyebrow. "I thought I needed to call 911 or poison control. Also, *not* funny."

Sophia added, "I remember you were bitter when he chose you last for a PE team in middle school. But to be fair, you had a broken arm and we were playing volleyball."

"I still had one good arm. And it was my dominant one." I held up my right index finger. "Oh! Let's not forget how we had a class presentation last year and I was already a ball of nerves, not eating breakfast or lunch out of fear of regurgitation, and in one of my Google presentation slides he changed the hyperlink and Rickrolled me in front of the entire history class. Jerk."

They both burst into laughter but then quickly composed themselves. I sighed. *Traitors.*

"There's more. Now I see him going to Platinum Gym at the far end of the mall all the time, lifting weights, studying himself in the mirror. Could he be any more vain? He is all about looks and swagger. So surface-level. I can't stand that kind of guy. I hate Peter Li."

And that kind of guy was the type everyone at school liked. Peter was great at all that "people-y" stuff, and he aced Model UN, and I was a little jealous of his student government pursuits. He was like an Asian Clark Kent. Charming and coy, but he also possessed the confidence, surefootedness, and attractiveness of Superman.

Infuriating.

Meanwhile I was on a different trajectory in life: one that involved immersion in arts and culture. Quietness and non-effervescence suited me and my future. Not making waves had kept me afloat so far, so why mess with something that worked for me? I was perfectly content in my non-risk-taking hermit-tude.

Elias said, "Hate is a pretty strong word. Can't we all agree that we just strongly dislike him?"

I shook my head.

"Detest? Abhor? Either of those active verbs, just to show some range in emotions?" He paused, then asked, "How about this instead?" Elias gave two thumbs down while spit-blowing a raspberry.

I shrugged. *That works, I guess.*

"Okay." Elias held prayer hands to his chest. "No more mentioning you-know-who. The entire senior class might be at that virtual um, thing that should not be named, and if we go to Santa's Village tonight we can get front-row views of the senior action! I've never been so excited to see Santa."

I had no clue the North Pole VR experience was having a special promo night. I didn't remember seeing any promotional signs or banners about it. Teens weren't exactly a moneymaker for our Santa Village photo business, but I bet a lot of them loved Korean food.

I abruptly ducked out of Sophia and Elias's conversation about Cheremy's dimples and pulled up the Canva app on my phone. I quickly made a senior night flyer for Kwons' Café: TONIGHT ONLY—BUY ONE MEAL AND GET AN APPETIZER OR DRINK FOR FREE. After fixing the font size, I showed Sophia and Elias my creation. "Thoughts?" I asked.

"Did you seriously just whip that up while we were chatting?"

Sophia passed the phone to Elias. "I swear, you better get into NYU. Or RISD. You're so talented."

Elias nodded. "This is so good, and Sophia and I will definitely eat at your parents' place tonight. Your mom gives us free appetizers and drinks anyway," he said with a gleeful grin. It was true, my parents loved Elias. He had the highest EQ of anyone I knew, he knew exactly what to say, and when and how to say it. Well, except when he was around Cheremy. Elias always fell to hushed silence when Cheremy was within whisper distance, partly out of fear of embarrassing himself by saying the wrong thing, and partly out of godly reverence.

I shrugged. "I'll get these printed out and handed out at the mall tonight." Also on my to-do list: sending a text to Mom and Dad to get their approval. I was sure they'd be okay with this one-day-only special event. Plus, this was celebrating the 200 seniors at my high school, so they should be on board, it being about school pride and all that.

Elias, Sophia, and I went back to our desks. After organizing his colored pencils, Elias asked, "Chloe, did you hear from the National Art Council yet?"

I shook my head. "Nope. Trying not to think about it." The National Art Council Youth Photography Competition was the most selective high school arts awards in the country. There was a fancy review committee with MFAs and PhDs from all over the world. It came with a one-on-one mentor meeting and a sizable cash grant. It was like winning a junior Pulitzer. I'd entered a few weeks earlier.

He smiled. "I'm just so happy you put yourself out there, Chloe. You shot your shot! Is that even how you say it? Or shooted? Both of those sound weird actually."

The likelihood of me being selected was approximately zero percent, but Sophia and Elias talked me into it, or more accurately, said they'd never talk to me again if I chickened out. And they, like me, were good at holding grudges. For me to win, well, it would be a miracle. And I didn't believe in miracles because they never happened to people like me. Even if I was talented enough, I was the type of person to get passed over. Someone else would always have more going for them than I did: they'd have studied in a renowned program or have had an endorsement from a famous artist. I didn't have things like that.

But I didn't want to disappoint my friends, so I did it. I entered. And my stomach was churning like one of those sideways slushie machines, knowing the results would be in soon.

"Even if you get it, or don't, let's go out somewhere, because we should celebrate our wins, and you taking a risk like this is a big deal," Sophia said, just as the bell rang.

"So, see you both tonight for dinner," I told Sophia and Elias. "I have to run to the front office to get some of these flyers printed." I waved bye and took off.

Mrs. Foster, the front office assistant, was my neighbor, and she loved me. I always offered to take her family portraits every year, which she gladly accepted. In exchange, whenever I needed something printed or copied, she was my go-to person. Another reason I liked stopping into the office: she had Dum Dum lollipops in a glass bowl on her desk. She knew my favorite flavors and always set aside the Hawaiian punch, cream soda, and green apple ones just for me; those were stashed in the upper right drawer of her metal desk.

After a pit stop with Mrs. Foster, I left the office with fifty flyers and a pocketful of lollipops. Feeling good about my plans for senior night, I thought it would be best to forgo permission and surprise my parents instead. They were always on my case about being more money- and business-savvy like them, so this was my big opportunity. My chance to shine. Maybe taking more risks wouldn't be so bad after all.

FOUR

CHLOE

JUST AS I PREDICTED, HILLCREST SENIOR CLASS NIGHT at the VR booth was more than they could handle. Over a hundred students showed up to take advantage of the school discount, and the system kept rebooting. While the line continued to grow at Peter's booth and the waiting masses grew angrier by the second, I offered coupons to tired and hangry students toward the end of the line who might want to take a dinner break and come back later, or maybe not return at all. It wasn't a benevolent swoop-in rescue of wary, starving souls. It was a calculated, 100 percent opportunistic play to get a ton of students over to Kwons' Café, and based on Peter's narrow-eyed glare, he knew it.

When I handed him a flyer, he snatched it from my hand. "I have to commend you for this shrewd, borderline-savage business move." He slow clapped, making the paper in his hand rattle as his hands came together.

"Bringing you satisfied, well-fed customers is my goal. You should be thanking me," I said with a huge grin, passing out the last flyer to someone standing right next to him. "Plus, it's just business. Don't take it personally."

He sniggered. "The design is pretty good, I'll admit that. It's also impressive you didn't spend any money on this."

I huffed, "How do you know that?"

A quick snort escaped his nose. "I saw you go into the office today without a stack of paper and then leave with one. You had them printed at school!"

"Actually, you're wrong. I had them *copied* in the office from the original flyer. And did you just admit to following me? Why are *you* so concerned with my whereabouts?" I crossed my arms, tilted my head, and puckered my lips. "Why so interested, stalker?"

His face flushed. I'd never seen him this flustered before.

The software notification at his kiosk dinged. "Oh good, we're finally back online." He flashed a smile at the group of four in the front of the line. "You're next, everything's working now."

My best friends came up to us. "Hey," Elias said to me, giving Peter a suspicious look. He then shot me a "why you talking to this guy we hate, does not compute" stare. And it didn't make sense: Peter and I were not in the same social circles, and we certainly weren't friends. He was squarely in the "athletes who made good grades" cohort. Elias, Sophia, and I ran with the artsy crew, if there even was such a thing. Elias was a bit of an exception—he was a floater. He made friends with everyone, and he was the fastest runner at our school, with the highest level of endurance I'd ever seen. He made it to state in both track and cross-country his sophomore year. At one point the football team tried to recruit him because they needed a new running back, but he said no, because he was in the leading role in the school musical. I wish I had even an ounce of his talent. We all did.

Elias grabbed one of my arms. Sophia came up behind me and took the other.

"Let's go to the food court, it's bustling over there." Elias waved over his shoulder. "Bye, Peter!"

I elbowed him in the ribs and whispered, "Why are you being nice to him?"

"Look, you were chatting him up, not me. And plus, he's friends with Cheremy. It's that simple. I might have to be more like Switzerland here if I want to extend diplomacy to the nation of Cheremy."

The line for Kwons' Café wrapped around the courtyard and spilled past Foot Locker and Claire's Boutique. I'd never seen the restaurant this busy.

Mom waved her hands toward herself. "Chloe-ya! Yeogiwa! Help me in kitchen!" She grunted a quick greeting at Sophia and Elias and dashed to the back.

"Did you tell your parents ahead of time about the promotion flyers?" Elias asked.

I sighed. "I told them about it over text when I arrived, and all they said was 'ok.' Maybe they didn't understand or even care? But why are there so many people here? There are only two hundred seniors at Hillcrest. And I only printed out fifty flyers."

Sophia looked at the line that seemed to be extending past Chico's now. "Can we help you? Or would it be better to get out of your way and come back in a few minutes?" Elias, Sophia, and I had been friends for over five years and they could pick up on my stress cues. The scratching of my face. My sighing. And then of course, my swearing and freaking out. I was at the sighing stage, so they knew what was coming.

"How about you two come back in thirty minutes? I'm going to try to do something about this crowd." They took off toward Sephora and let me handle the mess I'd created.

I scanned the line and was completely confused by the demographics. It was kids my age, which made sense given the special promotion, but there were also a bunch of grandma and grandpa types. I went up to one of them, a white-haired woman with a stylish Adidas tracksuit, and asked why they were standing in line.

The woman smiled. "Oh! Tonight is our nursing home's Silver Sneakers bonus workout day. It's five thousand steps around this whole place, did you know that? We heard from Mrs. Jackson's grandson about the senior discount, word travels fast, especially if there's a good deal. We're so excited to have a treat just for us. I've never had Korean food!"

My jaw dropped. My promotion was meant for *high school* seniors. Not senior citizens.

And now, because of this misunderstanding among the geriatric crowd, I'd need to tell my mom to apply the discount to anyone over fifty-five too. She was not going to be happy about that. The number of elderly dinner-goers in line was now larger than the high school senior count. I'd made a huge mistake.

With some quick back-of-the-envelope calculations, I figured out that the wait for the people at the end of the line was half an hour. The last thing I needed was to have our Yelp ratings tank because of the long wait, and some of these retirees had all the time in the world to complain. Mom and Dad were obsessed with their rating, making sure it never fell below four stars, because to them, anything below that meant that their menu, pricing, ingredient quality, or customer service was simply unacceptable. Some people rated Kwons' Café three stars with glowing reviews, and it always confused them. Dad always ranted about this. "Would you buy Amazon product or go to fancy restaurant with three-stars rating? Would you ride in Uber with three-star driver? Or get three-star babysitter? No! Why people say they love so much if it not four or five? Three star is like a C grade. Three point O grade point average. Why so stingy on star? If you love, give five. Or four if you very picky."

He was right. If I had an Uber or Lyft coming to pick me up and the driver had a three-star rating, I'd assume he or she was a serial killer and would smash the "cancel" button immediately. Yet here we were, with our amazing restaurant with prompt service and high-quality food, clinging for dear life to our four-star rating.

At the register, Dad input the orders and processed the payments while I made sure the orders fed into the kitchen on the display monitor and assigned them to the line cooks. When the line got too long, I carried a tray of meat and appetizer samples to the back of the line and helped answer any questions about the menu so when they got to my dad at the cash register, their meals were ready to go.

One of our most loyal customers had brought along a group of senior citizen friends who had special dietary preparation requests for their combo meals, which I took care of personally in the kitchen. Adding a small amount of sesame and canola oil to a large preheated pan, I took marinated beef from the fridge and added the slices of meat along with fresh-cut scallions, omitting the usual garlic and black pepper, per the customers' instructions. The bulgogi crackled and popped under the too-high heat. My mom noticed too. "Front burner need medium, not medium high." I nodded and turned the dial to the left.

Using metal tongs, I stirred and flipped the meat and scallions, allowing them to brown evenly on both sides. Although we had other dishes bubbling, cooking, and resting on the other areas of the stove, there was something about the rich and fragrant umami dominating the kitchen that made my mouth water even when I wasn't hungry.

When the meat was cooked through and slightly charred, I removed the pan from heat and used a spatula to transfer the bulgogi to take-out containers with pre-scooped rice in one of the smaller divided sections. Stir-fried fish cake and side salad were our only two banchan that didn't use garlic or pepper in the recipe or marinade, so I added those into the other two open sections. I walked to the front and called out the order numbers.

For a while, the processes had streamlined and things were going okay, until my mom yelled out, "Oh no! We running out of rice! Only few more scoop left!"

A Korean restaurant without rice? What kind of Yelp reviews would we get? "Mom, how could we be out of rice? We're an Asian restaurant!"

She barked, "We not buy as much wholesale rice... It's long story. But can you go buy some? We in big trouble!"

Where could I get short-grain rice in our small suburban town at 7:15 p.m.? My heartbeat raced as I ran to the North Pole Virtual Experience to find Peter. My chest tightened at the very thought of asking him for help. *Please excuse me while I go vomit.*

The lines at Peter's exhibit had waned, and there was a healthy-sized crowd with normal wait times. He was joking around with some of his senior varsity soccer buddies when I tugged his shirt and pulled him aside.

"I need to ask you for a favor. It's urgent."

He readjusted his Cubs cap. "Oh ho ho! *You* need *my* help for something? This should be good." He signaled to another coworker that he was stepping away for a minute. With a Cheshire-cat grin, he said, "And to what do I owe the honor, Princess Chloe?"

I sighed. "I'm serious. I need rice from your parents. Trust me, I wouldn't be here if it wasn't dire."

"Rice? What the hell? Did you all actually run out of rice? My parents have so many rice bags in their back room, they'll never run out even in an apocalypse. And nope, no deal."

Shit. "C'mon. Please? We can buy it from you. Non-wholesale. I'll pay retail."

"Sorry. My parents would love to see your 4-star Yelp rating drop. It's too good of an opportunity for them, they'd refresh the Yelp page while eating popcorn to see that go down like the New Year's Eve ball dropping at Times Square. There's no way they would give up rice unless they would get something out of this."

Jerk. We were running out of time. "How about we get your rice bag at $20 over cost?"

He smirked. "So let me get this straight. You want *my* parents to help *your* family out because of a bad call *you* made."

"Well...yes."

Was that a smile on his face? "Nope. No way."

Damn it, Peter Li. "Why not? It's a win-win. You get an extra twenty bucks. We get rice."

"Because...I'd have to explain all of this to my parents. That they need to help your parents...and c'mon. Like they'd agree to that? It's easier to just stay out of it."

He had a point. If I told my parents they needed to help Peter's mom and dad, they'd launch into a long tirade about their ten-plus-years restaurant turf war. I couldn't even bring up the Lis without dredging up years of history. And I couldn't dare tell them where the bag of rice had come from (they'd say it was low quality, or worse, poisoned), because frankly, they'd rather go bankrupt before letting the Lis help them.

I asked, "Is there any way you or I can sneak out the bag and have me replace it tomorrow? I'll still pay you some money even though it's technically borrowing. You don't have to tell them any of it is to help my family."

He rubbed his chin. "And what's in it for me?"

"I don't pull promotions out my ass like this ever again?" I squeaked.

"No deal."

I sighed. "And I'm nice to you for a month."

"And?"

I squinted. "You want more? Are you serious?"

He pressed his lips and nodded.

I gritted my teeth. *Damn it, I knew I shouldn't have entered a deal with the devil. Working with him was the last thing I wanted.* "Fine, I can do a photo session of you. For social media or whatever." Honestly, this was all I could offer. "That's it, though. I need to get back."

Peter pulled out his phone and walked down the hall to make a call. Eagerly waiting for his thumbs-up or thumbs-down, I paced the hall too, walking by the Rocky Mountain Chocolate Factory and stopping to stare at the treats in the window display. The store made the entire hallway smell like sweet milk chocolate heaven. There were candied and caramel apples showcased next to the chocolate-covered Oreos. Why would anyone in their right mind, with a normal functioning brain, pick an apple on a stick over chocolate dipped cookies?

Before I could contemplate this further, Peter wrapped up his phone conversation as he headed back in my direction. "Okay, bye!"

He flashed a charismatic, heart-melting smile. "We're all set. Got off the phone with one of the guys who works for my parents, and he'll help me sneak it out back and hand it over to you without them seeing. They're in a good mood and pretty busy, so it'll be easy. And you have to swear to bring back an identical one tomorrow. This will work out great as long as you get the rice back to us, no matter what happens, got it? One of the assistant managers at the VR booth is covering for me while I step away for this."

I managed to squeak out a thank-you.

He looked over at the chocolate store. "Oh wow, I'd love to eat one of those caramel apples."

What? *Sociopath.*

"Um, one more question, off topic."

Peter scowled. "I have to get your rice and head back to work. What else could you possibly want?"

I bit my bottom lip. Maybe this wasn't the best time to ask. But I was hungry, and I needed comfort food while dealing with this mess I'd made. Plus I'd been stressed out to begin with, waiting to hear about the photography competition. "You think we could do a dinner swap sometime? Spicy pork and mandu for you, shrimp lo mein for me?" God, what I wouldn't do for some shrimp lo mein.

His face broke out into a wide grin as we headed to his restaurant for covert rice retrieval. "Now you're talking."

"Then we have a deal." I thought about shaking on it, but went with an unsure nod instead. Hopefully I wouldn't regret this.

Mom didn't believe me when I said I bought rice at the local grocery store, but didn't press further, because she was preoccupied by the shrinking number of people standing in line. She cursed under her breath when she saw it was now ten people instead of thirty. She held out her index finger and barked, "Look! They going to Empress Garden!"

At first, it was a trickle. One person here, one person there. But then it was like watching an orderly trail of ants: a steady stream of people marching toward the Li restaurant, and some coming back to the line to relay information. Soon, the Empress Garden had the same number of people in line as we did. Maybe even more.

She left the cashier area and shouted from the back, "New rice ready in five minute!"

In an unexpected move, my mom reappeared and walked closer to the rival restaurant, trying to gather information on what was happening over at Empress Garden without the aid of binoculars. I trailed after her, explaining how I got the rice from Peter's family. I added at the end, "Peter did it to help me, Umma."

Mom turned to me with narrowed eyes. "Help you? You really trust him?"

Maybe? But I'd never tried to trust him before. Did I like him? Not really. But that didn't mean I didn't trust him.

With a shaky pointer finger, she gestured toward the counter. "Look! I told you I don't trust!"

Next to the cash register, a new Costco-sized plastic container of fortune cookies drew my eye. A handwritten sign read, "Extra cookie! Today only!"

This was in addition to the free drink and appetizer and

bonus lo mein that Peter had just added to their chalkboard with their daily specials.

Peter was one-upping our promotion! What an a-hole!

And I'd bought his rice for an overinflated price. Shame on me.

Shit. SHIT. SHIT! I hated Peter Li.

Mom growled, "Maybe we need to offer cookie too. Or two-appetizer promotion."

I completely understood where this need to escalate was coming from, but the food court was closing soon. "Mom, let it go. Let's get back to the restaurant and get through the rest of the customers. Get another batch of rice going so we don't run out. Plus, we all know your cooking is way better than the Lis'."

She harrumphed and headed back to Kwons' Café, where Dad was holding two trays of food, calling out "Order number ninety-four! Order number ninety-nine!"

While I took over the back kitchen supervision, Mom and Dad worked the front. They spoke to each other mostly in Korean but would randomly pepper in an English word because they couldn't think of the Hangul one. As the line started to die down, they did their usual gossiping about customers, thinking that the Korean language was like a secret code even though they used enough English words to reveal what they were thinking.

For example, several patrons in a row had embraced the latest fashion trend of metallic high-top shoes and bought limited-edition pairs at the pop-up shoe boutique around the corner. When a shoe aficionado, twentysomething white dude with dreads picked up his tray, Mom said to him, "Thank you for your business!" then quickly turned to my dad and said, "Geu *silver* shinbal bwass-eo?"

To which my dad responded loudly, "*Ugly space boot* gateun dae? Mot-saeng-gyeoss-eo."

I cleared my throat. "You both know that people can understand the English words you're saying, right?"

Mom and Dad looked at me, then each other, and stopped gossiping.

When the dinner traffic was back at a reasonable level, Mom told Dad about the Empress Garden "sneaking behind our back" with the appetizer and fortune cookie bonus. He shook his head but didn't speak. It was hard to tell if he was mad that the Lis had one-upped the Kwons or disappointed about how petty Mom was.

"Chloe-ya. Can you go to Costco to buy big bag of that pink gum I like? Probably faster to walk than drive." He pulled out his wallet and handed me his membership card along with a twenty-dollar bill.

Dad hadn't chewed gum in five years, maybe more, when he swore it caused intestinal gas.

"You want gum now? Don't you need me to help at the register?"

He sighed. "We need to give customer free thing too. Maybe free Dubble Bubble."

I laughed. "Wait, you think Dubble Bubble is going to sell Korean food? I made up this promotion...the free drink and appetizer...because of senior night at my school. It was just for one night, to take advantage of the crowd today." I sighed out of my nose. "This is getting out of hand, like an arms race. Now you want me to go to the store and buy a bulk quantity of Dubble Bubble so you can offer free gum to entice customers, even though we can barely get through the orders right now?"

Mom and Dad looked at each other.

Mom replied, "Yes."

Dad nodded firmly. "Everybody like Dubble Bubble."

Looking over at Empress Garden, their line was maybe fifteen people deep. Our was about the same. We were closing in an hour. No way was I leaving now.

Out of the corner of my eye, I saw Peter duck behind his restaurant's counter and walk to the kitchen. He stood next to the line cook, pulling handwritten order slips dangling from the window and assisting with assembling the orders. Maybe sensing my gaze, he looked up, and I quickly glanced away, grabbing an apron from under the counter and ringing up a few orders while Dad went to our kitchen to see how the cooks were doing.

Sophia and Elias stopped by to grab a bite just as the line began to wane, but I told them I'd catch up with them later when things were calmer. They looked like they wanted to stay with me. Maybe their ESP was telling me I was stressed out of my mind, but I said the one thing I knew would make them leave. "I saw Cheremy at the arcade." Their dreamboat. They left so fast I practically felt a gust of wind blow.

I'd managed to convince Mom and Dad that me walking the twenty minutes to and from Costco to get Dubble Bubble wouldn't have a big impact on the late dinner crowd. And sure enough, after fifteen minutes, the crowd dwindled to a normal midweek trickle. The senior citizens who had once swarmed the lines were now all headed to bed. The high school seniors went on to other places in or around the mall, like the Asteroid arcade, Lickety Splits bowling alley, and the Cineflix movie theater. And just like that, things were back to normal.

A few minutes before closing time, the late-night maintenance staff came through to eat before their shifts, along with the afternoon retail workers who had their oddly timed meal breaks. Mom and Dad knew all of them by name. Mr. Suarez. Mrs. Jamison. Mrs. Bartlett. Mr. Adams. I said hello and retreated to the storage area, where I grabbed a bottle of water from the Costco pallet of H_2O. Boxes of onions, garlic, and bags of rice were the only bulk produce and dry goods stored in there. Most of it was paper goods and utensils. A small pile of bills on my dad's wooden desk drew my attention, the top envelope with "LAST NOTICE" stamped in red ink across the front catching my eye first and causing me to stop mid-sip. It was from the landlord. Mom and Dad were probably late on rent, which happened every once in a while when they got too busy at the restaurant. Usually the landlord didn't tack on a late fee if they were behind only a few days.

My phone buzzed. A message from Peter. **You don't owe me for the rice, you can have it. A counter-promotion was something I had to do—it wasn't personal. Just business.**

There he was, mocking my words from earlier that evening.

Then he asked the unthinkable. **Still up for a late-night food swap?**

Was he serious? The nerve of this guy! I peeked outside of the storage room and saw Mom and Dad chatting it up with Gerry the security guard. Things had calmed down considerably. My stomach growled, like it was echoing my inner thoughts about my hostile feelings toward Peter. Meeting him for a late dinner would give me a chance to eat and bitch him out for his last-minute stunt.

Okay, outside in ten.

I unloaded the tongs, spatulas, and mixing bowls from the dishwasher and put them away, then reloaded with the dirty cooking utensils. After wiping down the counters with a mix of vinegar and water, I put together the spicy pork combo and threw in some extra mandu. They had been under the heat lamp all evening, so they weren't in the best condition plumpness-wise but would taste just fine. With Peter's meal in one hand and a fountain drink in the other, I used my elbow to open the back door. The wind made my long black hair whip around my head like kelp. I tried to blow it from my face, but all I managed to do was add spit to my voluminous mane.

"Uh, let me help." Peter grabbed the food and drink before I could react, freeing my hands to finger-comb my hair out of my eyes and mouth. Once I could see again, I looked down and discovered he had not only brought two folded seats for us, but he had also carted out a small metal patio table. "It's easier to eat food when it's on a table instead of our laps." He rubbed the back of his neck. "I guess that's pretty obvious and didn't require an explanation. And I'm sorry about the last-minute promotion at the end of the night. I needed to keep my parents distracted and busy from noticing the missing bag of rice. They had lower inventory than usual, which was really weird. They're overly freaked out about people stealing from them or cheating them, and their mood worsened when they saw all of your customers, so they'd notice it missing. The quick promotion was the only thing I could think of to divert their attention. They're so weirdly competitive toward your parents, I knew it would work."

Was he doing me a favor or trying to sabotage me? Was he being nice or being a dick? I couldn't tell. My gut wasn't telling me yes or no, it was saying *Can you please feed me already?*

The little bistro table was probably meant for one person: our two food containers plus two drinks barely fit. In fact, it was so small that when I sat down across from Peter, our knees touched. I jumped back, nearing toppling backward from my wobbly seat.

"It's just my knees, Chloe. Did I have static electricity or something?"

He was right, it was just two bony kneecaps. But what was this bodily reaction all about? It was like Peter zapped me. Or maybe I zapped him. My body did have a propensity to make static charges without any means of controlling it. This was my hidden talent. Like a Pokémon shock wave move, or maybe even thunderbolt, but with no points and zero wins.

Peter set right in to digging into his food and let the conversation go. I happily did the same. As requested, he brought me shrimp lo mein. And he got his spicy pork plus extra mandu we were going to bring home anyway. We sat in silence while we chewed and swallowed and drank and slurped. Before long, it was already time to help my parents clean up and close. Weird that he and I could just sit there and eat without actually speaking. It wasn't uncomfortable. If anything, it was relaxing.

He leaned back in his chair and patted his belly. "Oh man, I could seriously eat that every day. Every night too. You're so lucky."

"I was thinking the same. Lo mein. All day every day."

He pulled out a small brown sack. "I also snagged a sesame ball." Tilting the paper bag, I could see the sesame-seed-covered dessert. "It's still pretty hot, it just came out of the fryer. You can take it home for later."

A gust of wind came through and rattled the bag, which he placed next to my food. Our napkins rustled, threatening to disperse into the air, so he adjusted our drinks so they sat on top of them. "So when do we do the photoshoot?"

I narrowed my eyes. "You're not actually thinking I'd do the photoshoot after you pulled that shit on me, right?"

He shrugged. "We made a deal. I didn't make a deal that I wouldn't do a promo."

God, I hate this guy. "Fine. But it'll be quick," I muttered.

"And can I pick what the shoot is for?"

I crossed my arms. "What do you mean? It's not for you?"

He scrunched his nose. "Kind of? I need you to take updated photos of the restaurant and signature dishes for Yelp."

I was an artist, not a menu photographer. "Sorry, that wasn't part of the deal."

"Fine, I'll just tell your parents how you orchestrated the *entire* thing today, the good stuff *and* the bad—"

Instinctively, I grabbed his arm. He couldn't. My parents would never trust my judgment again.

I looked at my hand and noticed Peter didn't jerk back like I did earlier. "Please don't. I'll take the photos tomorrow after school, okay?"

He cocked his head and laughed.

Yes, you win this time, Peter Li. "Fine."

He eased into a smirk. "I can't wait."

FIVE

PETER

GETTING THE WIND KNOCKED OUT OF YOU IS THE worst.

But getting the wind knocked out of you on an outdoor basketball court in front of your entire PE class really makes that experience a million times more horrible. Especially because I was having a really good hair day.

A pasty, hairy arm reached down to offer "help." The same arm of the guy who knocked me down in the first place. If this were a real game with a referee, this would have been a blatant foul. Sean always played dirty. An angry person who was always in detention, he let his emotions out on the court. Lucky me.

I wasn't refusing his help, necessarily. Part of the problem was I still needed to catch my breath and, lying on the pavement flat on my back, it was taking effort to get air into my lungs. He had maybe fifty pounds on me, possibly more muscle in his upper arm than in my entire body, and he'd given me a well-placed shoulder check. I went down like a human domino, making the same sound as what you'd expect a human domino to make: a cracking-smacking sound from hitting the hard asphalt. I couldn't even sit up yet, and it'd been ten seconds, at least.

He put his hand down to his side. "Fine. Lay there in the middle of the court. Ruin our game." Sean snorted and walked toward the other basketball court. Everyone followed him. The freshman pickup game quickly disbanded as the upperclassmen continued without me on the adjacent blacktop area. I thought there was no one around so I could be solitary in my misery, but then Chloe's face came into focus, and unlike Sean, she wasn't dripping perspiration all over me. In fact, she was smiling.

It took time, but I caught my breath. Desperately and deeply, I inhaled and exhaled like my life depended on it. Maybe it did. Maybe Sean had punctured both lungs somehow and I was basically a deflated innertube with invisible holes in it.

Chloe's face disappeared. I turned my head slowly to see where she'd gone, but she was outside my peripheral vision.

Click.

Click-click.

I knew that sound. It was enough to make my upper body bolt upright.

"Are you taking pictures of me?" I whispered hoarsely.

She had her SLR pointing right at my face.

Click.

I cried out, "Hey! This wasn't part of our deal. And what sicko would take my photo in this dire state? Are you a monster?"

She gave me that scrunchy-nose, tilted-head Chloe look. "I'm an artist, this is what I do. I already took your menu photos last night as promised, which I'm still retouching by the way, but I'm more of a capturing-humanity-in-a-millisecond kind of photographer. Especially when opportunity strikes. And boy, did it ever. Your hair is pretty messed up now."

So she noticed. I coughed, then rolled onto my knees and pushed myself to a standing position. I needed to get up fast, to show Chloe I wasn't weak. Maybe she'd be impressed by my rapid recovery.

I smoothed my hair and repositioned my gym shorts, which had pulled up and fully twisted around, holding everything below the drawstring hostage. "And what type of humanity did you capture with me just now? Something dark and homicidal perhaps?"

"You looked surprisingly Zen laying down on the blacktop with your eyes closed. I had no idea that today's free activity time during PE would turn into something so entertaining. It's like you didn't even seem to mind that the entire school saw Sean take you down in one bump."

"That was hardly a bump. That was a shoulder bulldoze. I

can reenact it if you'd like. I won't hold back." She smiled, but a flash of worry in her eyes from her believing I might actually do it gave me so much satisfaction. "Don't worry, I'm too gracious and polite of a guy to do that. Plus, I'm too bruised to actually move. And I'm not hurt from him slamming against my body; I'm sore from landing on the asphalt."

Lifting the sleeve of my T-shirt revealed massive bruises forming on my upper arm. The raw scrapes on my elbow weren't bleeding, but they would need some cleanup. No torn clothes either, thank God. I was down to my last good jeans and couldn't bear asking my parents for another pair. They didn't understand that I couldn't just go to Marshalls and pick up any ol' jeans. It wasn't like buying Hanes sweatpants in bulk from Costco either. I'd tried on dozens of pairs of denim and the only ones that looked halfway decent were Sevens. The ones I was wearing didn't have any rips or scuffs yet, so their shelf life was at least another year, possibly two, with some expert-level patching and minimal washing.

Chloe looked over at the basketball game now in progress. "Are you going to rejoin the game?" She cocked her head and stared at me with a quizzical look on her face. Not judgy or condescending. Just genuinely inquisitive.

"Tough choice. Do I lick my wounds or save face by rejoining the game?"

She answered, "I think you should join. A lot of people saw

you take that hit. Sean does shit like that all the time. You didn't get a concussion or anything, you landed on your arm and elbow. If anything, you might be able to get a retaliatory shoulder slam or two in before the end of PE. I'm all about retaliation."

Well, that's hardly a surprise. While I agreed with her, part of me couldn't help but be suspicious that she was trying to get photos of Sean pummeling me. She probably had a photomontage on her wall of all my embarrassing failures in life. The one from today would be one of her favorites.

I tried to sneak a peek while she scrolled through her photo history on her SLR screen. She pushed her hand into my chest. Luckily I wasn't bruised there.

"I'll send it to you later. I can add it to your menu photos." Before I could protest her paparazzi moves, she pointed at Sean. "He just pushed someone else. I definitely think you need to show yourself. Let him know from your fast recovery he can't keep bullying."

I nodded and dragged myself toward the other basketball court. My entire body ached as I trudged toward Sean, but she was right. He needed to see me get back in the game. And I needed Chloe to see that too.

When I approached the sidelines, a few of my acquaintances clapped when they saw me get back on the court. The sophomore who had taken my place eagerly tagged out. He was tall, wiry, and no match against Sean's aggressive shoulder moves.

Sean's eyebrows shot halfway up his forehead. "You're back."

"I'm back." I nodded at Cheremy, who had the ball. He called out, "We have five minutes left. We're tied. Let's do this."

After a while, I didn't even feel the pain anymore. Sean tried to pass the ball to his teammate, but Cheremy intercepted it and threw me the ball. With an easy layup, I added two points just as the bell rang. I looked around to see who had witnessed my comeback. I smiled when I saw Chloe in the sidelines, snapping photos.

SIX

CHLOE

UGHHHHHH.

No matter what photo I took of Peter, he looked good. It was statistically impossible for him to not have any unflattering shots, yet I'd taken nearly two dozen, and he looked good in all of them. *Every. Single. One.*

There was Zen Peter, who looked calm and peaceful despite his awful basketball court surroundings.

Then there was Determined Peter, crouched down, hands on knees, focused. Patiently waiting for the game to resume after a timeout.

Alley-oop Peter. The guy who effortlessly dribbled, ran, and tossed the ball into the net like it was one fluid movement.

Then Dazzling Smile Peter. Who caught me red-handed,

taking a photo of his triumphant return to the game after he scored, resulting in his team winning the game.

I didn't even need to photoshop anything. He had no face blemishes. No weird lines or bumps. No physical flaws that I could zoom into with my high-res camera. Even when he got his left side flattened like a pancake and a little torn up, he still looked great. What human on this earth didn't need any blurring, smoothing, or spot removals?

Peter Li. That's who. And he was walking right toward me.

"You're going to run out of memory with all the photos you keep taking." My face grew hot behind my Canon camera.

"I keep my promises about taking your photos. I'm dedicated to my craft, what can I say?" Dipping my chin down, I clicked a few more times at Cheremy, to pretend I wasn't so focused on Peter. Sophia and Elias would be happy with these newest pictures.

"Can I see?" He reached his hand toward my camera, and I took a giant step back.

"No. You'll get the lens dirty." *Also, I don't want you to see how barfingly perfect you look in color, black and white, and sepia.*

He snapped his non-bruised arm back. "Okay, I'll wait." He sighed and winced at the same time. "I might need to go home early. I think my spleen exploded. And my whole body feels like it was meat tenderized. And then run over by a garbage truck."

What was amazing was how hidden all of his wounds and

pain were. If you didn't know where to look, you would have no idea he was so banged up. He was constantly kidding and smiling. So annoyingly upbeat. I thought about offering to take him home, or to a hospital or something, but two of his friends came over, hooting and hollering about his last shot. Kip, his taller friend, slapped Peter in the back, which made him wince. The last thing that guy needed was more physicality that day. Especially on his busted side.

Brach, his shorter friend, rumored to have been named after the candy company because his mom was obsessed with those yellow butterscotch discs, scratched his nose with his thumb and said, "When you took that fall, it was pretty embarrassing. But then you made the biggest comeback ever! And like, Olivia and her whole crew asked if you were okay. They're over there." Peter, Kip, and Brach looked over by the courts and sure enough, four girls were staring right at them.

Kip sighed the words, "Oh-livia."

Then Brach noticed me and said, "Oh, hey, Chloe."

Kip didn't take his eyes off Olivia and her friends for even a second. "Hey...Chloe." After the group of girls moved along, he was released from their spell and then ruffled Peter's hair. "Let's go see what Olivia and her friends are up to. Maybe we can walk them to class."

Kip and Brach sprung forward and met the girls by the doorway into the building. Peter shrugged. "I guess if I need a ride home, one of them can take me, right? Catch ya later." He walked over to everyone and grinned like he wasn't turning half purple underneath his clothes. How could he still smile and act like nothing was wrong? Was this impressive? Or deranged?

I'm late for art anyway, I thought to myself as I trailed them inside. I headed to my locker to get my portfolio and backpack and made my way to the studio.

As soon as class started, Mrs. Doyle peered at my latest set of photos for a good minute. Her reading glasses perched nearly on the tip of her nose, giving me the urge to push them back up to her bridge for her.

"Some of these photos are quite lovely."

Sophia popped her head over my shoulder. "Maybe she could use these after she officially gets accepted into the National Art Council Photography competition, right Mrs. Doyle? She's gotta be a shoo-in!"

In the corner of the room at the pottery wheel, Elias yelled, "Hell yeah!"

Sophia had always been my cheerleader. I, on the other hand, was a human Eeyore and Chicken Little hybrid, and didn't think past the competition application because I knew I wouldn't get in. Somehow, Sophia and I were compatible and were ideal counterparts. I grounded her. She lifted me. Together, we were a perfect complementary team.

Mrs. Doyle's deeply creased forehead suggested she wasn't

in full agreement with Sophia's cheery take on my photography portfolio. "Food photography still life is not easy to pull off, so I applaud this effort. But to win the National Art Council award, well, the work really needs to stand out. Tell a story. Pull heartstrings. Garner empathy. You get my drift. For a class assignment, this is great. For the National Art Council, you need to be exceptional."

Art really was the only thing I was any good at; specifically, photography was the one area of focus I could see myself in professionally. And now she was saying I didn't stand out at all.

Before I could Debbie Downer myself into a spiral of sadness, she added, "Chloe Kwon, you have potential to be exceptional. You turned in your class assignment early, so use the next week or so to explore composition, viewpoint, perspective, and narrative, so if you do get chosen for the competition, you'll be ready. It's all things you've studied, now it's time to put it into action."

She walked away and Sophia whooped, "Did you hear that? She gushed over you! She never does that. I heard she's the only arts and humanities teacher who has actually failed people. Can you imagine failing art?"

Mrs. Doyle was intimidating, with her towering height and wild gray curls. She was the only teacher who didn't accidentally mix me up with my sister Hannah, who had attended high school many years before me and had the exact same teachers. Mrs. Doyle never called me "Hannah-I-mean-Chloe," and I appreciated that.

I never thought of her as scary or too tough. To me, she was fair. And it was fair to say that my still photography wasn't exceptional. I was just an all around unexceptional human being.

When I started making Bs and Cs in pre-algebra, the teacher took me off the honors math track, saying I wasn't nearly as good as my older sister. Hannah went to college at Vanderbilt, where she majored in math and minored in French. She was a paralegal now and was applying to law schools, hoping the experience would get her into a top-tier program. She'd also spent a summer after college backpacking around France with her two best friends, trying to get better at speaking French. When I'd taken French in junior high, I was terrible at it, so I had no motivation to go to another country to remind myself of how badly I spoke it.

I was slightly better at speaking Korean, even better than Hannah, but no one seemed to care. The Kwons were too focused on academics and Hannah's future of becoming the first Asian American Supreme Court justice.

I restacked my photos and let out a sad sigh. I was good at being a mall elf photographer, but maybe that's all I was ever meant to be. I'd had other jobs around the mall I was good at too, like the associate at Color Me Mine, where I helped kids paint their ceramic plates, and as the Sears photography studio assistant. Maybe I'd peaked and this was the pinnacle of my photo career. Another heavy sigh escaped me.

"I don't think I'm good enough for the National Art Council

competition," I told Sophia. "Apparently they don't want a bunch of photos of Chinese and Korean restaurant takeout food."

Sophia pulled up a chair. She plopped down and wobbled; one of the legs had a rubber foot missing. "Okay, you clearly didn't hear Mrs. Doyle. She said you have potential and you need to work on the photography skills she mentioned. I don't know what they are, I'm a mixed-media person, but I know you have them. Or you can develop them."

Sophia's specialty was acrylics and wadded-up tissue paper. Her parents were artists too, so in her family, this wasn't weird at all.

"Maybe you can come over after school to help me out? Figure out my strengths and weaknesses? Help me evaluate my portfolio?" I asked, batting my lashes in the most cartoonish way possible.

"I want to come too!" Elias came over with a vaselike thing that resembled the silhouette of a snowman.

"Of course! Maybe with your help I can figure out which photos have the best uh...composition, viewpoint, perspective, and narrative. Everything I need to work on. I need to pull out all stops if I get this National Art Council opportunity. I need to get into NYU. I need to...what does your dad say again, Elias? That Nike slogan?"

"Just do it!" he battle-cried.

I laughed. "Yes! I need to just do it!"

"Yeah! You need to go to NYU so I can visit the city when I

go to RISD." Rhode Island School of Design was Sophia's destiny. A mere train ride away. Her parents met there, and her maternal grandmother went to RISD too.

"Y'all keep leaving me out. I want to visit too. And you better visit me wherever I end up. Don't abandon me." Elias jutted out his bottom lip and, with his index finger, pointed at his eye and swiped down his cheek. Elias was the brainiac, athletic theater nerd who was gunning for Yale. If we all ended up on the East Coast, it would be a dream come true.

"We need to stop talking about schools we haven't even applied for. We're going to jinx ourselves. We're only juniors, there's still time to mess things up." The other two nodded solemnly, as we all firmly believed in the sorcery of jinxing.

While Sophia and Elias spent remaining class time sketching, I searched online for the judges who would be picking the finalists for the competition. Some were commercial photographers, others were lifestyle ones, and then there was Lorraine Finch, the photojournalist I'd admired since I first became interested in photography. She'd won a Pulitzer a few years after she graduated from college, and now she was documenting "Lost America": photos of shrinking populations, small towns, and multigenerational family businesses. There was something about the way she documented history that fascinated me. I wanted to contribute to the world in a meaningful way, and archival history was one way to do that that really excited me.

Lorraine Finch might see my work. She was the be-all and end-all of grand prizes. And the ten grand cash award didn't hurt.

My eyes bulged when I saw a new prize highlighted on the competition landing page. "FINALISTS WILL RECEIVE ONE WEEK OF MENTORSHIP FROM A SELECTED JUDGE." Lorraine Finch's name was listed.

OMG Lorraine Finch could be my mentor. That would be a dream come true.

Elias snapped near my face. "So we'll see you tonight for our photo eval!"

Sophia clapped. "I'll bring desserts. This is going to be the best weekend."

It certainly seemed that way.

"Okay, please don't type on my computer with your Cheeto hands."

Sophia grimaced. "Sorry, I was going to lick them first, but I thought you'd be more mad."

Elias pulled out a pack of baby wipes from his backpack. "Gross. I carry these everywhere for exactly this reason."

I joked, "You have Cheeto emergencies?"

He handed over the wipes to Sophia. "I'm afraid that's classified information."

She pulled a fragrant cloth from the pack and removed

the orange dust crust from her index finger and thumb tips. Sophia continued to scroll through my online gallery, including some of the photos I'd submitted with my competition application, while Elias cracked open a can of soda and looked at the screen too.

I sighed. "You haven't said anything, and it's making me nervous. Is nothing good enough?"

Elias slurped his drink. "I see what Mrs. Doyle is talking about. Even from my untrained eye, I can see you're on the cusp on so many of these, but some of these you didn't show her, *wow*. You have some amazing black-and-white shots around the mall too."

I grabbed the plate of cookies Sophia had brought over. "What does that mean, exactly? On the cusp?"

He shrugged. "I dunno, it's hard to explain. It's like you're so talented and on the verge of a breakthrough."

Sophia sat up straight. "Okay, I've scrolled through like hundreds of photos now. I even went back to some of the ones you took last year, and the year before, to compare. You've grown so much as an artist. I'm jealous."

My face flushed with embarrassment. I was terrible at taking compliments. I had to get out of the habit of downplaying my successes and accomplishments. So rather than be self-deprecating or sarcastic as I'd been programmed to do, I offered a simple thank-you this time.

Elias chimed in, "I love the photos of the wooden bridge and the cityscape. You're really versatile. You should sell these as framed prints on Etsy. Or maybe even get them into boutiques around the city."

I swelled with pride as I took in their praise. "You guys think so? My parents are iffy about this whole thing. I've been trying to tell them I can make a career of it, maybe as a photographer for advertising or magazines. Lately they've really been on my case about finding a more stable career, with steady salary and good benefits."

Elias picked up my camera and scrolled through my images from the past two weeks. I hadn't uploaded to my computer to retouch them yet but was planning to later that weekend.

"Wait. How do you move these to your computer screen? I don't see a USB port. I want to see something."

I popped the memory card and inserted it into my external laptop drive. I'd taken 287 photos. Most of them were food photos from Empress Garden. While Peter was running to the kitchen or staging the food and drinks for the menu at some tables in the food court, I took some snapshots of Peter, his parents, and the line cooks with my zoom lens.

As the images appeared one by one on the computer screen, Elias left arrowed back to the people photos. "I think this is where you shine, Chloe. Look."

He paused on one that I barely remembered taking. Peter

laughing with a customer wearing a "Will Work for Chinese Food" shirt. Something about that moment was magical.

He flipped ahead. "Okay, that was good. But there are better ones. Don't kill me, but c'mon. Look."

It was a photo of Peter in an apron, pulling a handwritten order note from a clothesline. He and I both occasionally had to step in when the lunch rush got to be too big. So what if I'd captured this moment where he looked more realistically human versus perfectly handsome?

Sophia gasped. "And that one!"

Peter lying on the basketball court. The crumbling asphalt and weeds surrounding him as he smiled serenely, eyes closed. A juxtaposition of perfect and imperfect.

"Wait, you're telling me that my two best photos of all time... are both of Peter Li?"

They looked at each other. Sophia coughed into her single-serving Cheeto bag. "I mean, well, he's obviously photogenic and all, but these photos have that narrative voice that Mrs. Doyle was talking about. You're telling a story about Peter Li and his family. About his school life and their work life. The narrative is popping off the screen."

My stomach churned as Elias added, "Honestly, out of all of your photos, these are really, truly...exceptional."

How dare you. "No. No way. Nope. There's no chance I'd use photos of Peter Li for the National Art Council Award finalist portfolio if I got in. Absolutely not."

Sophia frowned. "Not even if it meant getting into your dream college?"

This was a fair and logical question, and I cringed at the thought. Would I be throwing away a potential opportunity to make my college application stand out next year? Was taking pictures of Peter Li and his restaurant the way to get into NYU? The National Art Council came with a decent monetary award too. I had a long list of things I'd love to buy, ranging from the practical (college tuition) to impractical (hoverboard). But I didn't want to get my hopes up.

Elias and Sophia flipped through the rest of the photos. They came back to the two of Peter. Sophia said, "Sorry Chloe, but these two are by far the best. Now the real question is, which one would you submit? I like Restaurant Peter."

Elias shook his head. "Pavement Peter is way better."

They both looked at me, like I would actually want to break the tie by choosing between the two Peter photos. I took them, yes, but were they "exceptional" because of my talent or because it was Peter as my muse?

Peter? *Gross.*

"I refuse to choose between two Peters. It goes against everything I stand for."

Elias asked, "Then why did you take the photos in the first place if you didn't want to use them for anything?"

Another good question. Why was I shooting photos of him

beyond what I owed him? When I grabbed my camera and focused on a subject, there was something interesting that caught my eye...something that through my camera lens could tell a story. The contrast in lighting. Vivid colors. Visual humor that could be captured in one click. Maybe there was something about him that was interesting or inspirational. Something deeper.

"Hopefully it's sheer passion of photography...and not stalker-y," Elias added, breaking my concentration.

Sophia shot me a sympathetic look. "Maybe you can think about it. He could be your ticket to a happier future."

Elias said, "Just eeny-meeny-miny-mo that shit. Pick a Peter."

Sophia laughed. "Or do that. We both think you have a shot at this competition. But you know, I get it. It's Peter Li. You can also try to take more pictures of other things, maybe something else will inspire you."

"Thanks. Maybe you're right. I'll think about it." My friends were honest and loyal, and I loved them to death. But they also knew one thing about me that would never change: there was no way in hell I'd let Peter Li help me with this, of all things. He could not be part of my future when I left for college to leave this place behind. I'd have to find another way.

The photo on screen was of a very handsome Peter (blech) but I noticed something in his hand that I hadn't before. Sadly, I was too focused on his coy smile and sparkling eyes to notice.

Tapping twice with my mouse, it was the same "final notice" envelope I'd seen on my parents' desk, right there in his hand.

There was no way both my family and his were both late on rent. It had to be something else.

"Thanks for the photo eval. Let's watch something on Netflix."

But before we started the miniseries, I added a reminder to my phone: *Ask Peter (ugh) about the scary landlord letter tomorrow.*

SEVEN

PETER

CHLOE KEPT GLANCING MY WAY, BUT SHE WAS certainly, definitely, positively NOT checking me out. Because every time I caught her looking over, Chloe's eyes rolled, and then she glanced away. It was unnerving because for the life of me I couldn't think of what I'd done to piss Chloe off so badly.

During my break from my VR admin duties, I came up to her between photo sessions to ask her what was going on.

"Spill it. Why are you mad at me?"

"I'm not mad at you. And I'm slammed with customers, so I can't talk," she grunted. "Time is money, gotta work. But we need to chat later about something important." She shooed me away and went back to attending to the family donning reindeer antler headbands.

Something important? Chloe thought she was done talking

to me, but she couldn't leave me hanging like that. I whipped out a "50 percent off" friends and family coupon from my wallet and handed it to the gatekeeper elf standing in front. "I'd like the digital-only package, please."

She typed up the order. "Fifty percent off brings you to the grand total of twelve fifty." After swiping my card, she grinned at me. "You're the oldest kid we've had come through today. Glad you're into the holiday cheer."

As the family ahead of me was wrapping up their photoshoot, the elf bouncer at the door waved me through. "Merry Christmas!"

Chloe didn't notice me approaching Santa's Workshop, which was good because I'd never seen her doing her work photography thing. She was always observing and lurking in the background, hiding from attention. But here, things were different. She was with a family of four plus a yippy dog, smiling, making eye contact, and reassuring them about their photo purchase. She shook the parents' hands and wished them a happy holiday season.

When they left, the look on Chloe's face when she saw me was the opposite of merry. "What are *you* doing here?" she asked, looking around like she suspected hidden cameras were planted all around us.

"I'm paying for a session. Because you won't talk to me otherwise. And I want to know what your dire situation is. Where do I go?"

Oblivious to the situation at hand, Santa gave me his regular holiday spiel. "Ho ho ho! Come here, young man! Let's take a photo and you can tell me everything you want for Christmas!"

I looked down at my "Ultimate Santa North Pole Extravaganza!" T-shirt and pursed my lips to hold back a laugh. "I'd like some new shirts, Santa." I leaned my shoulder on his overstuffed chair and smirked.

"I'm sure that can be arranged! Chloe, let us know when you're ready."

She took a deep breath in, and with an exasperated exhale, said, "Okay. On the count of three. One! Two! Say cheese!"

Click!

She took a look at the screen and groaned. "Okay, that's all we need."

I walked over. "Weren't you supposed to say *three*? The other sessions take over five minutes. You say you got it in one click?"

"It's fine. But we can do more if you want."

"Fine?" I cocked my head. I took a look at the image myself. Aside from the busy festive décor surrounding Santa and me, he and I looked great. Well, he looked a little drunk, and possibly high, but I looked, well, fine.

"Oh, you did get it in one shot. That's great. Now that you have all this extra time, will you please talk to me? I'm a paying customer, after all. You don't want me to leave a lukewarm Yelp review."

She cracked a hint of a smile. Thank God. We both shared the pain of hostile Yelp reviews, a common bond for restaurant families. "What would you possibly say in your write-up? 'Santa's Village felt unrealistic with the fake snow. One star.'"

"Probably something more like, 'Not for me. Santa was too way too jolly and predictable for me. Two and a half stars, rounded down to two because I'm in a mood.'"

She laughed. "Efficient elf only took one photo. It's not my fault I'm so photogenic. Three stars."

I laughed along but stopped abruptly. "Wait, you think I'm photogenic?"

Her face fell immediately. "Are you serious?" Her cheeks flushed pink as she showed me the photo again.

The gatekeeper elf's head popped past the wall. "Hey, we have a lull right now. I'm putting out the sign saying we'll be back in fifteen minutes. Let's take our break."

I focused my attention back on Chloe. "Oh good, now you *definitely* have time to talk with me. So you seem mad about something that you won't share. And now you're mad because you think I'm always photogenic." I had to admit though, that pic of me next to Old St. Nick was maybe the most epic photo of all time.

She shook her head. "It's not that. Well, it's kind of that. I might need your face and body for something."

"You need my face and body, makes sense." I raised my eyebrows and crossed my arms. "Admit it, you have a thing for bruised, banged-up guys."

She snorted and slapped my arm. "Stop it. I can tell your mind is in the gutter."

"You're the one who wants my body and face for free."

Chloe furrowed her brow. "You want me to pay you then?"

"That sounds like prostitution, when you put it that way. How about you just be straight with me and not talk in circles? Or cryptology. Or innuendo. Or whatever this is. I don't even know anymore. It might be insinuations, but I'm not smart enough to know how to interpret that."

"What are you even talking about now? You're being weird." Chloe motioned her head to come with her on a walk. So I grabbed a candy cane at the exit and trotted after her.

As I peeled the clear plastic from the red-and-white peppermint stick, she told me about the prestigious photography competition. That there were thousands of entries every year, and hundreds in the junior category. And that crabby Mrs. Doyle said her current portfolio wasn't strong enough, so if she was a finalist, she wasn't good enough to win. I could see why that would be a bummer, but none of this had anything to do with me. I waited for some obvious link to her hating me, but it never surfaced.

After a few steps of awkward silence, I just flat out asked her. "So why are you mad at me then? I don't get it."

"I'm not mad at you, Peter. I just..."

More silence.

The last thing I needed was my parents and hers to see us

walking around together. So I veered us toward Foot Locker, and we walked in with no intention of buying anything.

I grabbed an identical Vans shoe to the one I already had on and examined the price tag.

Chloe picked up a Chuck Taylor and put it back down. After taking a deep breath, she shot me a zinger. "I-was-wondering-if-I-could-get-your-permission-to-use-a-photo-I-took-of-you-for-the-National-Art-Council-contest-if-I-get-in." She said those words so fast it took me a few seconds to process what she wanted.

"You...want to submit the photo of Santa and me? Go for it."

Chloe scrunched her nose like she smelled something rotten. "That Santa photo? Are you kidding? No! I mean these other photos I took of you at the restaurant and on the basketball court."

Those photos? "Uh, okay. Same answer. Go for it. I don't mind."

The wrinkle between her brow deepened. "Really? There's like no chance I'll win, but I'd I owe you big if anything came of it."

On the tip of my tongue, the words, "Don't worry about it" formed, but luckily they didn't tumble out. I had leverage over Chloe now. She thought these photos were a bigger deal than they actually were. And now she owed me big for them. This was the best possible outcome.

I grinned. "How about you just owe me *small* then...unless

you win. Then you can owe me big." My wrist vibrated and I checked my watch. "I gotta get back. My break is over soon. Want me to walk you back?"

She shrugged. "Okay. Oh, there's one more thing I need to ask you." Chloe clicked on her phone screen. "You see this photo? This envelope, with the final notice warning...what is it?"

Squinting hard, I replied, "I don't know."

"You don't know because you opened it and read it, and it was confusing? Or you don't know because you didn't open it?"

"Honestly, I barely even remember you taking this photo, let alone what I had in my hand. It's my parents' mail. I didn't open it. Maybe we can go ask our parents about the letter, if it's so important."

"My parents got one too. Same scary FINAL NOTICE warning. I have a bad feeling about it now. Let's go."

She grabbed my hand, and the second she did, my body shivered.

Whoa.

I'd literally never felt tingling before, except when Sean knocked me down, but that was from killing off blood circulation. This was different. This was...nice.

And this was the first time I had ever seen Chloe Kwon run. At PE, for warm-ups, she walked around the track with her two buds, Elias and Soph. When we needed to break into teams for soccer scrimmages, she sort of strolled casually on the field. And when we had relay races, well, let's just say she never broke a sweat.

But there she was, dragging me by the arm with her hair whipping, cheeks flushed, and breathing hard. Whatever it was to cause this sudden change in Chloe's constant state of inertia was big.

Huge.

And that scared me.

EIGHT

CHLOE

I DROPPED PETER'S HAND AS SOON AS WE REACHED the food court. Strangely, I didn't hate having our fingers intertwined, running through the mall together, like one of those superhero movies where the main characters are trying to outrun an explosion. If the circumstances weren't so screwed up, I would have liked to savor the moment a little bit more.

But there was no time for that.

Leaving Peter behind, and without pausing to talk to my parents, who were both chatting with the mail carrier, I stepped past them and headed to the back room. Leafing through all the papers on the desk, I found the unopened envelope in a pile of bills to be filed away. Tearing the seal open, I skimmed the enclosed letter, glossing over phrases like "REGRETTABLY, DUE

TO FINANCIAL SETBACKS" and "NEWLY BUILT MIXED USE BUILD-
ING WITH CONDOMINIUMS," and "PREPARATION FOR DEMOLITION
BEGINS JANUARY 15."

In the mail pile was a document from the mall business
coalition. Some kind of tenant rights manifesto, with my mom's
handwriting scrawled on top "*ask Hannah*."

KNOW YOUR RIGHTS!

Lease Termination and Tenant Rights

*Landlord Pays for Relocation Costs: If the landlord chooses to
relocate you, put the onus on the landlord to pay for all costs associated
with the move or the demolition of your office space, including covering demolition/construction costs, real estate fees, moving expenses,
marketing, and other costs.*

*Time Constraints: Try to negotiate time constraints that apply to
the landlord for activating the Demolition Clause; the later the better.
For example, maybe the clause can only be exercised five years or ten
years into the lease term.*

*Increasing Notice Terms: How much advance notice will you
be given to exit the space? Consider the amount of time required to
relocate or rebuild your business without having to rush into a new
space that is not ideal. There is a big difference between having thirty
days to vacate and nine months to a year to vacate. Having time on
your side before you are required to exit equals more time to find an
ideal location and rebuild your business or storefront.*

Terms of Activation: Ask your landlord how much of the building will need to be renovated or redeveloped to activate the Demolition Clause. For example, perhaps it can only be invoked if more than half of the property is affected by the rebuild...

My entire body went numb as the legal jargon jumbled into a confusing mess inside my brain.

Our lease was being terminated.

But based on what I could comprehend, the mall was being demolished, not renovated. It wasn't a case of getting a new landlord and getting an HGTV-style face-lift. We were being evicted. Kwons' Café would be destroyed.

I walked out of the back room with the papers and took a photo of the page. I texted it to Peter, who was talking a lot with his hands to his parents across the food court. Lots of arm flailing.

I approached my parents, who were still chatting with the postman. Raising my voice, I barked, "We need to talk. *Now.*"

She replied in Korean, "Ah shikkeureo!"

"Be quiet? No, I will not be quiet. I saw the landlord's notice. I saw the coalition's documents. This affects me too." I'd spent thousands of hours working at Kwons' Café. I had the right to know what was happening to it.

Mom sighed. "Okay, calm your voice down." She apologized to the mail carrier on my behalf and turned to me. He smiled and walked away. "You wanting to talk? We talk now."

I began my inquisition. "This mall, is it really being demolished?"

My mom shrugged. "Everyone here say our landlord was going to sell to new landlord. But now they say they selling to a company who will knock down building and make condominium. We try to prepare for this little by little, maybe not fast enough."

I swallowed hard. "Can we fight this? Where would Kwons' Café go if the mall was gone?"

Umma didn't reply, so I repeated the questions, thinking she didn't hear me. But when she didn't answer the second time, I knew she knew what I'd asked. Mom didn't want to answer them. All she said was, "Let's go on a walk so you don't scare away customer."

She took off her apron and walked toward the west wing. We passed Build-A-Bear, where a line to get in wrapped around the corner for a limited-edition Paw Patrol stuffy.

Mom finally spoke. "Problem is everyone else here have stores. Everybody just pack and move inventory to another place. Restaurant people have kitchen, and sink, and air filter. Refrigerator. Stove. We have different concern. We have more problem with moving to another location or if they kick us out and—" She proceeded to throw her arms up and out and made an explosion noise.

I nodded in agreement. "Is there anyone in the food court who is speaking up for you all? For the non-store people?"

She shook her head. "No, nobody. Most of people in food court not speaking English well." Quietly, she added, "No one say anything. The papers they give us to read are not easy."

Chances were it wasn't just my parents who didn't understand these real estate documents. She was right. Maybe 70 percent of the restaurants at the mall were owned by immigrants. The gyro place, the Brazilian grill, the Mexican restaurant. They were all first generation owned. Since as far back as I could remember, my sister and I would have to read and interpret insurance documents, invoices, and bank paperwork for my parents. Hannah was always better at doing all of that, with her meticulous reading of details and ability to untangle and interpret complicated matters. And now this landlord issue had blown up big... Who knew if any of the restaurant owners understood the legality of any of what was going on?

"Why didn't you talk to Hannah yet? She's a paralegal!"

She shook her head. "She work so hard. And she always mad when I call about computer. Or bank."

Hannah was the techy, detailed one in the family. And yes, she got really irritated when you bugged her about software issues or installation glitches, but at the same time, she was the only I knew who actually read all of the iPhone's OS terms and conditions. I knew firsthand that she grumbled and complained when asked to do anything, but she'd always end up helping.

Still, given the severity of the issue and that she had a legal background, I needed to contact her immediately. I texted her to let her know we needed to talk.

That left me time to speak with Peter. Compare notes. Ask

questions. See if his parents had a better understanding of this situation, given that his mom and dad were born here and were fluent in English. Assuming he'd heard the same thing I did, we needed to figure out how to help our parents save their restaurants.

But then I got his text. From Mister crowd pleaser-sunshiny-optimism himself.

SHIT SHIT SHIT SHIT SHIT SHIT SHIT we're royally screwed

Shit.

If peppy Peter Li says we are royally screwed...we are doomed.

Doomed.

NINE

CHLOE

I GROUP TEXTED WITH ELIAS AND SOPHIA.

They're selling the mall. No more KWONS' CAFÉ. No more SANTA'S VILLAGE. And still no word from the competition 😔 😔😔😔😔😔😔😔😔

Elias initiated our video call. He had on a Korean face mask I'd given him for his birthday. "Chloe! I'm so sorry, are you at home? Can we help?" A grainy, frozen image of Sophia appeared and froze. Elias complained, "Soph, you really need to get better internet."

"I know, I know. I'm going to have to chip in to make that happen. It's weird how my parents are okay with low-quality internet from five years ago. I need Chase to convince them." Her older brother was at Purdue. The sole engineer in the family in the group of artists. I was the opposite: the photographer in the household of business-minded people.

Sophia cut off her video for a second and reappeared more clearly. "Is that better? I'm so sorry, Chloe. You were practically raised in that restaurant. Can we come over with ice cream and face masks?"

My skin desperately needed clarifying, purifying, and emulsifying (whatever that meant). I'd just walked through the door of my house and brought the phone straight into the bathroom. "Emergency mask time. I can feel the stress pimples forming." I ripped open the metallic plastic package, unfolded the drippy mask paper, and applied it to my face like a facial Band-Aid. My reflection in the mirror startled me: I was used to the white and black versions of these K-beauty facial products, but this one had honeysuckle essence, and the yellow made me look like I was wearing a jaundiced hockey mask.

Barely moving my lips like a ventriloquist, I asked, "Do you think it's possible to stop the mall demolition?"

Elias tapped his bottom lip. "I don't know, but you need to get organized. Fast. Maybe Peter could help. He has a lot at stake too."

I nodded. Peter, with his charm and good looks, could get others to band together.

Sophia chimed in, "Okay, I know your situation is dire, but I wanted to briefly point out that this is the first time anyone has brought up you-know-who's name without you going off on a long soliloquy like people do in those Aaron Sorkin movies or Shonda Rhimes shows." She leaned forward into the phone screen. "Oooooh, are you friends now?"

I thought back to the time he made fun of my elf-Yoda ears. "No." But...he'd recently paid for a photo session with Santa just to talk with me because he thought I was mad at him.

Confusing.

Elias squinted and pulled the phone to his face. "You're smiling, I can even tell through the mask. She's right, you always frown and curse when we talk about Peter. Why are you—wait. Do you *like* Peter?"

Four words I'd never heard in my entire life. Because it was a universally known fact that I did not, would not, could not ever *like* Peter Li.

Still, my face flushed with heat under my facial cover. It was supposed to have a cooling effect, but all it did was counteract the burning flush in my face to make my skin feel soggy and lukewarm, like a can of Coke that had sat out in the sun for an hour.

Sophia applied her mask and joined in on the teasing. "And you're quiet. You never miss an opportunity to bash Peter, telling us how annoying he was at school, at work, or at the restaurant. But really, are you sick or something? Do you need us to come over with emergency soup?"

"No, and no thanks."

Thank God for this mask fortress; they couldn't see my face contort like a wrung sponge. They were right about my lack of Peter eye-rolling commentary. When had this stopped? I'd done it for so long that it was practically part of my identity.

Elias said, "I think you have a crush. She thinks you have the flu. Is it possible it's...both? Ooooh, are you lovesick?"

I'd had enough. "Look, Peter's the same ol' Peter. And I'm the same ol' me. Can we just drop it? I need to figure out what to do about the mall. And making money."

"Okay, okay. It was just a joke," Sophia said. "But yeah, you have other serious problems at hand. Maybe you should go talk to the landlord on your parents' behalf. You'd need to dress more formally and be all businesslike."

Elias added, "Peter might be useful then. He's really good at chatting people up." He paused. "But you can be too, of course, but Peter's like a pro...he's...you know—"

Yeah, I knew.

Smart.

Charming.

Attractive.

Likable.

Boooooo.

Ugh.

"Enough Peter talk. It's time for a snack break."Elias went

off screen for a second and reentered the frame holding up a bag of M&M's. "I've done a ton of beauty ritual research, and M&M's and Skittles are the perfect face mask food." He inserted a green M&M into his mouth, chewed, and swallowed. "See?"

Sophia rummaged off screen and held up various bags of snacks. Cheetos. Pringles. Pocky sticks.

Elias shook his head. "No to Cheetos. You'll get cheese dust on your mask. Those Pringles are way too wide."

That left Pocky sticks. Elias and I both agreed it was a viable option. Sophia stuck a chocolate-covered stick into her mouth and muttered, "Success!"

Sadly, I had no treats. While they ate, I sat there thinking about the mall. A fleeting memory of Peter fake shoe shopping with me at Foot Locker flashed in my head and I tried to shake it out. *Not now.*

I said, "If I go see the landlord, it needs to be soon. I want to come prepared with a plan. Would you two look over a Google Doc I'll put together with some brainstormed ideas on how to handle all of this?"

Elias and Sophia both nodded and said "Yes!" in unison.

Sophia cleared her throat. "And Elias and I've been talking... We were thinking we might try to help your business out and help you make more money this holiday. We think we can bring Santa's Village to up-to-date Instagrammable standards."

"Really? How?"

Elias shook his balled fists by his cheeks in excitement and squawked, "We want to build a few fun, modern sets for you! And let's all three design new marketing materials because it looks like yours were just repurposed from the 1990s. We were going to have it be a surprise, but it seems like you could use some cheering up ASAP. Logistics-wise, we're thinking backdrops and cutouts on wheels so you can roll them around easily. At the very least, even if the mall closes, we can make this your most lucrative holiday season, and you can put more money toward your NYU college fund. Let's take money away from that North Pole monstrosity and out of Peter's pocket."

I teared up. "You two are seriously the best. Thank you."

Sophia replied, "You're very welcome. How's work going, though? Any funny or cool photo ideas we should be aware of while we create our final backdrop designs?"

"Uh, business is okay but a little worse than last year, so any sales boost would be great. Some of these kids really have a lot on their wish lists, so maybe aspirational in theme. Everyone's asking for Nintendo's latest games, electric scooters, one kid even said he wanted to stay at a five-star hotel. Who even talks like that?"

Sophia said, "Elias" at the same time he said, "I do."

We burst into a fit of giggles.

After I caught my breath, I asked, "Oh, by the way, what do you two want for Christmas?"

"Well, a five-star hotel experience, obviously." Elias peeled his mask off and with an index-finger-and-thumb pinch, tossed it into the trash can next to him. "And a trip to Paris. But the reality is I'll probably just get an Amazon gift card from everyone in my family. Am I really that hard to shop for?"

Sophia nodded so hard I thought her mask would fly off. "Are you serious? You're our best friend, and I still never know what to get you."

He scrubbed his face with a wet washcloth. "That's fair. I don't even know what to buy myself with those gift cards. What about you? What's on your wish list?"

She scratched her masked nose with her thumb. "I'd love a new iPad and stylus from Santa. I'm doing more digital art now and would love a better screen, my tablet is so old. Trying more of that instead of mixed media but it's hard without better pixilation. I love gift cards though. How 'bout you, Chloe?"

I'd heard hundreds of kids tell Santa all the things they wanted for Christmas. Ones who wanted big, expensive gifts for themselves. Or big, expensive gifts for someone else in the family. Some wanted world peace, ending homelessness, or good health. What did I want? Strangely, I hadn't really thought about it until now. Christmas was seven weeks away. I had to put my wish out into the world and will the universe to make it happen.

What did I really want?

To save the mall.

To get into the photo competition.

To be good at something. Scratch that. *I wanted to be* excep-tional *at something.*

This didn't seem like a wish I could share with mall Santa. Maybe it was even too personal to share with my best friends.

"Well, you know all the big wishes I have. Practically speak-ing, I need a new camera bag. There's a cool one I've been eyeing online and I keep hoping they'll offer a holiday promo code. And I could use some more memory cards. Depending on how the next few weeks go, my parents might only be able to afford to get me a session on one of those massage chairs near the Cinnabon. But I'd love to crash at a five-star hotel with Elias."

He laughed. "All I want as a middle child is to have that hotel room by myself. I need peace and quiet and unlimited Netflix. With unlimited room service. Get your own wish!"

"Okay, maybe I'd get the hotel room across the hall. But honestly, aside from keeping my parents' business afloat, if I could have anything in the world for myself, I know what I'd ask for." I knew. Now I needed to manifest this into actually happening.

I sat up straighter. "I want to not just get into the compe-tition, but I want to win that National Art Council contest so badly." It was the first time I'd really shared with them what I wanted in life, instead of being self-deprecating or deflecting. "I could get mentored by Lorraine Finch, and you all know she's my hero, and it would make my college applications stand out. I got an email saying I'll find out tomorrow if I'm in." I held my breath to hear their responses.

Elias beamed. "Ooooh I hope it happens." He opened his computer. "Send me over the Google Doc when you're ready. I have some ideas I want to add."

"You're so talented, Chloe, I really hope you get it." Yep, Sophia's superpower was making people feel like a million bucks.

"Thanks, you two." My greatest greatest skill in life used to be finding all sorts of ways to be down on things. But maybe, just maybe, it was time to channel positive energy. Maybe it wasn't too late to prevent the mall from being demolished. We'd set up a landlord meeting, meet with him about possible alternatives, and it would go over well. Maybe I'd get into the National Art Council competition too. Most likely not, because things like that never worked out, for me at least, but I could hope. It was the holidays, after all... It was time to make a Christmas wish and make it count.

TEN

PETER

"THINK QUICK!" I STOOD TWENTY FEET AWAY AND FLUNG a wrapped almond cookie toward Chloe, who was behind the register staring intently at her phone. She was supposed to catch it, not let it hit her face. It wasn't a wallop, but it also wasn't a little flick to her forehead either. It was just enough to bring out her instantaneous wrath. I instantly lifted my hands in surrender.

Surprisingly, her angry emoji-like face softened a few seconds after she saw the cookie was launched at her without harmful intent. In all honesty I didn't mean to hit her, especially in the face, but at the same time, I didn't want Chloe to bury her anger if she really was mad at me. That would be very unlike Chloe, who wore her emotions on her sleeve like badges of honor. And it would be something I would do: put on my "everything's fine" mask and play it off like no big deal, even if it really was.

The whole point of it all was I wanted to get her attention, which I did. I was a little early to our meeting, where we were going to brainstorm business ideas for a proposal to the mall landlord, and now she was waiting for me to say something to explain or justify my asshole cookie-to-the-head Ultimate Frisbee move. I kept my hands up and took slow deliberate steps toward the counter. "I have more of them if you want. Sorry about the throw. I wasn't trying to wreck your face or anything." *Nice one, Peter.*

Chloe muttered, "Uh, no problem." She went right back to looking at her phone.

What was so urgent that she didn't yell at me for my bad aim or threaten to sue me for nearly taking her eye out with a sugary discus? She never missed an opportunity to outwardly express her frustration with my very existence. Something else, something big was happening to distract her from her favorite hobby: hating me.

I took a few more steps forward. "Our updated menu looks really good, thanks to your photography. Mom and Dad even paid extra to get one of those QR codes to link to it. We updated our Yelp pages and website too. Really appreciate your help."

She pulled her gaze away from her screen. "That's cool. I'm glad it worked out. I need to do some for my parents' restaurant." With a sad-sounding exhale, she added, "But maybe it's not worth the trouble if they're closing anyway." She went back to scrolling and tapping.

"We need to think positively. But if you're busy now, maybe we could brainstorm later during another dinner swap? I'm here till closing."

She nodded but didn't disclose what was so important to steal all of her attention. Chloe looked over her shoulder at her dad, who was busy organizing the plastic silverware, napkins, and cups into precarious stacks and ignoring our conversation. "You want your usual later? Spicy pork?"

This time she managed to make lengthy eye contact. The longest I'd seen without any accompanying eye-rolling. "And I'll go with the shrimp thing again. It was really good last week." She paused. "Do you really think we can save the mall?"

I gave her the most optimistic smile I could muster, which was like maybe a seven out of a ten-point scale. "We can sure as hell try. And we have two of us."

She bit her bottom lip. "But even superheroes have ensembles. It's just you and me here."

My smile widened, easily a nine out of ten. "That's double the brainpower. Double the manpower. And we have complementing skill sets. You're artistically gifted, and I'm—" *How do I say this without sounding like an asshole*—"Business-minded. We'll be a good team."

Her eyes sparkled, making my stomach do a little flip. Chloe opened her mouth to reply but then her phone buzzed. "Oh God. Oh God-oh-God-oh-God. It's time." She did that thing that people did when they were watching horror movies in a theater and hiding their eyes, but also peeking. Chloe looked at her phone through her fingers, then with a wince, turned away, then glanced back again, hesitating, wincing, sucking her teeth.

I had to ask. Watching her was excruciating. "Can you tell me what's going on?"

"The National Art Council competition finalists have been announced. And I'm scared to see who made it." She tapped three times. "Shit! I think so many people logged in at the same time that the server crashed. It says the site is down for maintenance, argh!"

I looked up the National Art Council contest on my phone and refreshed a few times. "Mine's working," I said.

"Really? Can I use your phone? Please?" She glanced behind her to see what her dad was doing. He was still ignoring us.

The thing was, the Lis never crossed over the Kwon border. The last time I did it was for the rice donation, and that had me walking around like I was surrounded by trip wires and land mines. To do it again, and to let her borrow a phone no less, seemed reckless.

But Chloe's face. For the first time, she looked at me the way I wanted others to see me. I wanted people to see me as valuable. Genuine. And important.

My mom was talking to someone in the kitchen, so I used this chance to move closer to the Kwons' counter. I handed Chloe my phone.

"Th-thanks." She smiled and scrolled slowly.

Sooooo slowly. Did she not see how badly I was sweating from crossing enemy lines?

I wanted to tear the phone out of her hand and just use the find function to search for her name.

"Oh God. Oh God-oh-God-oh-God-oh-shit. Peter! I'm a finalist!" She beamed as she handed back my phone. Then she grabbed it back, took a screenshot, and AirDropped it to herself. Then she pretended to fling the phone toward my head and my arm jerked up in response. "Just kidding, I wouldn't do that. That's retaliation for the cookie incident." She smiled and handed it back.

I deserved that. "Congratulations, Chloe." My arms lifted with an instinct to hug her, but suddenly I was aware of her body's proximity to mine, and how sweaty I already was, so I brought my arms down and offered a double thumbs-up. *Good God, what is wrong with me today?*

I really did feel bad about the projectile dessert now, being flung at her face right before her big moment. It was supposed to be more of a peace offering but it could have ruined the progress we'd made between us. Before, we were like the Korean Jets and the Chinese Sharks, with the possibility of murder. Now, we were friendlier. Maybe even friends? I backed away while stumbling over an aluminum dining chair before I could ruin this good thing we had going on now.

She turned around to say something to her dad as I continued retreating to my original position several yards away. He nodded and turned back around to what he was doing—sorting the spices and condiments. Then Chloe called me, even though she was only a few feet away.

I picked up on the first ring. "Hey. Did you tell him about the competition? Mine don't usually care about stuff outside of academics so I don't bother. In fact, they don't actually care at all about any of my sports." I said that last part with a bitter taste in my mouth. Even though I'd made cross-country varsity my sophomore year, Mom had actually wanted me to quit, saying it was pointless to keep competing if I wasn't going to the Olympics. But when one of the kids we knew got into a good college with an archery scholarship and not a piano or academic one, she said I could continue varsity level as long as my grades didn't suffer. Gee, thanks for that, mom.

Chloe let out an exasperated sigh. "I just told my Dad and he just kind of—I don't know, acted like I'd just told him the grocery store restocked a new brand of toilet paper or something, like it was just an update. I don't think they get how big of a deal it is. There's less than a five percent chance of getting selected to be a finalist."

"Yeah, I hear you loud and clear. My parents are fixated on Sam and ignore most of what I do." Chloe was so lucky to actually be good at something though. My brother Sam was the smart one. He was the firstborn son, who came out screaming at the top of his iron-steel lungs, whereas I was the sickly, jaundiced baby in the NICU. I was always trying to keep up with my brother, be as good at him, or at least appear to be as good as him, but it was impossible. My parents' friends joked that I was Sam's Shadow, and they weren't wrong. I really did feel that way all the time.

I'd learned some few tricks from Sam, the master himself, who had done better in school than me with half the effort. He'd gotten drunk and high on graduation night and snuck home at 4 a.m. and entered my bedroom by mistake. In exchange for my silence, he'd told me the secret to his academic success: 1) always be agreeable, 2) don't rock the boat at home or at school, 3) chat up teachers after class and 4) be nice to everyone, nerds especially, because you never knew who you'd need to copy homework from in a pinch. Then Sam laughed and patted my back. "Lemme know if you ever need me to—" he said before passing out on my bed. I never knew what he'd offered. When Sam woke up the next morning he didn't remember anything.

Chloe's mood lifted as she chattered to me about her competition. I was happy for her to some degree, but I have to admit, I was jealous too. Imagine knowing exactly what you wanted to do in life. I wished I was talented like her. Meanwhile my entire existence had been centered on Sam, being like him, or better than him, so the only way to beat him or differentiate myself was through nonacademic activities. Where did that lead me? Spreading myself thin and by doing so many things, I'd opened myself up to more opportunities for jealousy and failure. I didn't even like art or photography, and here I was, feeling a little envious of Chloe, like I should have given this competition a shot too.

Chloe squealed, "Maybe I can request Lorraine Finch to be my mentor. How cool is this?"

"So cool." *Mental note, google Lorraine Finch.*

"Oh shit! I have to tell Elias and Soph! Gotta go."

Click.

As she ended her call, Chloe's mom walked through the food court, throwing me a death stare and frowning at the sight of me as she trudged past the demilitarized zone and headed toward Kwons' Café. Damn, she was so intimidating.

Chloe untied her apron, folded it, and stuck it under the register. She shouted, "Umma! You're back! I'm a finalist in that photography contest I told you about. Is it okay if I leave today to hang out with Elias and Sophia in a few minutes? I want to tell them the good news and to celebrate."

The food court was practically empty so it was easy to overhear Chloe's conversation. I filled the napkin dispenser quietly so I could listen to every word.

Her mom looked around the food court and nodded.

"Thanks, Umma!"

Chloe tapped her phone and stuck in her Bluetooth earbuds. "I have news! Let me add Soph to the call. She better answer... Are you ready for the update? I'm a finalist!" Chloe walked away toward the exit.

A wave of sadness rippled through me. She'd left me for her friends without remembering we had dinner plans. Not like what we agreed to was that big of a deal. We weren't going out on a date or anything. I didn't mind eating out a takeout container in the cold alley with her. In fact, maybe I enjoyed it.

But the dinner swap...spicy pork for the shrimp stir-fry special... We'd made a plan. She abandoned the plan. She forgot about me. Still, I was happy for her. But sad for me, and my stomach.

I guess it was possible to buy the spicy pork combo from Kwons', but my mom and dad would not be pleased. In fact, they might disown me if they even saw the "Thank you for shopping Kwons' Café!" plastic bags anywhere near Empress Garden.

I went back to work at my parents' restaurant and helped pack a few to-go items, stapling shut the brown bags to prevent outside tampering and to show which orders were completed. My parents were adamant about making sure the customers knew we took their order safety seriously.

After stapling and lining up six bags in a row on the counter, I noticed a Kwons' Café bag next to the register. I looked out to the food court to see if a customer had left it, but there didn't seem to be anyone who looked like they were missing their dinner. Everyone was already eating.

I smirked when I saw that the Kwons' Café folks didn't staple their bags closed like we did. I pictured my parents complaining about this incessantly: "Careless. Sloppy. Not good for their business!"

Without pulling out the contents, I reached inside the bag

and popped the container open. A familiar smell of spicy pork drifted toward me.

A text buzzed my phone.

Chloe.

> Sorry I ran out forgetting about dinner swap.
> Scatterbrained! Here's my part of the agreement.
> Soph and Elias want to take me to Coldstone
> Creamery to celebrate, I guess that's my dinner
> tonight. Raincheck on mine please?

She must've gotten my dinner together while I was working in the back. Before I could reply, she sent an animated GIF of a kitten with prayer hands.

I replied **I owed you for that never-to-be-spoken-about-again almond cookie incident from earlier, so we're even.**

I waited for her reply, which came a minute later.

What incident? She followed it with a winky face.

Free dinner and a winky-face emoji from Chloe Kwon? This day couldn't have turned out any better.

But then it did, when she wrote one more time.

> Brainstorm and dinner swap tomorrow?

ELEVEN

CHLOE

PETER AND I AGREED TO ATTEND THE MONTHLY MALL coalition meeting. Maybe there was already an effort underway to save Riverwood Mall.

The door to the community room was slightly ajar when we arrived. We walked in as two people stood and shouted at each other in front of the room. It was Mrs. Mishra from the incense store and Mr. Hall from shoe repair.

"We need a real lawyer now, this has gotten serious!" Mrs. Mishra scowled as she crossed her arms.

"Lawyers are expensive, and we don't have enough dues to cover legal fees! Where are these funds supposed to come from, a magical cash reserve? We barely have enough to cover basic marketing with our membership dues," Mr. Hall said with a raised voice.

Mom was in the back row, on the far opposite side from Mrs. Li, of course, with a stack of papers in her lap. I sat next to her and watched as she scanned words on the pages using the Google Translate app. Mom glanced up when I sat next to her and at first looked like she didn't even recognize me. She glared over my shoulder and made disapproving tut-tut sounds with her tongue.

"Why you come here with him?" she whispered just loud enough for the people in the row ahead of her to cause them to turn their heads.

Peter passed us and sat with his mother and texted me. I'll try to find out from Mom if they have anything planned. You do same and we can compare notes.

Good idea, I replied.

I know, he answered back. Why did he always have to ruin these nicer moments with his swaggitude? I swear, if he could just be humble for once...

"Your appa need me?"

My mind refocused on the present. She asked a logical question. Why else would I barge into a stakeholder meeting to find her?

"No, he doesn't. I came here because I need you to tell me what is going on. Is anyone here stopping the landlord from selling the mall?"

She looked up from the Google Translate app and instead stared at the ensuing argument between Mrs. Mishra and Mr.

Hall. They were still discussing whether or not the coalition should hire a real estate lawyer.

Mom sighed. "I don't understand."

I tried to grab the papers from her lap and she swatted my hand. "This is for parents, not for kids."

The heated debate subsided between Mrs. Mishra and Mr. Hall. They'd reached some kind of truce, agreeing that they should seek legal representation rather than keep using Mr. Hall's nephew to represent them and explain their rights. In their shouting match it had been revealed that the nephew attended law school but not only hadn't trained in real estate law, he also hadn't passed the state bar exam despite many attempts.

The meeting adjourned. Mom shoved the papers into her shopping-cart-size purse. "You wanting to talk? We can talk now."

Peter left with his mom. Hopefully he could get some truthful answers from his mom and dad.

I began my inquisition. "This mall, is it really being demolished? Is there any way to change the landlord's mind?" The crowd dwindled to just a few people lingering to pick at the Krispy Kreme glazed doughnuts in the back of the room.

My mom stood up and worked her way out of the row of folding chairs, her giant tote bag purse swinging and knocking some of the metal seats, widening my path unnecessarily. I opened the door for us, letting her pass through first.

"Everyone last year say our landlord son was going to sell to new landlord. But now they say he selling to a company who will knock down building and make condominium."

I swallowed hard. "They were talking today about getting a real lawyer. Does that mean you have time to fight this? Mrs. Mishra and Mr. Hall are pretty vocal. Is there anyone in the food court who is speaking up for you all?"

She shrugged.

No.

I messaged Hannah, who still hadn't replied to my "hey can you call me" earlier text. SOS NEED TO TALK ASAP.

Finally, she wrote back, saying she was out to lunch with colleagues and would be free in thirty minutes.

Then I messaged Peter. Lunch, take two? Same place, same food?

He wrote back immediately. I'm already waiting for you.

Though everything seemed dire, seeing Peter's face light up when he saw me made me feel better. Warmer. Calmer. Like maybe he'd heard something promising and hope was not all lost.

I sat down across from him and picked at my cold lo mein. "They're selling this mall, or trying to at least, and in the stack of papers my parents don't know I snooped through I found a memo that says there's a council meeting in late December for a final hearing, and on January 15 they'll pull demolition permits. Did your parents reveal anything else that can help us?"

He wiped his mouth with his napkin. "They told me the same thing, that they were hoping to stop the sale of the property, but the coalition was so disorganized that it was now getting to a point where they might be too late."

I put my chopsticks down. "But you're smiling."

"I am? Maybe because this spicy pork is even better when it's lukewarm. I love this stuff. Also, you looked pretty sad, so I tried to cheer you up." He grinned again, but this one seemed more forced.

"You're always so upbeat. Don't you have an off button?" His face fell, and I immediately regretted my words. "I'm sorry, I'm just stressed. It's this mall disaster, and the reality of placing as a finalist in the competition is settling in. How am I going to study for finals and get mentored and do the final project with all this mall stress? Anyway, taking it out on you isn't okay. I'm sorry. Thank you for putting up with me."

He said softly, "I'm stressed too. This whole thing is a disaster, and I have no idea why our parents didn't tell us their restaurants were in jeopardy. You're right, though. I should take this all more seriously. My parents started to pare down their menu, I just noticed. I'm sad to report there are no more sesame balls."

Nooooooo! Those were my favorite!

He continued. "If we're getting involved, we're going to have to be vocal and not be pushovers. That's way outside my comfort zone. I'm not that kind of guy. I'm always trying to smooth things over, laugh stuff off, and not rock the boat. It's my brother's key to success. It's how I get by."

I wanted to say *I noticed*, but offered an understanding smile instead. I was proud of myself for that. "Well, I'm the opposite. I'm Chicken Little. The sky is always falling around me." It was something I'd been aware of for a long time but wasn't something I actively tried to work on. It was the opposite of Peter's "can do" mantra. His positive outlook took you farther in life than my "can't do" attitude.

"I don't want to jinx anything, but...what would your parents do if they didn't have Kwons' Café?" he asked. "Would they open a new place? Do something else?"

I chewed my bottom lip. "It's hard to imagine them doing anything else. Or doing anything new. I honestly have no idea. I don't think they can." Pressure compressed my lungs, and my eyes watered at the thought of them starting over. *Oh no, no crying. Not in front of Peter.* I swallowed hard, hoping to push down my feelings. "Ever since middle school, I've had a real love-hate thing with this mall. Because of the restaurant, my mom and dad missed school events like concerts and ceremonies and plays. We don't go on vacations because no one would be here to mind the restaurant. It's always home, school, and the mall. Over and over again. I feel like I live on a spaceship or cruise ship and can't escape."

Peter frowned. When he did that, his dimple disappeared. I didn't like that, and I didn't like that I'd made him sad.

"I get it. All of it. I wanted so badly for my parents to have a nine-to-five job. That I could come home and there'd be a home-cooked dinner on the table or cookies baking in the oven. Everything in our fridge is from Costco or Sam's because that's basically the only shopping our family does," he said.

"And you know what else?" he added. "No, never mind."

I cocked my head. "Well, now I want to know."

"Fine. I felt bad because when I found out about this whole legal thing, all I kept thinking was...this is terrible...but then maybe my family can do something else so I can live my life my way and not always worry about my parents and their restaurant." His shoulders slumped. "But now I feel so shitty I thought that, and I'm freaked out about how they're going to make money. I don't know if they can weather this."

I grabbed his hand and then quickly let it go when a bolt of energy pulsed through me. Electricity flowed up my arm and through my body. It was like he'd zapped me.

He didn't let the hand thing bother him. "I'll be especially sad if it's the end of our truce." Peter looked at me and smiled, and my urge to cry vanished.

We ate in silence, politely nibbling at first, but then wolfing down our food as the outside temperature dropped by the second. Now that it was a couple of weeks past Halloween, we were officially in down jacket season. But not quite "see your breath as you talk or cough" season. I lifted my drink and noticed that it didn't even leave a ring of wetness on the table. That's how cold it was out there. I shivered in response.

That's when I looked down and noticed a small vase the size of a salt shaker, with one tiny purple flower placed in the narrow opening. "Did you bring that too?"

He blushed. "Yeah, uh, I did. I wanted us to have a nice meal and pretend we weren't at the food court, and pretend our lives weren't falling apart. But it's funny, now that Kwons' Café and Empress Garden might not be around for long, all I want to do now is to be at our mall, eating food court lunches at those aluminum tables and chairs that screech when you move them. They're always streaked with wetness from the table bussers who are constantly wiping everything down."

I leaned forward to examine the flower. It looked like a rose, but it was strikingly purple, in a way that a rose couldn't be. "Thanks for bringing the ambiance."

He laughed. "I stole it from the counter of the Greek place next to us. I'll bring it back later. They have like ten of them."

I couldn't help but to grin. He borrowed a flower for me. It was a thoughtful and odd thing to do. "I'll be honest, eating lunch and staring at this flower made me feel a little better. I'm not much of a flower person though, overall."

He furrowed his brow. "What kind of monster doesn't like flowers? Are you allergic?"

"Noooo, I just think they can be a hassle. How they bloom, then die. And then you have to dispose of these sticks of death while pouring out weird brown water that these dying flowers somehow produced. It's all weird if you ask me."

"*You're* weird. So what do you like more than flowers then?"

"Balloons over flowers."

"Interesting. I don't like balloons because they pop. Hate that sound."

"Not if you get the Mylar ones. Mylar over latex, hands down."

"Good to know. One more. Paperback or ebook?"

"Paperback over ebook."

He chuckled. "Okay...I lied, one more. Vanilla ice cream or chocolate frozen yogurt?"

"Those aren't even the sa—"

"That's the point. Vanilla *ice cream* or chocolate *frozen yogurt*?"

"How many more of these do you have stored up in that brain of yours?" I asked.

"Thousands. Maybe millions," he joked.

I couldn't help but laugh. "Maybe we should get back to what we were talking about and save those millions for another time."

"Fine. We'll pick it up later."

"I sent you a Google Doc with my own brainstorm. Sadly, I didn't have a lot of business ideas in there, and Elias and Sophia added 'sexy Santa year-round' as a joke. Could you add a few of your own in there tonight?"

Peter cracked a smile. "I'm hoping to think of some while I work out at the gym. I think better that way."

I rolled my eyes. "You and your daily iron pumping. Anyway, did your mom or dad tell you if the tenants were being relocated?"

He shook his head. "Nah, they said that there was that final city council meeting in a few weeks that they think will determine everything. But if you ask me, it'll be too late by then. Did you look at the older paperwork? It looks like the mall is selling because it's not as profitable anymore. Last year was the first time they actually lost money on the property because of wind damage repairs, which is kind of a miracle if you think about it, seeing as how all the other malls have closed. They have a developer interested, but they're looking to tear down, whereas the mall owner is also considering selling to a retail corporation who would put capital into renovating it. My dad says the landlord doesn't want the businesses to be evicted, but he doesn't want year-over-year declines either. It's all in the older coalition memos."

This was all new to me. My parents didn't tell me any of this or show me this paperwork. But at least now we knew the scope of the situation. Channeling some of Peter's positivity, I said, "We need to save the mall. We can do this."

"We? Like *us*? Like, me and you?"

I nodded. "Us. Like, me and you."

He smiled. "I have no idea how, but I'm willing to try. As long as you and I—"

My phone's ringer blared on full volume. A FaceTime request from Hannah. "I need to take this, it's my sister, *finally*. I'll catch you later."

"Okay, let me know what she says." He swaggered away, and I watched him disappear into the building.

The loud rings finally stole my attention away from Peter's backside. "Hey sis."

She closed her eyes and breathed deep. "I'm on a big case and don't have time to chit chat. What's so urgent?"

Hannah was scary. I couldn't even imagine how intimidating she'd be as an actual lawyer one day. "It's about Mom and Dad. Did you get my last text?"

Her face changed and she leaned forward. "I was busy. What's wrong? Are they sick? Did they get into an accident?"

"No, jeez, Hannah. Not any of those, thank God."

Hannah's nostrils flared, a sign of impatience. I had to hurry up. "The mall might be closing permanently. That means no more Kwons' Café."

She shook her head before I finished talking. "No, that's impossible. A couple years ago when I was there over Christmas break I helped them renew their seven-year lease. Or maybe it a few Christmases ago, I can't remember. You can't be right."

"Why would I lie about something like this?" *Ha ha, joke's on*

you, Hannah. I love pranking about our parents losing their business...
Happy Thanksgiving and Merry early Christmas to you! I explained,
"I don't know much about real estate law here in Tennessee, but
it looks like they have some sale-related paperwork they've sat on
a long time. And they didn't share it with us because they didn't
want to bother you or me, but now there's hardly any time to do
anything to stop this."

A woman walked by Hannah and whispered something in her
ear. I could only see a fragment of her right side, but she had on a
sharp gray suit and a light blue blouse.

Hannah sighed. "I need to go to a meeting now. Let me think
about it. If you have a chance can you email or take photos of any
paperwork they have? Maybe there are deadlines and requirements we can contest to buy us more time."

I knew she was the right person to ask. She was the smart and
strategic one in the family. "Yep, I'll do that in a few minutes. I'll
try to find out how to get us an appointment to see the landlord;
maybe we can propose some ideas to consider. Mom had a new
stack of papers today with tenants' rights information, I'll send
that to you right away. Thanks, Palindrome."

She cracked a small smile. "One day you'll get too old for
that joke, and it'll make me sad." In first grade, we studied
palindromes in school, and when the teacher said race car and
madam were some examples and asked us to come up with our
own, I realized Hannah spelled the same thing forward and

backward, and "Mom" and "Dad" did too, and cried because I wanted a palindrome name and felt left out. But then Hannah called me Otto for a whole week, and I shut up about that real quick.

Hannah always knew what to do. The right person was here now. Yay, Hannah, yay! Another palindrome.

My parents had an old-school metal filing cabinet stuffed with manila folders where they kept their important documents in their office. I found the memos about the mall closure, but a wave of nausea hit me when I saw that there was building sale–related paperwork dating back half a year. They had known about all of this for six months, maybe more, and not said a word about it to us.

On some of the earlier documents, Mom and Dad had both written notes in the margins: Korean translations of some of the English words. Thumbing through the pages, Mom and Dad had underlined sections and commented "*Ask Hannah*" and "*???*" on nearly every paragraph. In the most recent coalition correspondence, they hadn't written anything. Had they not had time to read any of it? Did they not understand and were they waiting to ask Hannah? Or had they simply given up?

I took photos of everything and sent them to Hannah, about twenty pages total. Then I logged into the office computer and checked the business email for anything I may have missed that came through electronically. After comparing the dates on the stack of documents to the opened emails in the inbox, it looked like Umma and Appa had printed everything out. When Hannah confirmed receipt, I turned off the lights in the back office and walked to the front, where Dad was helping a subset of the Silver Sneakers choose a meal. I whispered to him, "I talked to Umma. I know what's going on about the mall. We all need to talk."

A quick exhale spurted out of his nose. *Fine*, his nose replied.

"Why the long face, sweetie?" Estelle Chase was our most loyal customer and had supported our place for over ten years. Her pure white curls shimmered in the fluorescent light. It looked like one of those photos of Thomas Jefferson in his wig, but in this case, her hair was real...as far as I could tell at least.

My dad looked over at me. "Her face is not very long. It more like a circle. Like a pie."

"Thanks, Dad." He was smiling when he said it, and I knew he loved all pies, so I knew this was him teasing, and if anything, an actual compliment.

I chewed my bottom lip, unsure of whether it was okay to even mention the potential closing of the mall to Estelle. I had no idea how public of knowledge this was. I kept my mouth shut and answered, "Oh, the usual stress, plus the holidays." *And, you know, in what should be the happiest time of my life, me getting into the competition of my dreams, the restaurant that you've been coming to for over a decade may be smashed into bits by a wrecking ball soon.*

I looked over at Empress Garden, to see if Peter was still around. Only his parents were visible: his mom was writing the limited specials on the dry-erase board, and his dad was on the phone. A melancholy sigh escaped me when I focused my attention back on Estelle and her stark white Revolutionary War hair.

"Well, I hope it's nothing. Though I'd say looking over there, you have more than nothing going on." She pointed over her shoulder and as my gaze followed an invisible straight path, I saw Peter in the distance, talking to one of the other Silver Sneaker ladies, but staring right at me. My face flushed with heat. Estelle chuckled. "He's been looking over here for at least five minutes, and as much as I know I still got it, he's not lookin' at me, sweetheart!" She patted her curls on her shoulders.

Had he really been looking over here the whole time? I glanced over again and he didn't look away. Instead, he held up an almond cookie in a wrapper and mimed like he was going to pitch it toward me. I laughed but also instinctively ducked, in case he went through with it.

Estelle laughed. "Well, that's more like it. Nothing like young love to turn that long face into a smiling one."

Love? Was she joking?

Judging by her huge grin and wagging finger, she was not. Insert barf emoji here.

My dad ignored her comment. "Chloe is too busy for love. She has school and work and...some kind of drawing contest."

"National Art Council Youth photography competition," I corrected. Honestly, the fact that he cared to remember me doing anything other than academics was a win in my book.

"Oh Chloe, that's wonderful." Estelle was an artist, a sculptor in her retired days after a long career in corporate America. Out of anyone I knew, she would understand my creative passions and desire to go against the grain. "If you need any kind of recommendation, let me know. As a fellow artiste, from a family of doctors, lawyers, and financiers who still nag me about my career choices, I get it. We're one and the same."

I loved Estelle to death, but there were obvious things that set us apart, and not just because of the age difference. She was from old money. Like Vanderbilt family money. She didn't know what it was like to be a second-gen Korean whose parents came to the United States to live out their dreams, only to have one kid turn out to be an artist and see everything they built from the ground up literally demolished before their very eyes fifteen years later.

Another Silver Sneaker walker joined Estelle in line. She was approximately the same age, nearly identical length of curly hair, but her mane was dyed jet black.

"Estelle, can you get me a bulgogi bowl and a Diet Coke? I'll go find us a table." Her strong perfume lingered even though she walked away.

My dad said, "One bulgogi bowl. One Diet Coke. You need help to decide yours today, Estelle?"

Estelle studied the menu every time she came to our restaurant, and she always ended up ordering one of two things: the bulgogi bowl or beef mandu with side salad. This had gone on forever, even as we changed the offerings over the years. It was fine though, just funny that she'd pore over the menu, ask questions about ingredients and spice levels, but always pick combo 1 or 7. She had also told my parents that she liked their restaurant better than Empress Garden. Estelle was their favorite customer of all time.

Predictably, she ordered the exact same meal as her dining companion, and she dropped a five dollar tip into the glass container, as she always did. "Chloe, I mean it, if you need anything...a recommendation or advice or need me to contact anyone in the community, give me a holler." She handed me a business card. ESTELLE CHASE, ARTIST-IN-RESIDENCE, OLD FOLKS HOME. "My family hates it when I hand those out over the holidays during our fancy soirees. Speaking of which, I can't believe it'll be Christmas in almost six weeks!" She laughed and pointed to the glass doors. "Oh wow! It's already a winter wonderland out there!"

It looked like someone had shaken a snow globe and the mall was in the center of it. Just outside the exit was a life-size outdoor nativity display, now dusted with white, powdery snow. The religious organizations who put up the nativity sets every year came from all kinds of backgrounds, and as such the Little Town of Bethlehem at Riverwood Mall Display represented all different colors, ethnicities, shapes, and sizes. Black baby Jesus was swaddled in a manger next to Guatemalan Mary, being greeted by three older Wise Women who looked like Sophia, Rose, and Dorothy from the Golden Girls.

The snow covered the ground with gleaming sparkles. Everything outside looked so perfect and pristine, untainted by footsteps and car tire treads, which would soon come. I looked at Appa, and he looked back at me, offering a slight smile on his face but expressing distress in his eyes. When he offered Estelle, his favorite customer, a shaky and weak "Hope you enjoy. Happy Holiday," I knew why. He thought this could be our last holiday at Riverwood.

TWELVE

CHLOE

EVERYTHING WAS A DISASTER. THEN IT GOT WORSE.

"I'm withdrawing from the competition. It's a hell no for me."
I handed Sophia my phone listing all the finalist responsibilities.

Sophia glanced at it and scooped whipped cream into her
mouth. "Are you really that scared of public speaking? I mean, it's
only a five-minute presentation. And it says 'up to five minutes,'
so technically you could speak for ten seconds and run off the
stage and it would count. All you have to do is pitch your portfolio to the committee at the end of the program. That shouldn't
be too hard."

My stomach lurched. "It's in front of the committee, plus the
board, plus all the donors. And my future mentor." I looked up
past photos of the finalist event. "There are over one hundred

people in the ballroom! All wearing suits and gowns. No way am I doing this. I hate how I sound. How I look. And it'll take so much time. Nope."

"You don't think eventually you'll have to present your work to people? In college or grad school? I think you should see this as a prime opportunity."

I sighed. "A prime disaster-in-the-making. Okay, so let's say you're right, that this is a chance to impress people. What if I don't?"

I'd had plenty of opportunities to perform or speak in my past. Piano recitals. Class plays. Memorizing the prologue of the Canterbury Tales in Middle English and reciting it for a grade. All of them had my stomach tied in knots the night before, leaving my hands tingling and sweating. And then there was that one time I was the narrator of the school's theater production and I blanked on my lines. It was being recorded and streamed, and could very well rank as the worst day of my life. Of all the things that were challenging and unnatural for me, public speaking was the worst.

I really did hate how I looked on video and camera. I was the only person I knew who took makeup school photos and looked way worse the second time.

Elias shot me a sly grin. "Don't they say when you're nervous about speaking in front of an audience you should picture everyone naked?"

A harsh laugh burst out of me. "You know what's more

terrifying than reciting a speech in front of over a hundred people? Giving a speech to over a hundred nude people. So no. Not helpful."

Sophia asked, "Is there a way to still be a finalist and not give the speech? Have it pre-recorded? Like maybe you pretend you're sick or you lost your voice, get a body double? I'd do it for you."

Sophia and I shared the same clothing size and had roughly the same frame. There was one problem: she was two inches taller, her hair was a mousy brown, and she had translucent glowing skin with small freckles. Elias would have a better chance of passing as me. At least his hair was dark brown and he didn't burn as soon as he stepped foot out in the sunshine.

I hadn't thought about other alternatives. But I loved that my friends were not all "face your fears!" and "practice makes perfect," and were tolerant of my "to keep fears at bay, run away!" mentality. My brain nearly shut down when I discovered the link at the bottom of the congratulatory email, leading to more information about the local finalist presentations at the awards ceremony. Four of us had placed in our grand state of Tennessee. Two, including me, were from the Nashville area. One Gatlinburg. One Memphis. Even more people to be in the audience I was petrified of speaking in front of. Subconsciously I may have chosen art as my high school elective because it was the only thing that didn't deal with any kind of public performance. Band, chorus, and theater all did.

My competitors probably also didn't have the fate of a mall and their parents' livelihood dangling from a fragile lo mein noodle.

Sophia cocked her head. "I can see the wheels turning in your head. Stop being so down on yourself. Maybe you should take it in stride. Be a finalist. Get the mentorship. Then wait and see about the rest. Maybe you can find a way to work in the final project with the mall somehow. The speech is in like six weeks, right? That's plenty of time to figure out what to do. I can help. Elias can too. We got this."

Before I could stress how we didn't, in fact, *got this*, another email notification appeared on my home screen, with the subject *"FINALIST MENTOR PAIRING ANNOUNCED."*

I clicked. The first name listed, Mallory Abrams, was paired with my all-time-VIP-number-one-favorite photographer in the world, Lorraine Finch. My chest compressed so hard I had trouble breathing, and tears queued up in my ducts, ready to fall in a matter of seconds.

Scrolling down to the Ks, I saw my name. Chloe Kwon.

I grinned. "Okaaaaay...I think I'll stick with it, at least until I meet my new mentor. WHO IS. LORRAINE. FREAKING. FINCH!" Lorraine was the only one mentoring two finalists.

Sophia squealed. "Eeeeee Lorraine? The Lorraine Finch of *National Geographic*, *Smithsonian*, and the *Washington Post*? Oh my God!"

We hugged just as two texts appeared. One was a message from Peter. Dinner soon? Same place, same time, same spicy pork.

The second? From an unknown number with a 615 area code. Hello it's Lorraine Finch, your mentor. Very nice to meet you. I'm so sorry but they didn't give me your email address, only your phone number. Could you please respond with your email contact info at your earliest convenience? Have a wonderful evening.

Holy shit. Lorraine Finch had my phone number. Lorraine Finch texted me.

As I stood to bus my table, I showed Sophia and Elias my phone. "I'm a big deal now."

Sophia laughed. "You are."

Elias added, "And you're unstoppable."

Even if I needed to eventually drop out of the competition because of stage fright, or social anxiety, or from the mall demolition, I knew one thing: Lorraine Finch needed to be my mentor. No, actually, she WOULD be my mentor...because it was happening.

Lorraine Finch.

My mentor.

Wow.

THIRTEEN

PETER

"THERE'S NO HOMEWORK TODAY. C'MON, CAN'T YOU skip out on work after school just once? Play hooky one time?"

I don't know how many times I'd explained to Kip and Brach that I had two duties after work. The virtual reality job, which paid a little bit over minimum wage, and was how I earned spending money. Then there was my no-wage job of helping my parents close up their restaurant. Clean the grill. Wipe the counters. Take the trash to the dumpster. The easiest task I had was to make sure the receipts tallied every night, which took me no time, and was the most satisfying when the numbers balanced. Working at the restaurant was something I'd done my entire life. My brother was off to college now, but when he was living here we used to split the work or alternate days. Now the burden was all on me.

He picked a college three time zones away... I had to think it had something to do with wanting to get far away from all this.

I always did everything Mom and Dad asked. And my teachers asked. People said I had a great attitude and was a real team player. It was hard to say no to my friends, too, so it tore me up knowing I couldn't hang out the way they wanted.

But maybe a compromise would work. "Nah, I have to head to work and get in a quick workout beforehand. If you guys wanna hit the gym together we could do that, or we can go to the arcade later tonight. I could maybe take my break with you. The first round of Starshooters is on me." I hated to resort to bribery, but I also didn't want to lose my friends because I was constantly bailing on them and feeling like a flat third wheel when I did show up to things.

They looked unconvinced, so I added, "Olivia comes to the mall a lot. One of her friends works at that new ice cream place across the street in that new condo complex, the Scoopery. Or Scoop'd. Something trendy like that. I think her family owns it."

Both of them were in love with Olivia. She was new to the school, therefore super interesting to everyone because it was rare to have someone transfer in while the school year was in progress. Personally, I didn't understand how someone could fall for someone so hard without, you know, talking to them. She was pretty, sure. But what was it about her they loved? Her aura? Her ability to match clothes? Olivia didn't have any extracurriculars as far as we could tell, so they didn't even have common interests. It was purely based on hotness.

Don't get me wrong, if she asked me on a date, I'd go. And rub it in to Kip and Brach.

"Ok, let's hit the arcade and then go get ice cream," Kip said.

It didn't take Brach much convincing. He was already looking up the hours of operation at the ice cream place on his phone. "It's called 'Got the Scoop' and it's open late. Meet at the mall after dinner? Sorry Peter, no gym for me. It smells like feet in there."

That was perfect. I'd get in a quiet workout, shower, and start my shift at the VR station. Then eat my spicy pork dinner, play some video games with my buddies, and help my parents close up. Busy, but manageable.

I parked my car in the outdoor lot and stuffed my North Pole 3D Adventure black polo into a duffel bag. One thing I didn't love about my mall job was having to wear a uniform. I ended up buying a few of the same shirt, mainly because I worked so often, and laundry didn't get done anywhere near the same frequency.

Even though I had my puffy down coat zipped up to my neck as I walked a short distance to the mall's main entrance, my teeth still chattered. The heat of the mall whooshed around me when the automatic doors opened, and the welcoming scent of Annie's Pretzels made my mouth water. When I was little I used to love eating those twisted doughy knots, but my tastes changed. I was more of a savory and spicy (pork) kind of guy.

FIT YES gym was practically empty, aside from the few ladies from the Silver Sneaker crew hooting and hollering in the corner while doing bicep curls together with the smallest hand weights. I loved chatting with them, but because it was leg day for me, I was on the other side of the gym near all the machines. I pulled up my express routine on my phone notes app and got started.

4 Sets of
→ Squat–3 sets of 10,10,8,8 reps
→ Dumbbell Lunge–2 sets of 10 on each leg
→ 45-Degree Leg Press–2 sets of 15 reps
→ Leg Curl–3 sets of 15 reps
→ Leg Extension–3 sets of 15 reps
→ Standing Calf Raise–5 sets of 10,8,8,8,6 (heavy) reps
→ Seated Calf Raise–5 sets of 15 (light) reps

My upper half of my body was proportioned, but my legs were still on the scrawny side, no matter what I did. It had been that way since my jaundiced days in the NICU. Even in my baby pictures, my arms had ripples and rolls the size of King's Hawaiian buns, yet my legs were pretty thin by healthy baby chub standards. Sam was the naturally athletic one, and up to middle school he could outrun me, but I had the discipline to pursue sports where he focused solely on academics and played video games in all of his spare time. I'd finally surpassed him at something. My parents didn't give a shit about any of that, but I did.

I managed to get a quick run on the treadmill before showering. 1 percent incline. Easy walking pace, thirty seconds. Easy jog for five minutes. Picking up the pace with ninety seconds of running. Repeat intervals for fifteen minutes. Two-minute cooldown walk. Three minute shower.

When I got to work on the other side of the mall, I had barely put my gym bag away under the counter before a wave of rowdy customers came through. A bunch of guys from a neighboring school who had come around the previous week, claiming their experiences were unsatisfactory so they'd get free rides were back now, threatening to hurt our customer service ratings. Unfortunately, it was my turn to deal with these loudmouths. There were five of them and one of me, and as soon as my predecessor saw me walking up, she clocked out and said, "Good timing for me, bad luck for you. They're horrible humans."

"You guys want me to go over the different experience options or have you been here enough times to know them all by memory by now?" I asked coolly.

The biggest one stepped forward. He was the size of two of me.

"Sure, Shang-Chi. Tell us if you have anything new."

Was that some racist shit or did he think I looked like Simu

Liu, which would be a compliment? By the way he and his buddies were cutting up, I had to think it was the former.

Deep breath, Peter. Be cool.

We did, in fact, have a new "Twist-N-Turn spectacular" sleigh ride we just downloaded that wasn't rated yet because it was the most extreme ride in the whole portfolio. It was clear they had no intent on leaving, and they were there to make my life miserable. I thought back to when that kid Timmy, Chloe's little friend, insisted on riding something that was not suitable for him. It gave me an idea.

I said casually, "If any of you want to try a new session no one's tried yet, it's for the hard-core adventurer types. I personally can't handle the plunging, flipping, and whiplash, but maybe you all are more able to handle it more than moi." Did I really just say *moi*? What is wrong with me?

The leader of the pack spoke up. "I'm no wimp. I'll go first." He brushed me aside and took one of the seats.

The other four argued about who would go second. I made it easy for them. "We have five chairs and headsets. I see no reason why you can't all go at the same time."

They all whooped and hooted as they sat in a row.

"You look like a cyborg."

"I hope this is better than last time. I guess it can't be worse."

"Shang-Chi, if this sucks, we're blaming you."

I took their vouchers for free sessions and handed out the

headsets. I hadn't tried the Twist-N-Turn myself, but Robbie, our most loyal customer was the only one who had.

He'd even taken Dramamine beforehand, and he still stumbled out, a pukey green hue to his entire face, mumbling, "That was epic."

So maybe I lied a little. Someone had already tried it out. Oops.

The leader pulled his phone from his pocket. "Would you mind recording me on Instagram Live?"

It would be my pleasure, my friend. I took it from his Hulk hand and initiated the sequence.

"Recording!" I yelled as the five of them "whoa'ed and "holy shitted" as the program took them up, up, up into the frigid North Pole sky. Soon they'd nosedive and swoop up over and over, then zigzag, flip around and around, then do it all over again.

He didn't have many viewers, but there was enough of an audience to see these guys go from gung-ho to OH NO in less than ten seconds.

The guy with the curly red hair gripped the arms of the seat. "I—I think I need to stop." He waited a few seconds and yelled, "Oh-shit-oh-shit-oh-fuck," and released the headset. He immediately put his head between his knees. All of that made it on the livestream.

The other guys followed suit. One turned pale, tore off his headset, and ran to the nearest trash receptacle to get sick.

Another said, "I can't do this," and yanked everything off, and I swore I saw some tears. A gruff-looking guy with spiked black hair clawed at his helmet and eventually released it, but not without a boatload of expletives.

The last man standing was the leader. He stayed still and never started his sequence because he actually took a short nap instead. How? I have no idea. It had never happened before. When I poked his arm, he snorted and sat upright. Still unknowingly on the livestream and bewildered by his surroundings, he asked, "Mommy?"

And boy, did people comment.

So did his in-person friends. They would not stop with the mommy jokes.

While he tried to tell his gang he had passed out from extreme motion sickness, I couldn't wait to tell Chloe about this. I looked over at Santa's Village, but another photographer elf stood in Chloe's usual spot. As my shift continued, I snuck little peeks over at the photo area. *Chloe's not here because something big came up*, I thought to myself, even though we usually had the same after-school schedules, and she was definitely supposed to be working that day. After I made up all sorts of reasons in my head of why Chloe wasn't there (flu, family emergency, car broke down) and they increased in severity and absurdity (garbage truck collision, interstate pile-up, mall serial murderer, free tickets to Shen Yun or *Hamilton*). I got a text from Brach: **we're grabbing dinner then hitting the arcade.**

"Uh, sir?" Beside me, a kid wearing a manga T-shirt tapped my arm. "How much would it cost if I bought three rides if there's a buy one get one free special?"

I loved when these middle schoolers called me sir. I wanted to high-five him for that.

"Well, I'll be honest, I've never had anyone ride more than twice in a row. It's usually a lot of time, and people have their fill after two. Are you sure you want this?" I squatted a little so I'd be at eye level with him.

He scratched his curly head. "I got a bunch of birthday money from my nana, and she said I should spend it on anything. And this is the only thing I like besides computer games."

"How about this. You ride twice. Buy one get one free. And if you want that third ride, we'll give you a special deal. For brave three-peaters like yourself."

"Cool. I want to do the Santa Swing and Spin to start!" He dashed forward and plopped down in the nearest seat. "Your line isn't as long as it usually is. I'm glad I got my turn right away."

He was right about that. It was a slow day. I looked over at Santa's Village and couldn't help noticing the longer line. In the distance, Chloe's best friends pushed and pulled these enormous backgrounds around. Although they were large, the screens didn't look too heavy, and they were on wheels, which made it easy to set up. A few brightly colored Christmas backgrounds caught my eye, but they had also built backdrops for other holidays too.

Sophia rolled around a Thanksgiving-themed one covered in cartoon turkeys, and Elias unveiled a Hanukkah one with lots of glimmery shimmer, as well as a red, green, and black Kwanzaa backdrop and a glitzy New Year's display. I had to hand it to them, they had really upgraded and modernized the photo experience, and customers were responding by admiring the background options and props. Even Santa had fun optional accessories, like sunglasses, a cigar, and a gaming headset.

Elias waved at me, and I offered a small nod hello. He caught me staring at them, admiring their work, and looking for Chloe.

"Uh, sir? Can I do that one again? It was the coolest! I liked it better than the 'Dashing through the Asteroids' one from last year. That was kinda weird."

It was. We discontinued it because it was not only unpopular, but angry STEM parents didn't want their kids to think asteroids could be in the earth's lowest atmosphere without burning up. Of course, this was all ridiculous seeing as how they were okay with Santa Claus and eight reindeer flying a sleigh.

As I started his second session, I got a message from Chloe.

Food later? Out back?

I checked the time. **OK will let you know when I'm on break.**

"Uh, sir? Can I do a different one now? Which do you recommend?"

This kid was my favorite type of customer. Besides the sir thing. He wanted my opinion, and I never got asked that enough.

"Wellll, if you want a roller-coaster effect, I'd go with Rudolph's Rollicking Ride. It's a lot of drops, so if your stomach can't handle it—"

He nodded vigorously. "I rode the Matterhorn this last summer. Is it scarier than that?"

I tapped my finger on my chin. "Well, if that's the case, I think you'll be able to handle it, champ."

While he rollicked with Rudolph, I kept checking the time. As soon as the next staff person came by to give me relief, I could meet up with Chloe.

My little buddy scooched down from the seat and handed me the helmet. "That was way better than any roller coaster. Will you be around next week?"

"We'll be here through the holidays. And then next year we'll see."

"Cool. This is my favorite thing at Riverwood. I'm Griffin, by the way. I'll see you next week."

His mom was a few feet away and waved at me. I waved back. What a nice family.

My replacement came up behind me. "Hey Petey!"

A blow of moist breath entered my left ear. Gross.

"Hi, Tanner. I'll be back in an hour." He took a stick of mint gum from his pocket and unwrapped it. I wish he'd chewed that before he talked into my ear.

I handed over the iPad to hot-breath Tanner. "The payment

app wasn't working right, so I had to reboot the OS. Should be running fine soon."

To my surprise, the owner of the VR franchise showed up at the booth too. I hadn't seen him since I'd started working there over a year ago, and honestly it was surprising to see the bigwig slumming it with an hourly employee. "Hey Stanley." I reached out my hand. "Long time no see." Maybe he was checking in on my performance. Maybe that group of guys complained about me and he was there to reprimand me. Or maybe it was none of those things and I was overthinking it...like Chloe being involved in a garbage truck accident on the interstate and then murdered on the way to see Shen Yun.

Stanley shook my hand, pumping it hard. "Yeah, we had two mall locations close down just in the past few weeks. It's not even an issue with our business, VR is still an area of growth in the economy. It's that the two malls nearby officially shut down, and because we're currently only located in shopping centers, well, we're screwed. A sad but real truth, we'll need to change our business strategy soon. Some of the staff is picking up shifts here though in the meantime, and one of the employees is coming now so I can show her how to close up for the night." He paused. "I'm sure you've heard about this mall closing. But I guess it's not as lucrative as it used to be, and the owner wants to sell before it becomes a money pit like the other malls around here. They were talking midyear, but now they're saying the developer who's interested is pushing to vacate all businesses starting right after the holidays."

I nodded and shoved my hands in my pants pockets. We had less time than I thought we had. "My friend and I are trying to get organized and meet with the landlord and pitch some business ideas. Hoping he'll reconsider the sale."

He barked a harsh laugh, which didn't feel so good to the ol' Peter ego. "For Ricky Junior, the ideas will need to be easy to implement. I went to school with him. His dad owned a lot of real estate in Riverwood, and he took over when his dad retired. His dad was such a nice guy, and really good with money. I think Ricky still lives in the family mansion with his parents, mooching off them. I'm a pretty shrewd businessman myself, but Rick's dad was like a lowcapital, bootstraps Warren Buffett. He didn't have much money, but he turned what he had into pure gold." He studied my face. "Well, if you and your friends are serious and want to give this a shot, who knows, maybe you have what it takes to talk some sense into him. From what I heard he's pretty set on selling, so it would take a lot to change his mind."

Pulling out his phone, he looked something up and wrote it down on his business card. "You probably have his general office number, but this is his direct extension. He's better in face-to-face meetings." Stanley sighed as he handed me the card. "I don't know if his dad is involved at all still, but this was the first place he bought. Surely it has some sentimental value to him. If you call and get through to his admin assistant, tell her you're a friend of mine."

"Thank you." This guy was a wealth of information. I held out my hand, and Stan grabbed it and pulled me in for a bro hug.

"Good luck, man. Honestly, if you can pull this off and save the mall, it'll make a great story one day when you tell your kids about it. And this would look great on your college applications. These days you need anything to help you stand out."

I hadn't really thought about this as a means to get into college, but yeah, he was probably right. And saving the mall was something Sam would never do. It was one way I could show my parents I was special after all.

With Stanley closing up, it meant I could leave a little earlier than planned, which was okay money wise even though I didn't get much in the way of tips. Plus I was eager to get some food in my stomach before I met up with Brach and Kip.

My parents were both at Empress Garden. Dad was talking with a customer, and Mom was explaining to the newest line cook how to stir-fry their signature dish, Triple Delight. But since the customer had asked for no shrimp, she only used beef and chicken. A double delight.

She tapped a little cornstarch into the sauce for the meat. "Not too much, not too little. Just a little sprinkle. Stir. Sprinkle a little more."

Mom placed the beef with cornstarch coating into the wok

bubbling with oil. With tongs in one hand, she added layer after layer of beef and chicken. The meat popped, crackled, and eventually turned golden brown. She held a piece up for the kitchen staff to see. "Nice and crispy, cooked through all the way." She removed the fried meat slices and placed the pieces on paper towels. As they cooled, she stir-fried scallions, mushrooms, carrots, ginger, and garlic, browning them. Before removing them from the heat, she added the beef, thickened oyster sauce, and a dash of sesame oil.

Mom's family had been in the restaurant business for over thirty years. My maternal grandparents had come to the United States when they were in elementary school, so that made my mom a second-gen Chinese American, but really it was more like third gen. Dad was too. Penny Li and James Li. As American as Chinese chicken salad.

And that made me basically fourth gen, as American as the individually wrapped fortune cookies at Panda Express. We celebrated Lunar New Year and ate Chinese food often. I'd been to China once in my lifetime, but had no family there to visit. Everyone we knew was in the United States, specifically in New York and California. I didn't know any Mandarin. My parents spoke the language when they were little but had forgotten most of it.

Looking back over at Dad, he was still with the same customer, using his own version of sign language to tell a little

Chinese grandma that they were out of special number one. She was switching between Mandarin and Cantonese, hoping he'd understand at least one of them. I felt bad for him. And her.

When she saw me walking over, she asked me a question in Mandarin, something that suggested that I help her translate. When I used similar sign language to my Dad's, she realized we were both no help. My heart tugged a little when she walked away with the paper menu.

Dad shrugged as she exited the mall. "I guess my Duolingo Chinese lessons aren't paying off like I'd hoped." He smiled at me. "But that's why we're hoping you can take Chinese in college. Get some of that culture back."

What my parents didn't seem to understand was how terrible I was at learning foreign languages. I'd taken three years of Spanish, yet it was more booksmart learning than intuitive. Recently in the mall, a Spanish-speaking customer stopped me to ask where he could buy fútbol shirts, which I knew was soccer, and I replied back that he should go to Sports Lobby in Spanish, or what I thought was Spanish. He repeated the question three times before he said, "Gracias," and then used a voice-activated assistant on his phone to ask the same question.

Mom wiped her hands on her clean apron. "Let's hope you can still get into a good college with your Spanish grades."

Ooof. Okay, so maybe she did understand how terrible I was at languages. My other grades were good and keeping my overall

GPA afloat. But I'd probably quit Spanish so I didn't have to suffer through APs.

Dad handed me a container with air holes cut into the corners as vents. "You always ask for shrimp, so we saved you some before it sold out."

They hadn't figured out that Chloe was the shrimp girl actually. I was a pork guy.

"Thanks," I said. After glancing over at Kwons' Café and only seeing the Kwon matriarch standing at the register, I sighed and asked my parents, "Mind if I eat this out back?"

They looked at each other. "Fine if you don't want to hang out with us uncool parents. We won't take it personally." The crinkles around their eyes and their laughter made it clear I had their permission.

I texted Chloe. I have your food. Heading to alley.

To my surprise, she immediately wrote back. OK.

I looked over at Kwon's again. Still only the mom there. I didn't dare penetrate the pulsing energy wall fueled purely by the Li and Kwon animosity. Other than the almond cookie day, I never tried to breach the perimeter while they were there. I wasn't about to try again anytime soon. Way too scary. It was like how kids knew not to go to the creepy, run-down, boarded-up house in the neighborhood. It never turned out well.

Pressing the door's metal bar with my back, I pushed myself straight into the forty-degree climate. My temperature usually ran warm, but it was clear that this was uncomfortably past my own comfort boundaries. It was cold as fuck out there. Before I could run back inside and grab my coat, I caught a glimpse of Chloe. Or rather, her ears. Chloe's elfin Yoda ears were mint green and hard to miss.

She jerked her head up when I was in her peripheral vision. "Hey, don't throw any cookies at my face."

Well, hello to you too. "I wouldn't dare. I still have this dinner transaction to make. I wouldn't risk sacrificing spicy pork."

She asked, "No table and chairs this time?"

Crap. I knew I'd forgotten something. "I can run in and get them."

"Nah, I need to be quick." She bent down to pick up a container. "Here's the pork. You might need two hands, I really packed it in."

I handed her the shrimp takeout. "Yours is heavy too."

We both retrieved each other's dinners one-handed, but had to act fast because the eco-friendly packaging did not do well with lopsided pork or shrimp weight.

"So just to warn you, I might need to take a call while I'm out here. I've been waiting for thirty minutes for my mentor to call. She said she'd try to reach me this evening, and I didn't want to be working at Santa's Village when that happened. I called in a favor and took the evening off." She opened the container and picked at the lo mein with her chopsticks. "I'm way too nervous to eat."

Well, I wasn't way too nervous to eat. I shoveled the Korean food in my mouth and grew a little concerned when I'd wolfed down half of my meal without her taking a single bite. Should I have waited?

"Did I get you the wrong thing?" I asked. She loved our lo mein. My heart sank... She wasn't into our food anymore.

She sighed and closed the top of her food container. "No, I just don't think I can eat before I talk to Lorraine. Hey, can you tell me what you think of her message? Maybe I'm interpreting it wrong."

"Okay." Did I have to stop eating or could she read it while I ate? I didn't want to sound rude but...I was starving.

"This is what she sent: Let's talk later."

I waited for her to continue, but she didn't. "That's it? Let's talk later?"

She nodded, her eyes widening, eager to hear my assessment.

"Are you being serious? She's going to talk to you later." Was there confusion in those three words? Mental note: never say LET'S TALK LATER to Chloe.

"But...she means tonight, right? Later means later in the same day? She sent the text at 4:55 and it's what...almost 7:00 now? She'll call me before bedtime, don't you think?"

I didn't know what to say. Later meant, well, later. Like, when Brach said "I'll pay you back later" meant he'd give me money in one minute, or an hour, or like, never, because he forgot. Probably best not to tell her that example, come to think of it.

"Did she send you other texts earlier to provide context of time?" I couldn't believe I was indulging her with her overthinking this. I shoveled rice and pickled cucumbers into my mouth in quick succession.

As she shook her head and frowned, I put my nearly empty food container on the ground and looked at her screen as she scrolled up. The other texts from Lorraine were friendly and were all about how excited everyone was about Chloe's participation in the contest. But sure enough, after the last "Let's talk later" text, she dropped off the face of the planet. Not cool.

I leaned in closer just as Chloe pulled her head back. Her Yoda ear went into my mouth.

"Ppppuh!" I spit out the green lobe and Chloe's frown literally turned upside down. I'd never seen her laugh so hard, not even when that kid threw up on my shoes.

Her woodpecker-like laughter made me crack up. We both got a few belly laughs in and for a brief moment, we smiled like we understood each other. She took off her green ears. "I don't even know why I was wearing those off duty. I keep forgetting to take them off."

The cold air made Chloe's cheeks and nose rosy, and with her eyes shining and smiling in the corners, I'd never seen her look this way. Cute. Attractive. Kissable.

I wanted to kiss her so badly, but we had other things to discuss. Urgent things.

"Hey, Pete! We've been looking for you. It's arcade time!"

Damn. Kip's booming voice was unmistakable. Sure enough, when I turned, he and Brach were walking straight toward us. "Oh. You're with Chloe." He glanced at her like he looked at the Impossible Burgers under the school cafeteria heat lamps. Zero interest. Zero enthusiasm. "Hey."

Brach was a little friendlier. "Hey there, Chloe."

Chloe wasn't in my social circle, so all she probably knew about these guys was that they were on the lacrosse team with me. And all they knew about her was she was a yearbook photographer and one of those artistic types at school. The last time my friends and I did anything remotely artistic was in middle school, building Minecraft world shit.

Her phone rang. Her attention snapped to me. "It's her."

"You want me to be with you when you answer it?" I asked without thinking or looking over at my friends to make sure it was okay with them. This would ultimately mean delaying our arcade outing. But this was more important. And she looked like she needed a friend.

She glanced at Kip's bored face. "Nah, it's okay. I'll manage. Have fun at the arcade! And we still need to catch up about all the other stuff." She headed in the opposite direction down the alley and answered the call. "Hi, Ms. Finch. So glad you called."

Brach turned to me. "What was that all about? You two best buds now?"

I didn't know what we were. We weren't really all that friendly, well, with the exception of our dinner arrangement. Though we didn't avoid each other anymore or roll our eyes when the other person was within a ten-foot radius. "I guess we're not...*not* friends."

Kip raised an eyebrow. "That sounds like friends."

Brach added, "I thought you hated the Kwons."

These guys had heard me complain about Chloe and her family for years. The Li-Kwon rivalry ran deep and wide. It wasn't something that could be waved off with a superficial truce because well, as the age-old Mandalorian mantra goes, *this is the way*. The best we could do was skirt around the fringes of the decade-long unspoken agreement between our families and have secret dinner swaps and be ambivalent toward each other all the other times.

"She's okay," I mumbled, as heat crept up my neck all the way to my ears. "We swap dinners a few days a week and do it out back so our parents don't know." I didn't want to keep talking about Chloe and me, so I shifted the topic. "Have you tried their spicy pork, though?"

Their faces lit up. Brach said, "We should try it. How spicy though? You know I can handle Mexican and Thai food heat. I've never tried Korean food."

Kip cocked an eyebrow. "How have you not had Korean food? I have it like once a month."

I let out a slow exhale as they bickered about why Brach only likes to eat burgers and pizza, and Kip joke-threatening to end their thirteen-year friendship if he doesn't branch out more. They were distracted, and that was good for me. Maybe they'd forget about—

"Hey Pete, so you and Chloe? Yes? No?" Brach hadn't forgotten. And I couldn't think of another way to divert attention. I took a long sip of Coke instead.

Kip smirked. "I think him avoiding answering is enough evidence for me. Make sure I'm the best man at your wedding. Brach would be a disaster."

God, there wasn't anything I could say or do to make this go away. If I stayed quiet, they thought it was because I liked her. If I protested, they would say it was because I liked her. Damned if I did, damned if I didn't. Was that how that saying went? "Can we just go play some games? They have that new VR Alien shooter. I'm ready to kick your asses."

"Let's go," Brach said.

"Yeah," added Kip. "It's cold as fuck out here."

We walked inside, and I could hear Chloe's voice drifting through the ventilation grate. She sounded upbeat. That was an excellent sign. Good for her.

The blinking, blipping, and dinging sounds echoed around us as we entered the neon-popping arcade. It was how I imagined Vegas to be, but with no smoking, drinking, or boobs.

As we waited at the Aliens Invade! game behind two guys

finishing up their turns (read: dying over and over and running out of credits on their game card), I texted Chloe. **Good luck with Lorraine!**

She replied pretty quickly. **Wrapping up. Went good I guess** 🙇

I knew Chloe well enough to know that was her jumping for joy.

Can't wait to hear more.

"We're up!" Brach motioned for me to step forward. "You and I can go first, then Kip."

I shoved my phone into my back pocket and smiled to myself as I lifted my astro blaster to blow up the descending alien colony ships. I got off work early and had my favorite dinner, my friends were here, and Chloe hit it off with Lorraine. All in all, a great night.

FOURTEEN

CHLOE

MY VOICE CRACKED WHEN LORRAINE SAID HELLO.

Actually, it squeaked. I squeaked a hello back and then couldn't stop the cracking, squeaking word-vomiting. "It's a pleasure to finally chat with you. Like not text chat, but chatting on the phone. I've followed your work for so many years and just being able to speak to you is a real honor. I hear you live close by, not that I googled your address, I read in the local paper that you had a remote studio location that you used to foster your creativity."

I was astonished and mortified by my own incessant chatter. I immediately shut my mouth and clasped it with my hand, with the hope that I could muzzle myself and let her have a word in edgewise.

Lucky for me, a tinkling of laughter echoed through the phone speaker. "I love your enthusiasm, Chloe. Your photos have a certain energy, and I haven't seen that before in someone so young. Your photography portfolio was quite impressive. I'd love to speak with you about your inspiration for your submission and discuss my mentorship, specifically in the field of photojournalism. The way you capture expressions, moments, human emotion... you have a bright future in journalism if you'd want to go that route."

I pulled my hand from my mouth to say, "Thank you." Lorraine Finch, world-renowned photographer, was complimenting my work. *My. Work.*

She continued. "I've just kicked off a new project I'm doing for the National Archives about the evolution of the dwindling suburban mall culture. As you can imagine, the timing of your submission couldn't have been any more perfect. Most of my focus for the exhibit has been on the actual mall buildings, so your image of the workers in the kitchen really grabbed my attention. I saw some of your most recent work on your website and would love to know more about the story behind your Empress Garden restaurant photograph. Do you have a connection to that business?"

I looked up the image on my phone. It was a landscape orientation, in color instead of monochrome. And it featured Peter Li, front and center. Did I have a connection to that business?

Yes...my parents made fun of it all the time, using Korean swear words. How could I even explain to Lorraine that the history between the Lis and Kwons was full of grudges, bad feelings, and jealousy? Honestly, I didn't understand the origin of the animosity, and I was so little when it first manifested that I'd never even questioned it. It was a bitterness so deeply ingrained from my childhood that I couldn't see past the "sworn enemies" of our families to even be all that friendly with Peter. Were we friends-ish now? Friends Lite? Could we be more? I enjoyed his company, mostly, and appreciated the fact that he didn't seem to know how annoyingly good looking he was. I wouldn't swap dinners and risk getting caught for just anyone.

I chose my words carefully. "I was considering this image for my finalist portfolio actually. I took that photo to capture the hard work that goes into a restaurant. There's a lot happening behind the scenes, and so many things that could go wrong, if you're not on top of everything."

She said, "That's so interesting to me. Could you give me any examples of this?"

"The Wi-Fi can cut out, the fryer can break down, or the software glitches so you can't ring up customers. We're old school and handwrite orders on tickets to pass to the back. Empress Garden does this too."

"Oh, I didn't realize your family was in the restaurant business too. I can only imagine how hard it is to keep a business in a mall afloat. I've studied malls across the country. The population in our town is changing, and the younger generations aren't as interested in coming to the local mall every weekend, and this is consistent across the United States. And studies show they do most of their shopping, especially their holiday buying, online. It's a shame."

I could have just as easily taken photos of my parents working hard at the café, scrubbing the grill, hauling in wooden crates of vegetables from the alley drop-off. Owning a small restaurant was no walk in the park.

I whispered, "And we just found out Empress Garden, along with my parents' restaurant, will be closing. They're demolishing the mall."

Lorraine sighed. "Oh dear. I'm seeing this across the country too. I'm so sorry this is also happening to Riverwood."

Not wanting to bring the mood down, since she was calling me about the mentorship, I said, "We're trying to do what we can to save it. But in the meantime, let's get back to how lucky I am to have you as my mentor."

She replied, "Yes, going back to your photography, you were able to capture one of the workers there so beautifully. His intensity. His seriousness. His pain. All with a click of a finger." I'd taken a few shots of him from far away with my fancy lens and was able to zoom in thanks to the high resolution. I pinched and widened the photo from Empress Garden. Now that she said it,

I could see Peter's intensity, seriousness, and, now that she'd spoken about it out loud...his pain. It was a busy day and we were shooting the menu items in a walled off area of the food court away from our parents' restaurants. I'd also taken photos of Peter and the staff with my long lens when he wasn't looking. Peter was going back and forth, helping me and running back to the restaurant to make sure takeout orders were prepared correctly. If they weren't, his mom would bellow his name, "*Peterrr!*" and everyone in the food court could hear it. No one wanted to listen to that. Especially not the Kwon fam. And especially not Peter Li.

"That's Peter, his family owns that business. He doesn't work in the kitchen that often. He sort of pops in wherever he's needed, like maybe a substitute teacher. Or actually, more like a helicopter parent."

She laughed. "I see. So you took a photo of him in a moment while he was in the kitchen with the staff. This photo pulls my heartstrings and makes me want to know his backstory. It speaks to me on many levels. The flicker of vulnerability in his eyes." While she talked, I pinched the photo and expanded his face. God, I hoped Peter didn't sneak up on me while I was enlarging his body parts.

This picture spoke to my art teacher and Elias and Soph, who insisted I enter it into the competition. And honestly, it spoke to me too. I knew what it was like to have parents whose second home was at a restaurant. The nine-to-nine daily grind, including some holidays. The missed birthday parties, the absence from school events, and the limited extracurriculars because of my side job, being the restaurant apprentice. Some of my friends growing up asked if I got paid to clean the grill, mop the floors, and bag the takeout. Chop the meat and vegetables, wipe down the counters, and scrub the employee bathroom, which was the worst job ever. I laughed and joked it off, saying it was an internship for entrepreneurship. I never answered the truth: we didn't have money to spare to pay me a living wage. We were barely getting by. And I was worried. And scared. And this was all before I knew the mall was shutting down.

This photo was a mirror.

Peter knew my life better than anyone. He basically had the same existence, even though he had more friends and activities. Peter was always hustling, doing a few after-school activities that would require no parent involvement, and taking a bus or driving to the mall afterward. Even when we weren't at our photo studio and VR jobs, we were usually at the mall after school anyway, doing our homework at the tables in the food court or in the back rooms of our restaurants. Every once in a while I would catch a ride to my house—I did homework and made my own dinner there—but I'd gotten so used to being at Riverwood that I actually preferred it now, even if it meant I would end up restocking napkins and cutlery, cleaning the stove top, and washing pots and cooking utensils when my homework was done instead of bingeing the latest new streaming releases.

Maybe it wasn't preferring that way of life after school. It was more like resigning myself to it, because I knew it was what my parents needed.

I studied Peter's photo with a less subjective "Ugh...Peter" lens. A serious expression replaced his usually jovial face for once. I could see it now. Wearing a shabby apron over his crisp school clothes made him look older. A slight shoulder slouch acknowledged that this was the way our life was. We weren't like the other kids in our school. We were different from them in so many ways.

I swallowed hard. Yes. I could see. Peter was me.

"I'm glad the emotion came through visually."

"It most definitely did," she chirped. "Well, as you know, we have a mentor session and a final presentation in just over four weeks, where you'll share your inspiration of your submission to the finalists committee along with a short essay. Everything we just discussed...I think it would be wonderful essay fodder. There's also a Q&A with the judges, so they can ask you questions about your portfolio and future plans. You can also provide other supplementary visual materials such as videos, storyboards, and infographics. Can you come to my studio for our mentor session next week? We can discuss photography technique and inspiration. And, if it's okay with you, I would love to get a personal tour of Riverwood Mall. Then I could see where the inspiration for your contest entry came from, and it might help me understand your point of view."

Wow, this was information overload, but all of it was good. Well, except for the essay and Q&A parts. But being mentored by Lorraine and giving her a tour of the mall, basically my second home, sounded great! "Should we meet for mentoring first or would you like to see Riverwood beforehand?"

She paused before answering. "Let's go see the mall, if that's all right with you. Would this weekend work for the mall tour? I'll email you the parent permission and waiver form."

"That works. I'll get the permissions signed. Let's meet at noon on Saturday at the food court, next to Christie Cookies and Orange Julius." Those were easy to find, and they also smelled good.

"Looking forward to it! See you then."

We hung up and I clutched the phone to my chest. At age sixteen, my dreams were coming true. How was this even happening?

FIFTEEN

CHLOE

I ONLY NEEDED ONE PARENTAL SIGNATURE ON THE permission form. A quick scribble of the pen was the only thing left to do. I had filled out all the preceding information and yellow highlighted the area for Mom or Dad to sign.

As for the parent who would give the least resistance? Dad. He was more easygoing and would better understand why I needed to do this. Mom would tell me it was a waste of time, not practical, and to not bother with something nonacademic. She signed off on school field trips, summer enrichment camps, and books. Dad approved the fun stuff. He was the one to sneak me extra dollars when I went to see movies (at the mall of course) or went to an occasional concert with friends. He bought the photo printer from my wish list last year and convinced Mom that photography was a better teen pastime than vaping and drinking with the wrong crowd. She agreed...reluctantly.

Mom was talking on the phone with the meat distributor when I pulled the slip of paper from my messenger bag. "Appa, can you sign this? It's for a prestigious mentorship opportunity."

He pulled his reading glasses from his shirt front pocket. "Mentor...ship? Who you mentor?" Squinting at the page, he skimmed the disclaimers as I told him all the exciting details about the National Art Council. Umma and Appa knew I'd entered and was a finalist, but they thought it was a school thing and I'd bring home a cheesy certificate or a cheap shiny ribbon. They didn't know how life changing this opportunity was for someone like me.

"So this Lorraine lady, she teaching you how to take photo? You already know how. Click. Snap-snap." He held the paper in one hand and mimed taking a photo with the index finger of his other hand.

I nodded. "Yes, but she's an expert, and she'll give me career advice. If I win, I'll get ten thousand dollars."

He pulled out a pen from his other shirt pocket. "Why you not say that first? Ten thousand dollars is big money!" Scribbling something that looked like three waves of an ocean, he handed me the form. "I hope Lorraine lady help you win the money."

Mom hung up the phone. "You need me? You look over at me a few time and it look like you sneaking something."

I shot Appa a worrisome look. She was in a sour mood.

Dad cleared his throat. "She ask to go out with her friends and I said maybe tomorrow."

Mom nodded and walked to the back storage area.

Appa smiled at me. "Good luck."

Saturday, 11:52 a.m., the elderly Silver Sneakers speedwalkers whizzed by me, marching in perfect sync. Elbows out, with matching red tees, they headed to the main entrance of the mall, where they would march outside in the parking lot and reenter in JCPenney. As long as I could remember, the Silver Sneakers had walked around the mall on Saturdays just before lunchtime to get their winter exercise. In fact, the carpet was even a little more worn in certain areas because they had walked the same path for so long. In a couple of weeks it would be Thanksgiving, and they would don festive feathered turkey hats, which was always a treat. Most of them were grandma types, with big, polite smiles and "good mornin's" and "pardon mes," but even so, no one dared walk near them because they gave an occasional stink eye to anyone who ran across their speedwalking path, or blocked them by stopping to tie their shoes along their route.

"Howdy Chloe!" Silver-haired Patricia waved at me as she walked by, as did a few of her friends. After their weekly walks, they had lunch in the food court and usually at least one of them ate at my parents' place. Mom and Dad frequently threw in a free soft drink or extra appetizer, because they were such loyal customers. This type of red-carpet treatment was usually reserved for other Koreans in the community who stopped by the restaurant. This was my parents' way of showing them that after years of patronage, they regarded them highly. Patricia and her entourage were their people.

While waiting for Lorraine, I added a few questions for Hannah on our shared Google Docs. She had been looking over our paperwork, and in the past few days I'd been talking to the Silver Sneakers crew about mall improvement ideas: ones that would help the mall get more foot traffic or grow revenue. Peter was put in charge of getting lease agreements from his parents and other tenants to see if there was something we could use in them. I needed to send him the lease for Kwons' Café before the end of the day.

I perused the cookie options behind the nearby plexiglass. Christie Cookies was my favorite dessert place of all time; occasionally, they offered free samples when they had a seasonal offering. Southern butter pecan was my favorite. There weren't any bits of cookie pieces out to try, which was a bummer, because I'd skipped breakfast out of fear that when I met Lorraine, I'd regurgitate everything with my clackity nerves. And stress eating was something I could easily do right now, with the mounting pressure of the mall closure and the National Art Council competition both going on at the same time.

When I'd worry about one thing, my brain would flip over to the other and I would get even more stressed out. How was I supposed to speak in public under duress? Put me in elf ears in front of kids and parents with a camera around my neck, and I was comfortable. Ask me to talk in front of a crowd or to someone I idolized? I lost my shit, but not in a good way. Lost it in a vomit-y, call the janitor way.

How was it even possible for me to win this competition? How were a couple of kids and a paralegal supposed to save the mall?

"Oh there you are! I'm Lorraine!"

I'd watched so many YouTube videos of Lorraine I had no problem recognizing her when she approached. I smiled as she greeted me. Lorraine looked impeccable in her Burberry scarf and crisp black wool coat. On her shoulder, she wore a brown, buttery-leather camera bag that I wanted to touch so badly. She looked like an Oscar-winning movie star with her grandiosity. With her arm outstretched, she said in a silky smooth, calming voice, "It's great to finally meet you in person."

The way she lit up, it was like she was in awe of meeting me, whereas I knew it was completely the other way around. When I reached out my hand and shook hers, words were stuck in my throat and my mouth didn't move. I was dumbstruck. Or starstruck.

Lorraine-struck.

We stood there in silence, mainly because she was awaiting a reply from me, and I still had no idea why my brain was screaming "Say something! Tell her you like her coat! Say nice to meet you too! Pleeeeease!" but it didn't neurologically connect to my mouth, jaw, and vocal cords. Oh, and my breath. You hear about people taking your breath away, but this was literal proof that it actually happened.

A puberty-hormonal-change squeak vibrated the back of my throat before I managed to utter a weak, "Hello. I'm Chloe, you must be Lorraine." Well, at least some of my neurons were firing again, even though all I managed to do was state the obvious.

Get it together, Chloe. First impressions mean everything, including but not limited to world-class photographers.

"So, shall we take a tour?" she asked.

If there was anything to get me talking, it was Riverwood Mall. I walked in the direction toward the closest flagship store and she trailed close. "You'll see a mix of brand-name stores and small locally owned businesses. Here's an airbrush T-shirt shop that only opens in the summer and holidays. Down the corridor over there is where I use my photography skills to work during the holidays, in Santa's Village. There's a chain jewelry store to our right that no one ever shops in but has still managed to stay in business. Maybe it's a drug front, with a worldwide footprint."

She laughed at my commentary. "I have to say, it would be the least likely place the authorities would look. At a place that sells tennis bracelets and solitaire engagement rings. It's genius really." Lorraine smiled as she pointed to the next few stores. "Shoe repair, frozen yogurt, and a candy store. All of these been here a while?"

I nodded. "Most of the smaller, niche stores have stayed, mainly because of loyal local customers' repeat business. It's the bigger shoe stores and sports-themed outlets that seem to have the most trouble. The anchor stores have been in business since the mall opened, but we're worried about them with the decline in foot traffic. Some of the newer and nicer malls they built across town a few years ago are two stories high. Riverwood is all one level, and people don't like to walk."

Just then, the silver sneaker pack emerged from JCPenney and headed our way. Bobbing silver hair and elbows out, these ladies looked like they were ready to do the chicken dance. They passed by us, whooping and cheering.

"Okay, *they* like to walk, but they're like the only ones." I gestured at all of the middle-aged and older men and women sitting around the central fountain looking at their phones.

Lorraine pulled her SLR camera from her bag. "I've visited almost every major mall in the Middle Tennessee area, and this is the first time I've been compelled to snap photos." She took photos of the clientele around the fountain, the Silver Sneakers posse, and the small toy store having a liquidation sale because it was closing. For years the store had barely held on thanks to clever promotions: they were full-service, offering wrapping, packaging, and local delivery. Lorraine was capturing the special energy of Riverwood. We weren't the fanciest or coolest mall by any means, but we had a good mix of stores. Obviously, the food court served the best cuisine around too.

We walked and talked as she snapped photos of what she called "the mall energy."

Click. A picture of Belk department store with vintage lettering on the entry sign being replaced by their newest logo.

Click. Photo of a girl at Claire's getting her ears pierced, visible from the store window.

Click. A group of skateboarders getting chased by a mall cop on an electric scooter, whizzing by the kiosk that only sold wind chimes. I had never understood who was buying those things. There were two kinds of people in the world: wind chime people and normal people. That business had been there for five years, maybe more, and there was always someone browsing. Unbelievable.

"Fascinating," Lorraine said as we walked back toward the central fountain. "This mall has evolved and changed in a direction I haven't really seen anywhere else."

The past week, Riverwood Mall had undergone its full holiday metamorphosis as we entered the second half of November. In the middle of the fountain on a temporary platform was a twenty-foot teddy bear in a red and green vest lip-synching to the holiday music blasting from the speakers surrounding it.

"This fountain has been here since the mall opened in the early nineties, before I was born. It's a wishing fountain, and every year they drain it and collect the coins. It's donated to the local toy drive, and the store owners match the donation." I pulled some coins from my cross-body purse. "Would you like to make a wish?"

She grabbed two pennies and a nickel from my palm. "Thank you!" With an underhanded throw, Lorraine flipped each of the coins, flicking them from her thumbnail and launching them high in the air. They somersaulted and landed in the water like an Olympic-trained diver, gracefully and elegantly, with an ear-pleasing "bloop" sound as the metal disc made contact with the water. She smiled as the coins sunk to the bottom. "Oh darn, I forgot to make a wish. Maybe I'll double up on wishes next time. It's your turn!"

The only coins I had left were a couple of dimes, which of course didn't provide a lot of aerodynamic heft. Also, I had a weak throw in general, and to make up for the lightness of the coins, I chose to underhand throw them...hard. One hit the mechanical bear smack in the nose and then plopped into the water. The other one sailed directly into the bear's mouth, which would have been even more impressive if I was actually aiming for it.

"Oh...no." The bear's mouth struggled to close. When the lips almost met, it sprung back open, and a grinding metal sound replaced the holiday soundtrack. After ten seconds, the coin must've fallen out or worked its way through because the bear's lip-synching systems restored to normal. Well, as normal as a giant robot bear singing Mariah Carey's "All I Want for Christmas Is You" could be.

A stern voice flooded the fountain loudspeakers. "Hey! Don't throw anything else at the bear or we'll call security!" My face flushed with heat as bystanders stared at me. The most horrible thing was that the bear lip-synched the entire scolding word for word.

Lorraine didn't even flinch in embarrassment on my behalf. She motioned for me to follow her. "How about we go get a corn dog on a stick? I love their lemonade."

Once we were out of earshot of the fountain crowd, I deadpanned, "I forgot to make a wish."

She chuckled and her eyes smiled. Thank goodness she didn't want to drop me from my mentorship. I couldn't blame her if she did... Was any other mentee causing robot bear mechanical failures?

I waited for our corn dogs and drinks while Lorraine walked around the area and continued taking photos of the mall's local, chain, and franchise businesses, like Auntie Anne's, Sbarro's, and Hot Topic, as well as the locally owned Froyo Yolo, Country Craft House, and the Asteroid Arcade that Peter and all his friends went to all the time.

A sense of urgency filled me while we walked back to Corn-Dog-on-a-Stick. "Would you like to see where I work, at Santa's Village? And my family's restaurant? We can see if Peter's around, he's the dude, um, I mean subject, in my photos."

She took a sip of lemonade. "That would be a perfect way

to end this tour. It's amazing how mall culture across America is essentially the same, but also different. There are some variations, like outdoor malls, mega malls with rides, outlet malls, and I'll be going on tour soon to photograph those types of venues this upcoming spring. I'm so glad I got an opportunity to see Riverwood before it closed."

I chewed my bite of corn dog and swallowed. "There's a final hearing with the city council on the eve of Christmas Eve, December twenty-third. This is when they'll be proposing to pull permits for the mall demolition. We're hoping to make a case with the landlord to save the mall before then though. So there's still hope."

She spoke with caution. "Oh dear. I believe the twenty-third is the same day as the local National Art Council Gala. I can double-check, though, before making you worry."

Too late. The anxiety of the two events converging on or around the same day sent my heart racing. Two big events, both determining my future, both needing a win.

How would I be able to handle both huge deadlines looming like a black cloud above my head?

While I checked the city council date on my phone, Lorraine scrolled through her calendar. "The gala is the twenty-third but in the evening, at 5:00."

I breathed heavily from my nose. "The council meeting is in the early afternoon, but the time hasn't been set. It'll be tight."

Lorraine offered me a reassuring smile. "It'll be tight, but I have faith that you'll do great. Maybe we can add new photos of the mall, juxtaposing against the old."

This gave me an idea. "What if I created a video for the competition to show the mall's history, and all the people who make up the mall community? Could you help mentor me with something like that?"

Ideas flooded my brain. I'd go through Mom and Dad's old restaurant stuff to see if there's anything photoworthy. When the video was finished I could share it with the landlord. We could pitch something to the local paper or come up with a social media campaign that highlights the mall's history and roots. Peter could do the same with his parents' old keepsakes, and he could ask some of the older stores and restaurants because he was good at all the people-y, talk-y stuff. And it allowed me to stay behind the camera, engage in the world the way I was most comfortable, all while giving me an opportunity to build my narrative voice.

"This is a wonderful idea, Chloe, and I know you'll knock it out of the park. I can see that your idea lit a fire under you and you're busy thinking of options, so I'll just hang out here for a bit while you go do what you need to do. Looking forward to our mentorship time. I can't wait to see how you pull everything together. I'll message you the details about our next meeting."

If Lorraine Finch believed in me, maybe anything was possible.

SIXTEEN

CHLOE

MOM AND DAD KEPT MOST OF THEIR OLD PHOTOS IN A broken metal lockbox in their closet. It contained their personal treasures; maybe not things of huge monetary value but keepsakes that they'd run back inside the house for if the whole place was on fire. I pulled the box off the shelf and walked it over to their bed, then flicked on the lamp so I could see better. Unclasping the dual latches, the smell of aged paper, fading photographs, old documents, and mix of old leather and metal mementos wafted toward me. It smelled like history.

Mom and Dad didn't like me going through their belongings, especially when it came to things they purposefully hid away in their closet. But this was a special situation, one that required me to act quickly, begging for forgiveness instead of asking for permission. I needed to find something—anything—that I could use from their past to help others see that this restaurant was more than just a place of business. It was our past, present, and future.

I especially loved looking in their lockbox to examine the jewelry. There were watches, brooches, and rings. Thumbing through their old passports and letters written in Korean, I wondered if my mom and dad had always dreamed of owning a restaurant or they'd had other plans in mind when they came to America.

For the papers and documents, my parents had organized everything by date. My hands trembled as I lifted the top page on the pile, the newest addition to the stack: a printout of the National Art Council junior photography finalists, my name accentuated with a bright yellow highlighter. I hadn't even known that my parents cared about the National Art Council. Any time I'd mentioned the competition they simply nodded and went back to what they were doing. No "good job." No smiles or praise. No acknowledgment or reward. It was as if I'd announced a new weeknight bedtime.

I hadn't even printed this out for them. They searched for this announcement on their own. They printed it. Highlighted it. And put it in the special box. All without my help.

I wiped my eyes with the back of my hand and took a deep breath. This entire time I'd assumed they were so disappointed in me. Hannah could fill up an entire lockbox with her own accomplishments. Maybe even two of them. Her National Merit Scholarship notification letter. National Honor Society pin. Spanish achievement ribbon. Phi Beta Kappa medal. The list was endless.

Yet, my National Art Council finalist announcement was right there, along with Hannah's top achievements. Maybe this was the start of something for me. Maybe I was late bloomer. My desire to have something of mine cherished and tucked away in their treasure chest wasn't clear until now, and I was annoyed at myself for weighing my self-worth with a dumb sheet of paper enclosed inside something that could be mistaken for a heavy-duty fishing tackle box.

A message on my phone buzzed. Through my tears, I could barely read the text.

Mom and Dad still at restaurant, doing late inventory check. I'm with them right now trying to keep them distracted. Any good photos or articles in the lockbox?

Hannah. I'd told her about the plan, and she was my lookout.

I wiped my eyes once again and placed the National Art Council article on the bed. I continued to place the rest of the contents in little piles.

The majority of the papers inside were of little value for what we needed: school enrollments, achievement test scores (ugh), and vaccination cards.

The second layer of yellowing papers and documents further down were foreign to me; I rarely reached them when I snooped in there. And honestly, they looked pretty boring. Little did I know there were so many hidden gems: historic documents from before I was born, when my parents had given birth to Hannah and to their second baby, Kwons' Café. I was baby number three.

Folded newspaper articles were held together by thick metal paper clips and binder clips. It was hard to believe that everything remaining in the box was older than I was. My fingers trembled as I loosened the clasps. What if I pulled too hard and the papers ripped? What if I couldn't replace everything to their original state and my parents found out I was digging into their sacred personal belongings? I'd probably be grounded through the end of the school year. Maybe longer. Maybe forever.

After a few minutes, all the newspaper pages were freed and for the first time, I was able to see what my parents had stored away all these years. Excitement swelled inside me as I unfolded the first new-to-me article.

"Grand Opening of Riverwood's First Korean Restaurant." Bingo. This was exactly what I needed. A short few paragraphs announcing the public launch date of Kwons' Café. I laughed out loud at the photo. The only thing that had upgraded was the cash register. My parents hadn't changed anything else in about fifteen years. Even the tip jar was in the same place.

The second newspaper clipping was more coverage on the restaurant from its first year. The headline read "Voted The Best Restaurant by the Riverwood Community." My parents barely smiled for the camera. Mom held me in her arms while Hannah clung to Dad's left leg. Umma and Appa looked so young, with their jet-black hair and smooth, wrinkle-free faces. The restaurant business had really worn them down. Or maybe we did... or I did, by placing stress on them by not being exactly like their other ideal child.

Another text from Hannah. **SOS! Mom and Dad are coming home! Hope you found something useful.**

I did find wonderful treasures, and all I needed to do was scan them and with some Photoshop magic, then sharpen and adjust these articles to use these in our campaign.

Although I had all the source material I needed, something drew me to the last sheet of newspaper folded into quarters. This was the largest keepsake of them all, by far the biggest when fully unfolded.

It took me a few seconds to read and reread the headline: "East West Wok Opens to the Public." The profile piece was lengthy, and I didn't think I'd have time to read it. My gaze was immediately drawn to the large photograph at the bottom. Dad and Mom were on the left. Umma had a big pregnant belly, and based on the date of the article, that little watermelon was Hannah. To the right of them was another Asian couple: a man and woman holding a baby. Both couples were standing next to a few other people, probably customers.

An overwhelming sense of familiarity sent a jolt down my spine. The man, barely looked out of college, looked just like Peter Li. Bringing the article closer to me, I could see that this was Peter's parents standing right next to mine. They looked... happy-ish? Like they weren't willing to murder each other. What the hell was going on?

My jaw fell open as I read the article. The Kwons and Lis owned East West Wok together, and they brought "Eastern exotic cuisine from Korea and China to Riverwood." They had been business partners! The article included a sample menu...sesame chicken with broccoli and marinated bulgogi beef didn't sound all that exotic to me. There was only one main dish on the list, a fusion delight called kkanpungi, that my parents described as "spicy and sweet unique fried chicken" on the menu. How ridiculous that the journalist took liberties in describing their food and culture in a way that was nothing like their reality. Maybe they should have added descriptions of "exotic fortune cookies" and "exotic fried tofu" to the story.

Did the Li and Kwon family warfare start when they ran a restaurant together? I took all three articles to my room and scanned them on the highest-quality setting. Mom and Dad would be here soon. My duty was to scan, reassemble, and return everything back to normal. When that was done with that mission, I could go ahead and freak out about what I'd just learned.

On my tiptoes, I slid the lockbox back to the original position just as my parents closed the front door. Using the hats and scarves as coverage, I put things back to the earlier state, thanks to the photos I took of the crime scene before I pulled everything down.

While Mom and Dad came up the stairs, I ran to my room, closed the door, and let out a frustrated, exasperated sigh. The rift between the Kwons and Lis went way back, and the chasm between them had widened for fifteen years. Was it even possible to repair their relationship? What happened to East West Wok?

I messaged Peter. SHIT! SHITTT! We gotta talk soon, and I need to show you something important...early dinner exchange tomorrow ok?

He replied Studying now, big test tomorrow. Sounds good, well, except for the shit part.

See you tomorrow. Good luck.

I knew how important Peter's grades were to him. And I could wait twenty-four hours before I turned his world upside down too.

SEVENTEEN

PETER

I MAY HAVE GONE OVERBOARD WHEN CHLOE ASKED me to get photos and historical mementos from the other store and restaurant owners. After school, I introduced myself to every single store and shop manager in the entire mall. Aside from a few ornery people, they were really excited to have someone try to do something about the mall closure, since so many jobs were at stake. Everyone offered to pitch in, whether it was by contributing photos, or talking to their friends in the local government, or volunteering to help on various committees. I wanted this video to be the best it could be.

I even snagged some old menus from my parents. But when I asked them for old photos or other mall-related keepsakes, they said there weren't any. This was weird because they'd kept every single terrible childhood photo of my brother and me, in either buzz cuts or bowl cuts, over my entire life span. And they took great pride in our family photos—which were framed and placed throughout our living room—with my mom and dad's hands placed awkwardly on our shoulders, our faces not quite smiling at the camera. There were multiple years with braces and expanders too. My brother had 20/20 vision, but I ended up photographed with my value frames from Lenscrafters and Costco all through elementary and middle school before I wore contacts. There was no way Mom and Dad didn't have keepsakes from the early restaurant days.

If I kept pressing though, they'd both be angry with me for questioning them. Clearly they didn't want me to dig anymore, and it wasn't like one of them was calm and the other hotheaded, like good cop/bad cop parenting, or that Mom was the yin to Dad's yang. They were identical. Both fiercely private, stubborn, and impatient. Compatible because they were so similar that it was scary. And this meant that when they yelled at me, it was always two of them against one of me.

But I had everything I needed to give to Chloe. She was running late, and her noodles were getting cold. The temperatures had dropped to a brisk thirty-five degrees, but in the back alleyway it was maybe low fifties thanks to the heat from all the restaurants blowing through the grill vents, just barely above teeth-chattering levels. My stomach growled, and her shrimp lo mein tempted me, but I held out for the Kwons' Café combo.

"There you are!" Chloe exclaimed as she burst through her restaurant door and plopped down in the chair next to me. She slid a takeout container toward me and pulled the lo mein to her. "Oh God, I have so much to tell you, you won't even believe... wait. Did you do all of this?"

Her gaze traveled from the lit candle, to the nice paper dinner napkins, to the white tablecloth, then over to the small rose floral arrangement I'd gotten from the Riverwood florist at the other end of the mall. I couldn't tell from her surprised face whether she liked the little added touches to our usual dinner hangout, so I backpedaled. "It's to celebrate that I scheduled a meeting with the landlord, thanks to the help of my boss. It's December first. The florist offered his arrangements to thank us for trying to help the mall. He gave this to me for like, a huge discount." I didn't bother telling her it took me nearly fifteen minutes to pick out the perfect flowers for her. It was too embarrassing. "I know you're not super into flowers, but I thought these were nice."

Heat rushed to my face as I stuffed spicy pork into my mouth.

She looked at me, then back at the flowers again. "I don't know what to say. Thanks for setting up the landlord meeting. And...no one's ever actually gotten me flowers before. Thank you."

"Mur melcom!" This was what I got for stress-eating Korean pork. Lack of dude confidence and the inability to enunciate. I swallowed and chased the spiciness with a few chugs of Sprite, then tried again. "You're welcome." *Much better, Pete.* "Now, you want to tell me what you found? I got you everything you needed." I handed her an overstuffed accordion folder. "I have tons of photos, videos, magazine and newspaper articles... It's great. But it's weird, my parents were acting shady—"

She grabbed my hand and my heart nearly stopped.

"That's what I needed to talk to you about."

Chloe was holding my food-shoveling hand. I wasn't competent enough to use chopsticks with my other hand, and although I was still hungry, I didn't dare disrupt Chloe's hand on mine. It was like admiring a butterfly: you didn't want to startle or disrupt the moment of simple beauty, especially when you knew the moment was fleeting.

To my surprise, she also grabbed my other hand. "You HAVE to talk to your parents. They might open up to you." *What was she talking about?*

She let go of both hands to dig into her messenger bag. Booo. See? Fleeting. Bye bye butterfly.

Chloe showed me newspaper articles and photos she had scanned. None of it made any sense. When were our parents actually at one point in their lives...*not* hating each other? Their body language in the photos didn't scream "*RIDE OR DIE*" but it definitely didn't suggest that they were destined to be mortal enemies. They didn't look like people who would eventually ban the other couple and their offspring from coming within ten feet of their eating establishments. In fact, this was the only time I'd seen my parents in any photograph...sort of smiling. Even in photos of my baptism, my brother's graduation, and my brother getting into med school, they always appeared stoic and stern. I had to think Chloe's parents were the same way.

"What do you want me to do, ask my parents about East West Wok? They won't even share anything with me other than old Empress Garden menus, and I tried. I don't know how to get to the truth from them."

Chloe's crestfallen face said everything. She was always so sure of who she was and what she wanted out of life, so it yanked at my heartstrings to see her like this. It was like my whole body was unraveling.

I had to think of something. She needed me. And I needed her.

Without overthinking it, I scooted up next to her and placed my hand on her arm to comfort her. My pulse quickened the second we touched. "There are some restaurants that were here around the same time as East West Wok. Want to look through these piles of history with me? I separated it by business and put everything in chronological order. It shouldn't be that hard to find. Then we can talk to the owners who were there and see if they remember anything from back then. Maybe they knew our parents."

She gave me a meaningful look and nodded. "Okay."

Reluctantly removing my hand from her arm, I grabbed the

accordion folder and handed her a few piles of artifacts grouped together in gallon-size ziplocks. "Don't mess anything up or they'll kill me."

"Of course."

After a few minutes, I waved a newspaper clipping in the air. "Hey! I found something!" I showed her an article from the Hamburger Palace. "They were next to East West Wok back then! Let's go talk to Mr. Fry, the owner."

She squealed and grabbed the page out of my hand. "Yes! This is so perfect. I could kiss you."

Blood pounded in my brain. Kiss me?

Why not?

I took a deep breath and leaned forward, then pressed my lips onto hers.

Spontaneous, electrifying, tingling. Wow.

I fell back into my chair. Chloe's eyes widened, then crinkled in the corners from her wide smile. "Well, that was better than flowers."

She stood from her chair and I rose from my seat too. *Peter, don't ruin this. Please don't go trying to be your scaredy-cat crowd-pleaser self. Just kiss her again.*

She pulled my collar and as my head dipped down, her lips crashed into mine. I closed my eyes and kissed her back with equal force. A door creaked open, causing both of us to jump back and separate, but it turned out to be the wind pushing open the back entrance to the gyro place. We laughed and held each other in a tight embrace as delivery trucks sputtered and grumbled by, her arms wound inside my coat and around my back, my arms draped on her shoulder. Surrounded by honking and beeping and warm restaurant vent air, standing next to the white tablecloth table with roses I bought for Chloe, we were in the most romantic of unromantic places. It was perfect.

EIGHTEEN

CHLOE

HE KISSED ME.

And I kissed him.

It terrified me that we had done something so fundamentally forbidden. Yet I couldn't stop thinking about his warm lips pressed against mine. If I didn't have the final presentation for the National Art Council and the fate of the mall to worry about, I'd just replay that moment over and over in my head—my lips tingling from the contact, the jolt from his arms around my body—until the next time we kissed. I wish I had that luxury.

Instead, Peter and I sat at a food court table while I tried to interview Mr. Fry about his knowledge of East West Wok while he complained about his arthritic back, the global warming conspiracists on Facebook, and how his good-for-nothing kids take-take-take from him all the time.

"...when did pomegranates become a superfood? Who gets to pick what the superfoods are? When I was your age..."

"...and have you seen these gas prices? How is it that we have a state as big as Texas drilling and yet we're still so dependent on the Saudis? I thought electric cars were supposed to fix this!"

What was it with older people and gas prices? My parents' number one complaint was about the prices at gas stations. Every time we drove by one, they remarked, "Waaa! So expensive here! Four dollar?!"

"That's highway robbery! Near us is cheaper! Five cent cheaper each gallon."

"Unleaded so high! Why so high? Maybe because this neighborhood too rich."

They could have an entire radio show solely about gas prices and have people like Mr. Fry call in. He'd jump on his "These gas prices are an abomination! We were promised flying cars by now!" soapbox and people like my parents would egg him on.

Maybe this could be their backup plan if we couldn't save this place.

Well, we really couldn't save Riverwood Mall if Mr. Fry never got around to helping us because he was knotted up in his random thoughts. Peter must've had the same thought. As soon as Mr. Fry paused for a breath, Peter asked, "Could you talk about the time Hamburger Palace was next to East West Wok?"

"Whoa son, that was ages ago." He chuckled. "Were you even born yet? Let's see, that was maybe fifteen years ago, maybe more. I remember there were two little ones running around, a boy and a girl. Not related though. One was from one family and the other was from the other one."

Hannah and Sam.

He jutted his chin stroked his beard. "Maybe it was two boys, it was hard to tell them apart. Not because they were Asian, but because they both had the same bowl mullet." Mr. Fry pointed his index fingers to his forehead and moved them back past his ears and down to the shoulder. "Maybe it was a trend or something in those days. In any case, that business fizzled pretty quick." He exhaled out of his nose and just stopped talking. So after all that chatter, he had nothing to say now?

I asked, "Wait, so, do you know what happened? Why did it fizzle?" The large clock on the wall read 7:35 p.m. Hannah lived across town and was meeting me soon so we could confront our parents together. I needed answers, and all I'd managed to gather was that Mr. Fry hated inflation, superfoods, and Toyota Priuses. Honestly, he was a man after my own heart.

Mr. Fry cleared his throat. "They never told us what happened exactly, but there was speculation. I don't like to spread rumors." Mr. Fry stopped speaking again, and I was about to jump in to tell him we really needed to hear what he'd heard and that spreading rumors was okay by us, he quickly added, "You didn't hear it from me, but it was over finances. A third friend, a business partner, who either loaned or stole money, I don't remember all the details. There's no one else to ask because everyone else around those days has come and gone, sadly. And that guy skipped town from what I heard. And if the mall closes, there goes all the history..."

Mr. Fry's mouth trembled. He sat upright and composed himself. "Let me know how else I can help you two. It seems like you're trying new things to keep Riverwood around. I like that. Keep up the good work. You're entrepreneurial, like the bunch of us." He gestured to the restaurants behind him. "Some of these guys are franchisees, but they got hustle too."

I pulled out the only photo I had of East West Wok. "Do you know anyone else in the photo?" I'd thought the other people in the picture were customers, but maybe not.

He lifted his reader glasses from his chest pocket and put them on. "Oh wow, this is a blast from the past. Look at our old signage!"

The Hamburger Palace in the far background looked exactly the same to me. But that was part of its charm: it had a genuine retro feel and the price were reasonable. Probably had something to do with Mr. Fry's aversion to hiking up the cost.

"Well, those are your parents of course." He pointed at our

moms and dads. "Goodlookin' bunch. Maybe it was you kids that gave 'em the gray hair." He winked at us, and Peter and I both smiled. Mr. Fry was a good guy, even if he was rough around the edges. Riverwood's own real-life Oscar the Grouch.

He tapped his fingers on a man standing off to the side. "That's him. He's the guy that blew up the business."

I pulled the photo closer to Peter and me. I had no idea who that lanky guy was. He had black hair and appeared to have a cigarette in his hand.

Peter gulped. "Shit. That's Uncle Joe."

NINETEEN

PETER

UNCLE JOE WASN'T OUR ACTUAL UNCLE. HE WAS A family friend.

Was.

Past tense.

He was our neighbor, once upon a time. No clue where he was now, and I hardly remember him even though there are tons of photos of me in his arms as a wee baby.

He wasn't Chinese either.

Joe Brewer. A name too common to be googleable.

"You know that guy?" Chloe's brows drew into a concerned, deep V expression.

I ran my hand through my hair. "Uncle Joe used to be a friend of my parents. He told everyone to call him Uncle Joe. I don't know what happened to him. I never really asked, and my parents never talked about it." My head swiveled toward Mr. Fry. "You mean Uncle Joe was part of East West Wok?"

He bobbed his head up and down. "I'm not one to gossip," he leaned in for full effect, "but I *heard* he was skimming off the top." Motioning his head toward my family's restaurant, he said, "I think you better confirm with your parents though."

Was Uncle Joe the cause of the chasm between the Lis and Kwons? Did he screw them over financially?

There was only one way to find out.

I eased into a smile. "Thank you for your help. And thank you for making the best hamburgers in town. I could eat them all day."

Chloe shot me a look. Like if her rolled eyes could groan, this would be her perma-expression toward me.

Mr. Fry stood up. "I saw in Hannah's email that you all were going to meet with the landlord, and one of the ideas you had was doing an international food festival. It's a great idea, but how about broadening it a little so I can cook something up too? I'm not international, but I can do BBQ like no one's business. Might be nice to try something a little different, you know?"

Chloe's face lit up. "I love this idea. Riverwood International Food Festival was the original concept, but you have a point. Maybe this could be a bigger food festival. Oh! Maybe we could make it like a street fair!"

I asked, "You'd have vendors outside?"

"I was thinking inside. But maybe both." She laughed and clapped her hands. "Maybe we can bring in food trucks and other craft vendors here, like a pop-up event. You know, I've always wondered how they got those brand-new car models inside the mall. There doesn't seem to be an entrance wide enough for the SUVs, yet there are always cars, trucks, and SUVs inside this place. Do they drive them down the corridor or are they towed in? I'll ask." She pulled out her phone and wrote herself a note. "Oh wow, my to-do list is getting so long. The landlord better love these ideas."

It was great to see Chloe this way. Full of ideas, energy, and confidence. I wanted to hug her, but as weird as it sounded, I was worried that by embracing her I'd suppress her radiant light somehow.

"Well, let me know. I'll be happy to help however I can or even cater an event. And that street fair idea, as my grandson would say, it really slaps. Or is it claps? Whatever, you know what I mean." Mr. Fry stood up and wiggled his back. "Damn arthritis. Anyway, good luck, you two." He walked toward the direction of Hamburger Palace but then took a bathroom detour.

I knew what needed to happen next, at least for me. Chloe probably had a million things running through her mind, but I had just one: to find out what the hell Uncle Joe did to cause so much hate. Tapping lightly on Chloe's hand, I said, "I need to go find out what went down at East West Wok. My parents are both working now, and I can ask them both at the same time."

She didn't pull her hand away. The length of time my hand rested on hers was directly correlated to the level of heat rising in my neck. "If you can get to the bottom of it, maybe there's a way our parents can put aside their differences, even if it's just short term, to work together and with us to help save Riverwood."

My dad walked to the bathroom just as Mr. Fry exited. "I'll just catch him when he comes out. It's weird when people have full-blown conversations at the urinals." I shuddered while Chloe laughed at me. "I'm serious! When someone talks to me, wanting to be all chit-chatty at the stalls, I don't know where my eyes are supposed to go. There are no good options. You either look at the other person, or look down at your own—"

She cut me off. "You know, I don't need to hear anymore. I used to think there was a lot more social pressure on girls than guys, but maybe I was wrong." After chatting about school a few minutes, Chloe pointed ahead. "Look! Your dad just came out of the bathroom. Call or text if you find out anything."

I jumped to my feet and jogged over to my father, walking alongside him as he headed to Empress Garden. "Do you have a second to talk about something important?"

Dad's brows furrowed as he stopped in his tracks. "Here?"

Standing between Victoria's Secret and Chico's? Uh, no. "Maybe back at the restaurant?" I headed to Empress Garden, and Dad

followed suit. "I have some questions about things I heard from—"
I heard Mr. Fry's gruff voice echoing Kwon in my head...*I'm not one
to gossip...You didn't hear it from me*...I couldn't throw old man Fry
under the bus after he gave us so much valuable intel.

"You heard *something* from who?" Dad asked.

"I saw it in some newspaper clippings. About your restaurant." We entered the food court area where some of the Silver
Sneakers walking club were having dinner and a few harried moms
and dads had cranky toddlers and infants with them, trying to find
a way to eat a meal while keeping an eye on their little ones, who
wanted nothing more than to crawl or teeter-walk away.

Dad went behind the counter and put on his apron. "You saw
something in the *Tennessean* about us?"

Mom came out from the kitchen. "A review in *Nashville
Scene*? Maybe someone's giving us a Best of Riverwood award?"
She pointed to the wall next to the register covered with wood
plaques with bronze placards. "I was hoping we'd win again!"

I shook my head. "No, it's this." I took the printout of the
scanned article from my pocket and unfolded it. "You two used
to own East West Wok. Co-own it actually, with the Kwons. What
happened? You were friends, once upon a time." Handing it to my
mom, I looked behind me to make sure there were no customers.
This might take a while to sort out, and my parents would use a
line of hungry patrons to defer or deflect the issue. I tapped my
index finger on Joe Brewer's face.

All Mom said was, "That's Uncle Joe. He's not welcome here."

Dad said through clenched teeth, "He doesn't live in Tennessee anymore. You don't need to worry about him."

I knew that by not responding to my earlier point, about being in business with the Kwons, that meant the joint business part was true. "So you *were* in business with Chloe's parents. What happened?"

Mom shook her head. "It happened a long time ago. Don't bring up old ghosts."

Dad confirmed. "Leave it alone."

"But I'm just trying to understand. Is Uncle Joe the reason why you and the Kwons aren't on speaking terms?"

Mom clucked her tongue. "Uncle Joe was a snake. He ruined our business, and it was hard to get another loan for this place. We were lucky to find a bank, but they gave us a high interest rate. The Kwons are lucky to have their place too. This doesn't concern you. It happened a long time ago. It's over now."

"But it does concern me. And it's not over. Normally I wouldn't care if you were giving another family the cold shoulder, but you and the Kwons are part of this mall community. If we're gonna save this mall, we need you to work together."

Dad raised his voice. "We don't ever want to work with them again."

"But—"

"There's nothing more to say." Mom exchanged looks with

Dad, her lips pressing together and shaking her head no, a warning not to disclose any more information to me. "Now go home and study."

My dad slammed the napkin holder on the counter. This lack of communication between them and me was sometimes a relief. They'd never ever given me "the talk" about where babies came from or asked questions about any nights I stayed out past curfew. As long as my grades were good, they pretty much left me alone. But this time it was infuriating. It was like them telling me I was too young to understand. That I wasn't adult enough to handle it. That I didn't deserve their respect.

I messaged the only person who would understand.

Chloe.

They won't tell me ANYTHING.

She replied, **Hannah's not going to make it here, we can't ask my parents about it together. Maybe I'll try by myself?**

Good luck, I hope you get more answers than I did.

Three-dot reply bubble. Then nothing. I looked over at Chloe across the food court. She was chatting with her parents and the getting the same results. Fallen faces. Crossed arms. Heads shaking no.

A message from Brach vibrated my phone. Shooting hoops, playing Overwatch, ordering pizza at my place. You in? The only answers are yes or hell yes.

I needed to get my head on straight, and hanging out with my friends would help me take my mind off things. I threw on my backpack and slipped out the back of the restaurant. Exiting the covered loading dock, I walked toward the employee parking lot where snow had dusted our ratty red Corolla, giving it a very holiday look. Turning on the ignition, I looked in the rearview mirror to see a steady stream of smoke from my exhaust pipe rise into the frigid air. With my hand on the gear shift, I moved the knob to R, but didn't back out. Instead, I shifted the gear back to park and messaged Chloe.

Text when you're done with your parents. I'll drive you home. Want to make sure you're OK.

No three dots. No reply yet. But I'd wait until I heard back.

TWENTY

CHLOE

DAD BARELY LOOKED AT THE PHOTO BEFORE HE handed it back to me.

"That's long time ago. We don't want to talk about."

Hannah would be so much better at extracting a confession. Umma and Appa took her more seriously.

I tried another approach. "We really need you two to get over your differences, for the sake of this Riverwood community. For the sake of Hannah and me."

Mom rolled pennies into a fifty-cent stack for the bank. Without making eye contact, she muttered, "We don't like Li family."

No shit, Mom.

"Who is Uncle Joe?" I asked.

Mom and Dad's heads both snapped up, like I'd just threatened to conjure evil spirits with the mere mention of Uncle Joe's name.

"Who is he? Why is this man in this photo?" I handed my mom the newspaper article.

Dad pressed his lips so tight I thought they might disappear forever. "We never say his name here again, okay?"

"Okay...but can you please just tell me who he is? Or what happened at East West Wok? Anything to make sense of this hatred toward the Lis?"

Hannah and I never questioned their warnings to stay away from the Lis. It was a fact, and we took their word for it. Like being told the burner was too hot to touch, or the tales of caution to never to pour fat down a drain or drink clumpy milk. We took them as truths we didn't dare defy or question.

Mom sighed. "Tell her. Maybe she stop talking so loud and scare away customer."

Dad raised his eyebrows. "Jjinja? We tell her?"

She nodded curtly. "Not much story. Li family is bad business partner. End of story. Stop hanging around with Li boy."

My stomach fell to my feet. Had they seen Peter and me together? *Together* together?

Dad added, "We know everything. What you doing. What you sneaking around. We see you."

Ohmygoddd.

How was I supposed to respond? I wasn't sorry Peter and I had gotten closer. An apology wasn't something I was willing to offer them because there was nothing to be ashamed of. So what if they were rival families? I'd fallen for Peter. We held hands. We kissed. Hannah would be the type to call it off to please my parents. But I wasn't Hannah.

"I don't regret what we've done. And I'm not going to stop." Had they seen us kiss? The thought made my stomach sink.

Dad tilted his head and eyes bulged. "Okaaay, but if you keep taking Li family noodle for exchanging spicy pork, can you share? I love lo mein."

Mom slapped his upper arm. "Don't tell her that. She need to stop swapping spicy pork for traitor food."

So this was all about...the dinner exchange? They didn't know about Peter and me? I almost burst into laughter, but that might lead them on a fishing expedition. Biting my lip was the only thing I could do to suppress a smile.

Dad shrugged and winked at me. Clearly Dad wasn't exactly on the same page as Mom. Maybe he was the one to butter up for more information.

Umma sighed. "Appa always thinking with his stomach." She lifted a small box from under the counter and opened it with a box cutter. Hundreds of salt and pepper packets.

Dad announced, "Chloe, can you take that box to back room to stock up?"

Grabbing the package from Umma's hands, I did as I was told. While I was sorting the salt and pepper into separate bins, Dad came to join me.

"Li family make the best Chinese food in town. I miss eating." He sat on a wooden stool. "We meet them when we first move here. They live on same street as us."

I knew if I kept quiet, not interrupting with questions and letting Dad go on, it was my best chance at getting more answers about the past.

But then a grimace passed over Appa's face. "Okay, when you done, come back for another box." He stood up.

"Wait!" I had to choose my words carefully. "What were the Lis like back then?"

He sighed. "We young then. We just have Hannah. They have big dream of owning their business. We do too. Umma and me looking at business like car wash, dry cleaning, corner market, laundrymat. We go into business together, we think we work less if more people owning place. Big mistake."

"East West Wok was busy?"

"Yes, and we fighting all the time. Like our name, Umma and Appa want 'The Wok.' It simple. Cool sounding. Hip."

I tried to not cringe at Dad saying the word "hip."

"Li family want Golden Wok. We argue and finally choose name." He paused and looked wistful. "Business was good. Then Uncle Joe, Li family friend, he has a small business accounting and bookkeeping company and say he can give us discount. He live on our street too, in big house. Corner lot. We thinking he so successful and we were so honored he want to help us."

My mom called to the back. "Yobo! Yeogiwa!"

Dad shot me an apologetic look. "Umma need me. Uncle Joe steal a lot of money from a lot of small business and then he leave town. Police never find him, they say he maybe leave country." His eyes watered, and mine filled with tears in response.

"We trust him with our life then. Now we trust nobody." He patted my shoulder and added, "Don't be accountant."

Mom and Dad weren't thrilled when I wanted to be an artist, but it turned out accountancy was worse in their minds. For some parents, that would be a dream job for their kids.

As soon as Dad left the room, I searched for Joe online, and while he was hard to find at first, his name came up with articles about East West Wok and "Joe Brewer embezzlement." He was a small-time swindler, but since he'd scammed so many individual immigrant entrepreneurs, for nearly twenty businesses in the state of Tennessee, and evaded taxes, the collective fraud really added up. He started small, by overcharging for bookkeeping and accountant tasks during tax season, then moved up to embezzling from payroll systems. He got caught when he got greedy and opened a new credit card attached to one of the restaurants he did the books for and used it for personal purchases, then paid it monthly using direct bank payments. It was all small charges, like gas and meals, that went undetected for years. And like Dad said, Joe was never caught because he disappeared into the wind. He skipped town and took millions of dollars with him. He had no known family. Maybe Joe wasn't even his real name.

I texted Peter and let him know I'd be calling him with this newly discovered information. It was way too long to type out.

What had happened to Mom and Dad all those years ago weighed my heart down, like someone placed a weighted blanket on my chest. They had so much pride and honor. Coming here from Korea after college, trying to live the quintessential American dream, owning a restaurant and then having someone take advantage and scam them... I could see why they'd be so distrustful and regretful. Their hate was directed at the Lis, when they were actually more angry at asshole Joe. But the Lis were clearly hurting too. Maybe there was still hope for the two families to reconcile.

Or at the very least, maybe for once they could let bygones stay in the past. Could we convince them that saving the mall came down to the whole community coming together? Could they forgive, or even agree to be civil, for the sake of working toward the same goal?

My parents harbored grudges all the time; it was part of their DNA. It ran in the Kwon family. They never liked to admit they were wrong, even with insignificant things like accusing me of leaving the lights on or not replacing the toilet paper roll when it was actually one of them. Or Hannah.

Maybe these extreme, special circumstances would help Umma and Appa come around. Maybe the Lis would come around too. And then maybe after all of this was over, Peter and I could do as we pleased.

TWENTY-ONE

PETER

I'D SPENT THE WHOLE NIGHT LOOKING THROUGH MY parents' business paperwork instead of studying for midterms. My grades were high enough to be able to balance out less-than-stellar exam scores, plus I was pretty good at hitting up the teachers in their office hours, which always seemed to help my GPA in the end. Sam had taught me that: teachers and professors like it when you stop by. It shows you're interested in the subject and they're more likely to remember you when it's time for final grading.

Mom and Dad told me not to ever bother Sam, because he was so stressed out in med school. But I didn't know if this constituted an emergency and their wishes could be overruled. This was eviction we were talking about...it was an exception, right? I'd looked over all of the landlord and mall coalition correspondence by myself and maybe 50 percent of it went way over my head. The other 50 percent I understood on a line-by-line level, but putting it all together I had no idea if my parents had any legal standing at all. My parents probably had a better grasp of what was going on than other business owners since English was their first language, but it was their refusal to talk to other people in the coalition, plus their stubbornness and pride, that would hurt them more than anything. Over the years, they'd burned a lot of bridges. And not just burned them...they'd detonated them with a shitload of C-4. They had a reputation for arguing about employee parking spots with mall management, complaining about food odors with their neighboring restaurants, and they accidentally let a curious crow in the back door when it was propped open this past spring. Crows were smart and sneaky assholes, and one got in and this one wreaked havoc. For weeks, no one could catch him and he ate through hundreds of dollars of food supplies at night. I was able to lure him outside with a trail made of bits of Sbarro pizza crust. When he saw the grand prize, an entire triangle slice of pepperoni pizza just beyond the door, he couldn't resist.

Everyone hated my parents after that. I begged them to offer lunch to everyone for free, to ease the tension, but they said no way. Specifically, Mom barked, "That's too expensive," while Dad shook his head and muttered, "This is the other restaurant owners' problem for not installing a good fan above their stove. That's why we had the door open. Why should we pay?"

That's how it always was with them. Always someone else's fault.

Before they went to sleep, I knocked on their bedroom door. "Come in!" Mom and Dad were both in bed, watching the local news.

"I don't understand... Why didn't you ever tell me about the mall closing? Or take any of this as seriously as you should have?"

My mom took off her glasses and put it on the nightstand. "The coalition said they'd work with the landlord. They should have made it all easier to understand. There was a lot happening, talks about relocation and buying us out. Even maybe expansion of the mall. But we waited and waited, and now everything changed. And time is running out." She sighed and pushed a gray lock of hair out of her eyes. "No one kept us in the loop. They should have. There's a meeting next week, the day before Thanksgiving, maybe there will be more news. Maybe it will be good this time." Then Dad reached over and clicked off the lamp by his bed, making the room go pitch black. His way of saying, "Bedtime. Conversation over." I found my way to the door after stubbing my foot on the dresser and feeling my way around the wall.

Back at my desk, I pored through the paperwork again. As much as I hated what was going on, the landlord Rick Jones Jr., a.k.a. "Jones Realty LLC" came across as a reasonably nice guy who had inherited a lot of commercial real estate from his dad. Rick Senior was the original lessor to my parents, and in the landlord communications he'd been very open and forthcoming about his plans to hand over his real estate to his son. Junior had stated that "nothing would happen until after the holidays" in his latest memo dated November 1. So there was that at least.

It was two a.m., and I hadn't even studied for AP Bio. I sent Chloe a message: Want to meet up after school?

I was too tired to explain why or where or any other pertinent details. What surprised me was her immediate reply. Yeah I'll find you at your locker.

It was nice that I wasn't tripping all over myself about what to say or how to say it with Chloe. She was warming up to me, but still acted in her own Chloe-like way. And the thought of that made me smile. I tried to wipe it off my face by relaxing my cheeks and opening and closing my mouth like a giant bass, but even after I logged into the school science portal, looking for AP bio practice exams to take, the grin was still there.

Brach slapped my thigh so hard it made my eyes water.

"Why'd you do that?"

"You are shaking the entire row of bleachers with your fidgety leg. Stop! Don't make me do the pinch and twist."

Brach punished Kip and me by pinching skin on our upper arm and twisting the fat. I thought that when I gained muscle definition in my arms, he'd have trouble doing it, but no, he always found a way. Brach used his torture sparingly, but when he did, it was effective.

"What are you so anxious about?" he asked, holding out a pack of gum. He was addicted to Trident, but that was a good thing for me, because it meant he always had gum in his possession.

I took one, unwrapped it, and popped it in my mouth. "My parents."

"So, the usual."

"Sort of." I'd told Brach and Kip about the landlord issues while we were playing Overwatch, but they were barely listening and honestly, I didn't divulge all of it. They had their own suburban white-collar, white-guy family issues—with divorces, remarriages, and various medical problems plaguing their genetic pool. Complaining to them about money issues, my parents' stubbornness, and their ability to hold grudges like it was their actual job never felt right. And plus, my parents never talked to anyone outside the family about private stuff like money issues, and it was implied that we shouldn't either.

We watched Kip run around the track with his arms high above his head, like he'd already won this race. Brach and I had completed our relay for PE and were watching the next heat.

Brach elbowed me. "Isn't that Chloe?"

Yep, he was right. She was on another team, a few lanes over from Kip. And while Kip was kicking up dirt and running Olympic-level speeds, only to be slowed down by his own idiocy with his victory arms, she was doing what she always did in PE. Walking. Or actually, strolling. She didn't even seem to feel any pressure to go any faster or that she'd be letting her team down. Chloe didn't give a shit about that stuff. I wish I could be like that. And I wish I could run up and kiss her again.

"You think she'll finish the lap before the bell rings?" Brach asked.

"I'm guessing not." I waved to her, my right arm shooting straight up and hand swaying left to right, but she didn't see it. I hope she wasn't ignoring me. It wasn't the kind of wave that I could play off by running my fingers through my hair and acting like I was trying to smooth out my cowlick. Her lack of response made my cheeks flush with embarrassment.

She was only half done when everyone else had disbanded and was going back to the gym lockers to change clothes. But rather than follow my buddies back inside, I jogged over to Chloe to walk the rest of the lap with her.

She startled at my sudden appearance. "Oh! It's you. Hey Peter."

"A penny for your thoughts?" I fished in my gym shorts pocket and found an extra stick of Trident. "Or gum instead?"

She accepted the offering and smiled. "Sorry I'm a little out of it. I was thinking through my video edits for the competition and worried about us getting our asses kicked to the curb in January. All this has my brain working overtime. And there's no time to talk about...or explore...us. You know?"

The shadowy circles resting under my eyes, plus all my constant yawning, were evidence of that fact. "Yeah, I know. It's a lot. It's been hard to focus on anything."

Chloe nodded. "You still able to meet after school? My sister is coming over, and she's going to share what she's figured out so far. Hannah's the smart one who can make sense of all this and she'll save the day. She works at a law firm as a paralegal. I don't know if you knew that."

I knew Hannah Kwon. She and my brother were huge rivals in high school. He was not a fan. Like he still talked about it with his high school buddies, how he got screwed over for the top spot in the class because she took Honors Spanish and he'd taken Latin but switched to French after two years and didn't get the GPA benefit of Honors or AP foreign language like Hannah did. Chloe was nothing like her sister, whereas Sam and I were alike mainly because I tried to emulate him but never could quite cut it. I kept waiting for my moment to shine, and I hoped that I'd wake up with some kind of aha moment of self-discovery, with some certainty of what my purpose in life was. But that day hadn't come. Maybe it never would. But if we could actually save the mall, it might help me stand out and change the trajectory of my life.

The right side of the double doors to the indoor gym was propped open by a makeshift doorstop made from a folded piece of cardboard. Everyone was already in the locker rooms changing and showering. Chloe and I squeak-walking on the glossy, newly polished floors echoed in a way that was especially loud and awkward for just two people.

She reached out and touched my hand. "So I'll catch you later then?"

We stopped in the far end of the gymnasium where the locker rooms for girls and boys were on opposite corners.

My body shivered as her touch sent cold tingles up my arm. I couldn't speak coherently, so I nodded instead.

"I'll make dinner for all of us." Even in her oversized school logo tee and baggy mesh gym shorts, she looked adorable in her roomy outfit. Her cheeks were still flushed from that lap she took, which was funny given how little effort she put into it. She offered me a shy smile that made my insides warm. "Don't expect anything fancy though. It might be leftovers from the restaurant plus stuff I make. See ya!" She continued grinning and backed up, smacking into the cinder-block wall. "How'd that get there? Uh, see you later!" Her glowing cheeks turned brighter red as she ricocheted into the girls' locker area.

"Think fast, Yao Ming and Jeremy Lin wannabe!"

A bright orange ball flew from Sean's hands straight toward my face. And I was not thinking fast, I was thinking about Chloe and savoring that brief moment we just had alone. A wide hand shot in front of my nose and swatted the basketball away. I recognized that hand... It had saved me from other varsity sport mishaps and frequently pulled me up from off the ground when Sean body checked me in basketball and PE soccer.

"Thanks, Brach."

"That piece of shit really has it in for you." Brach stood next to me while Kip exited the locker room and wandered over to us.

Sean narrowed his eyes and pressed his lips to a flat line. "So Jeremy Lin, wanna do a three-on-three pickup game after school?"

The answer was no. No, I did not want to do a pickup game with Sean and his Sean clones. I had to be somewhere after classes ended. But that wasn't an acceptable answer.

"Or do you have to go to the mall, like you always do? Aren't there child labor laws in China now?"

I laughed without even thinking about it. Mainly out of habit, because for my whole life Sam had taught me to go with the flow. That was how he handled adversity and it worked for him. "I have plans actually."

He cracked up, like I'd just delivered a sidesplitting punchline. "Sorry, I'm trying to picture you having other things going on other than being a nerd and making kung pao chicken."

I wanted to tell him we didn't have kung pao chicken and

never did because of my mild peanut allergies, but it didn't seem like the right time.

Brach elbowed me. "We'll be there. How about an hour after school so we can get some homework done and play a quick game? Show him a second time what losing is like."

I added, "Yeah, okay."

Sean glanced at his two clones on either side of him. "That works for us."

The trio just stood there as I walked past them to change and get my stuff from my locker. Kip and Brach followed me in to make sure there wasn't any more trouble. As soon as we were out of earshot, Kip asked, "Why does Sean have it in for you? I don't get it."

I shrugged. "Some people are just assholes. He's had a rough life, and for whatever reason he's taking it out on me." For years I'd try to stay out of Sean's way, to let him do his terrorizing elsewhere, but this year he had a target on my back. His Jeremy Lin and Yao Ming jokes were predictable and unoriginal, like he'd downloaded middle school racist jokes from the internet circa 2012.

"Well, I don't know what he's trying to prove, but I hope we win this afternoon." Brach fished a pack of mint Trident from his front pocket and offered it to Kip and me. Kip grabbed three sticks and shoved them into his mouth one right after another. This meant he wanted to pop bubbles. Which meant he was stressed. Kip rarely got stressed. Just the other week he nearly failed his driving test and his heart rate barely crept above his resting rate. Bubble popping was a bad sign.

And that made me more anxious than ever.

I skipped last period so I could look through more leases. I knew Chloe would be on my case about abandoning her that afternoon, so I wanted to have everything reviewed before I went to her house.

The only good thing to come of this experience was that I had some new life clarity: I knew I didn't want to be a Realtor or lawyer when I grew up. Not only had I spent so many late nights reading tedious leases and legal correspondence, I still came up with nothing. Nada. Zilch. This was nothing like what you'd see in like a *Law & Order* show, when lawyers find a smoking gun. I didn't even have a squirt gun. When I compared our seven-year lease to Chloe's family's lease, they turned out to be identical.

I took a sip of Monster drink and rubbed my eyes. It was quiet in the school library, and none of my friends were here, so it was easy to concentrate. The librarians even left me alone and didn't come over when my energy drink can hissed and fizzed as I opened it. God bless them.

From my backpack, I pulled out the lease I'd gotten from

the "vegan leather goods" store next to my VR place. The store carried pleather goods, or animal-free leather, as they marketed it on their store signage. It was vinyl, but that didn't stop the trendy high school and college kids from happily forking over money for plastic clothes. My guess was the plastic they used wasn't the recyclable kind.

I offered the owner five free VR sessions in exchange for a copy of his lease agreement. The toy store owner got the same deal. Chloe would probably be pissed, but I also threw in a free photo with Santa if they sent it over by email. Both of them did it.

My constant yawning caused my contacts to blur, which made it hard to compare these boring-ass leases side by side, line by line, word by word.

I muttered, "Just one more page" and took another swig of caffeine.

It was the next page that made me yelp. In the fake leather goods lease, there was a "demolition clause" that permitted the owner-slash-landlord to sell the property and boot the tenant out. I flipped through more pages. Same for the toy store. The shoe repair business too. And the Driving Me Nuts! store that always smelled so good.

But the Empress Garden lease didn't have this section.

I texted Chloe. I found something!

She wrote back immediately. Is it good news?

Yes? I think? May need your sister to double-check
but yes?

She wrote back **Good news! Omg I could kiss you.**

Deal!

Then she added **it better be really good.**
It was. I found the smoking gun.

TWENTY-TWO

CHLOE

PETER WAS ALREADY AT MY LOCKER WHEN THE BELL rang. I was worried about him being late, but he was early. There he was, with his back against the lockers, one leg lifted up so his foot was pressed against one of the bottom metal doors. His head dipped down, and that made his hair sweep forward in a cute way as he looked at his phone. I wanted to take a photo of him looking like that, but my nice camera was at home.

A few of Peter's friends including Cheremy the school hottie came up to him, causing me to halt in my tracks. No way did I want to walk up to Peter and pull him away from his buddies. And what would I say exactly? *Hey Peter, we have to hurry to my house and come up with a game plan to save our parents' businesses from*

*ultimate destruction. Oh hi Cheremy, Brach, and Kip. Nice to see you.
I love how your hair swoops.*

Sophia came up behind me pointing to her tablet. "Hey! Check out this new background design, it's all anime-themed! I just need—"

"Shhh." I subtly motioned at the hot guy gang swarmed around my locker.

"Are they waiting for you?" she whispered, her eyes as round as frisbees.

I couldn't help but laugh. "Uh, not exactly. I need to meet with Peter about the landlord stuff. And Kip and Brach are always hanging around him. But Cheremy...no idea."

"Cheremy..." A dreamy look crossed her face as she stared straight at him, not even being subtle anymore.

I lowered my voice. "You're actually drooling."

Her hand flew to her mouth. "Oh no! Are you serious?"

I cackled so loudly that all four of those guys looked over at us. *Shit.*

Peter cleared his throat. "I'll catch you guys in an hour then. On the blacktop." They did a round of half-hug, half-backslapping as they left, leaving Peter alone again by my locker. Sophia's gaze followed the trio out the door as she slowly moved toward her locker across the hall from mine.

I scowled at Peter as I approached, making his charming grin fall away. "You need to be back in an hour? Like how are we supposed to come up with a mall plan in that short amount of time?"

He rubbed the back of his hand on his chin. "I know, I'm sorry. But I can't let these guys down, they're depending on me. Actually, they can't let *me* down. Cheremy's going to sub in for me until I show up."

"What are you even talking about?" My hands holding my backpack straps moved down to my hips. "Where do you need to be that's so important? More important that your parents and mine losing their restaurants? *They're* depending on you? Well, we are too."

He took a deep breath in and out. "Trust me, I don't want to be anywhere else but with you." Peter looked a little mortified and added, "You know, strategizing. And helping. But Sean, you know Sean... He challenged me and my guys to a three-man pickup game. You wouldn't understand, but I have to do it. But we're wasting time chatting here, can we go to your house now? I'll show you what I found, and I already worked overtime today to make up for it."

I really wanted to strangle him. He was going to play basketball? "I hitched a ride this morning with Elias. Can you drive us?"

He nodded. "I have a hard stop at 3:40." It was 2:45.

Hannah texted. **Just got home.**

"Fine," I grumbled. "I hope you drive fast. And you're the designated note taker."

He stood up straight. "Yes ma'am!" He saluted me and exaggeratedly marched down the hall next to me. I rolled my eyes as we exited to the parking lot.

Hannah looked at Peter like he was day-old guacamole. With hesitation and mild disgust. "You must be Peter. You look just like your *brother*."

Peter was handsomer and nicer and funnier than Sam, but I didn't want to say all that to her.

He held out his hand. "And you're Hannah. Hi. You're exactly like Sam described."

Her brows knitted close together as she returned the handshake. I tried not to laugh—he shook Hannah in a way she didn't expect, and she didn't want to ask him what he meant by his comment because it would show she cared what other people thought. It was so nice to see someone stand up to her. My respect for Peter shot up, but it didn't make up for the fact that he would be ditching us in half an hour to go shoot hoops.

Hannah led the way to the dining table, which was where she had set up her work area. Stacks of leases, landlord correspondence, and real estate law books filled every square inch of the wooden surface. "As you can see, I've already gotten started here. Take a seat."

With no time to spare, we sat and waited for further

instructions. Hannah always knew what to do, and she did everything well, so I knew we were in good hands.

Hannah remained standing and tidied up a small pile of papers sitting on her laptop keyboard. "I have no idea what to do."

It took a few seconds for her words to sink in. "Whhh—what do you mean? The coalition meeting is in a few days. We need to share something!"

Peter shot me a look of concern. We both thought today would be a brainstorming meeting, maybe come up with legal strategies and fundraising ideas. But she was already starting off with the message *All hope is lost. Abandon ship, mateys!*

"I've been looking through all of this while I'm also finishing up law school applications, and I've been staying up till three or four in the morning, so maybe that's part of it. I'm not seeing a way to save the mall. Legally at least."

None of this sounded like Hannah. She was my dog-with-a-bone, here-to-prove-you-wrong sister. I lost every single argument with her. Or, at least, felt like I did. Mom and Dad often let Hannah get her way because they were tired of arguing with her, which was also what her teachers and professors did when she contested their grading policies. *Ugh...change the channel, I don't care anymore... you're so annoying! Fine, you can go to the movie with your friends. Okay, okay, you can get partial credit for that answer on the exam.*

Who was this person standing here in front of me, telling us she didn't have a plan B? Or her typical plans C and D?

She sat down and flipped through the closest stack of papers, many of which had Post-it tabs at the top. Hannah shook her head as she came across a page in the middle of the pile. "Did you know Mom and Dad didn't even open up some of these envelopes? They were sealed in a milk crate under the desk in their office." Her hand flew to her forehead. A light face-palm.

I asked, "How can we help? Should we look through these piles?"

She let out an exasperated breath. "No, I have them in a specific order. I have more to go through. But could you two unseal that stack of envelopes, unfold the documents, and put them in a separate stack?"

Peter cleared his throat. "I'm here to help, but is that really the best way to use us right now? I mean, we could help you in other more strategic ways, and I think I found something with the leases."

She sighed. "I'm sort of in the middle of something."

He looked at me, then looked at Hannah. "Yeah, let's divide and conquer. Maybe Chloe and I could go to her room so we don't bother you."

Hannah shrugged and went back to reading.

"My room?" I squeaked. I hadn't planned on having anyone go upstairs, especially a boy I kissed. I knew Peter would probably be coming over so I tidied up the living room and kitchen and hid away some embarrassing things my parents kept around the house, like wooden backscratchers, boxes of Band-Aids, and random tubes of ointment. I Swiffered and vacuumed. Stacked and folded. Fluffed a few throw pillows. All downstairs.

I even put up our Christmas tree, which my parents had gotten from a summer yard sale from one of our elderly neighbors who was moving to Florida to retire. It was one of those wiry silver vintage ones that you couldn't find anymore. These days, artificial trees were green or white, and preloaded with lights, and sometimes music. Most of our paper and clay ornaments were handmade, from our preschool days up to maybe middle school, pre-Pinterest. The string of lights we usually hung up every year were burnt out or unintentionally flickered due to neglect and old age, so we hung our outdoor lights on the tree instead, weaving them in and out of the tinsel-y branches. The large, multicolored bulbs dominated the tree and the room, but also added cheer and festivity to our otherwise drab and boring home.

He tapped his watch and smiled. "I only have a few minutes. We should get going."

"Um, okay. So let's go to my room then, I guess, for only a few minutes, then you can get going." I bellowed this, hoping to throw Hannah off about Peter and me. But then it came off as super weird and awkward, drawing attention to the two of us instead, the opposite of what I wanted. I pushed myself away from the table and he did the same.

I avoided eye contact with my sister. "You can follow me, Peter." Rather than wait for him, I darted up the stairs so I could pick up some of the mess along the way before he could see it. When I entered my room, I shut the door immediately behind me. I scooped up my exercise bras, nightshirt, and socks from the floor and tossed them into my closet. I grabbed the box of Kotex teen winged pads that was sitting on my nightstand and threw it under my bed. I peeked to make sure the box wasn't sticking out when I heard Peter knock and ask, "Hey! Can I come in?"

Flustered, my voice squeaked again. "Yes, sir!"

Yes, sir? WTF, CHLOE.

He took cautious steps forward, like I'd boobytrapped the floor with my barely worn crumpled jeans and hoodies. Peter put his backpack down on the ground next to my easel. "So where should I sit?"

I glanced around the room. My desk chair had clothes on it. My bed had clothes on it. My hamper had clothes on it. This was not a guest-friendly, sitting environment.

"I'll just stand, I guess," he said with a smirk.

"No, no. Hold on." Like a snowplow, I used both hands to push heaps of stuffed animals, notebooks, pens, and pencils on my bed to give him enough room to take a seat. He cocked an eyebrow when I stood and held out my hands toward the bed. "Ta-da!"

He stared at the spot but didn't move.

"Is something wrong?" I asked, bracing myself. I mean, there was a lot wrong with my room—everything from my taped-up elementary school art, to the multiple water bottles lining my desk, to the towers of folded clothes on my dresser that should have been put away—but at least he had room to sit now. But having a cute guy in your bedroom which was an actual disaster zone, well, this was something movies and novels didn't really help people like me navigate.

Oh God.

Peter Li. Was in my disaster of a room.

Would we kiss again? Was there time? And if we did, would it be magical like the other night? If we didn't, would the spark between us fizzle?

Peter Li was now sitting next to a heap of loosely folded underwear, seeing me at my very worst.

"Nothing's wrong. Just thinking I didn't picture your room to look this way."

Heat rushed to my face. "I wasn't expecting y—"

He continued, "I mean, it's bad. But it's actually in the same condition as mine, if you can believe it."

I couldn't believe it. I always associated my clutter and messiness with being right-brained. Mom and Dad always scolded me for not being more like Hannah, and this was one of the ways. She was tidy and took pride in how she presented herself, including the appearance of her bedroom, which was minimalistic, or looking at it another way, boring and sterile.

Mine had the energy of a preschool's finger-painting room. A whole lot of oomph. And by oomph, I meant shit strewn everywhere. Yes, it was a problem. Yes, I knew it was and would occasionally clean up to the point of it looking nice, but it would all unravel back to a state of disarray within a few hours, so what was the point?

"I enjoy my cluttered chaos. Plus, I know where everything is."

He asked, "Where's your laptop?"

I pointed at my desk, where books and notebooks were piled up. A silver case peeked out toward the top of the stack.

"And your science homework?"

I pointed at my backpack. Which was sitting on top of an upside-down wooden crate I'd meant to sand down, prime, and paint last year.

"Okay. Where are *you* going to sit?"

The usual plan was sitting on my chair, on top of the barely worn clothes, with my back pressed against the hoodies and sweatshirts hanging off the back, but I didn't feel comfortable doing that in front of him.

"You could sit next to me." He scooted over and patted the mattress with his right hand. There was technically room for me there, but I'd have one inch, maybe to two inches, tops, of separation from him. As I mulled over my options, he added with a coy grin, "I mean, there's always my lap."

My jaw fell open. Peter was so...

"I was kidding. Wow, the look on your face. But seriously, I don't bite. Just sit so we can get started." He stood up, pulled a laptop from his backpack, and went back to the bed. I knew he was joking, but for a second I pictured myself there, on his lap, and my entire body heated up to the point where I began sweating. *No, Chloe, no. You need to focus.* Wiping my forehead with the back of my hand, I plopped down on the clear area on the bed next to him, causing me to bounce a little, then lean and smash into his arm and thigh.

He didn't even flinch. It was like girls fell into him on beds all the time. No big deal.

I slowly sat more upright, but him being heavier and so close to me meant that the only way I could *not* touch him in any way would cause a great deal of strain on my core and glute muscles. And using my muscles for anything wasn't exactly my forte. He really didn't seem to care though. He tap-tap-tapped away on his keyboard. So I let gravity do its thing. My body pressed into his, and he excitedly showed me his restaurant's scanned lease documents.

"Here, look! So my parents' latest lease is for five years, and signed four years ago. Everyone else's are five-year leases too, but they're all fairly recent, like in the last one to two years. I don't really understand why the lease terms would change over time, to be honest."

I chewed on my bottom lip. No idea what he was talking about. Zero clue.

He asked, "Do you think this might have something to do with when the son took over the family business? Do you know when he started getting involved with the mall?"

I nodded. "He started popping up two or three Christmases ago." That was around the time the mall holiday potlucks stopped and the white elephant holiday gift exchange was scrapped. The retired dad was all about *community*. The son, not so much.

He continued. "Anyway, our leases are the only ones that haven't been converted to the new lease language. We still have just over a year left on it. It's so weird, your parents and my parents signed nearly around the same time." A sudden feeling that my head was too warm distracted me from his words. Being so close to him caused my face to flush, warmth now spreading to other parts of my body. "Our lease is missing a section the newer ones have. Or rather, the newer leases have a section added that we don't. Something called a demolition clause. That's as far as I got, but I think it's relevant. It says that they have the right to tear down the building and evict everyone, but that's not in our lease. It's in everyone else's, but not ours."

I jumped to my feet. "Hold on, let me look that up." *Anything to stop this rapid overheating of my body.*

Opening my laptop on my desk, I typed standing up. *Clickity clack.* Pause. *Click.*

"Okay, I just googled *demolition clause*, and this is huge for us. They put the clause in those new leases so they could boot tenants out when they sell and demolish the building, I think you said that. But if ours didn't have it...was the rest of the lease wording the same?"

He nodded. "Yeah, pretty much. The only real difference was the demolition clause."

"I bet the store owners didn't even notice that section."

He continued nodding.

I plopped back down next to him. My body crashed into his. "You really pulled through today! You're so...so..."

My brain tried to form words, but my body was also acutely aware that my left arm and thigh continued to touch his right arm and thigh.

"Resourceful? Attractive? Genius-y? Is that even a word?"

I pushed his arm. "You're not who I thought you were. I thought you had abandoned me today, but you didn't. You're pretty okay, Peter Li."

"You're pretty okay too, Chloe Kwon." He smiled and for a second I thought we'd kiss again. I hoped we'd kiss again. But he dipped his head and continued pointing at a few clauses in the documents on his screen.

My brain still couldn't focus. Unimportant thoughts swirled in my head. *Does he like Tide original scent? Or is that Ivory soap? Is he getting warmer to the touch?*

"So what do you think?"

Think? Think about what? His lips? His sly smile?

Say something. "Uh, let's run it by my sister?"

He peered down at me through his long black eyelashes. "Okay." Though his face read serious, his mouth turned upward. "I expected more...arguing."

I sat up straight, pulling myself away from him. "Arguing? Really?"

"I don't know, we always you know, bicker."

"Bicker?" I huffed, pulling my back into a vertical line.

"Uh, maybe it's banter?"

"Ha! *No.*" Banter was *not* something we did. That was something grown-ups did in romantic comedies on Netflix, or two chatty BFFs did on mainstream TV shows. It wasn't how two Asian kids who worked at a dying mall in Tennessee with competing businesses interacted with each other.

He laughed too. "Okay, fine. We can call it intellectual discourse. Happy?"

"It's more like healthy conversation between two people, where one is always right and the other is Peter Li."

"Ha. Fine, you win." Peter's eyes crinkled around the corners as he laughed. He had this charming way of hanging on to my every word, never glancing at his phone, to make me feel like I was the most important person in the world. It seemed genuine. I'd never felt this way before, and to my surprise, my body relaxed and toppled into Peter's right side again.

He didn't flinch. I didn't either.

As he powered down his laptop, I had an idea. "Hey, can you print this demo clause section from one of the leases? You think we can get the leases of even more people? Maybe the bigger sample will help. Maybe more people have an older lease like us."

He bit his lip and said, "It might be hard to get any information from other store or restaurant owners. My parents aren't exactly the type to make friends. But...I'll try."

"Well, my parents love burning bridges too. They come with accelerant, heavy-duty matches, and a giant fan for the flames. You know, to blow the smoke into the faces of everyone they've alienated." *Including your family. Sigh.*

I added, "Well, maybe we can go together and ask around. We can try to rebuild those bridges. And you can use your Peter charm to win them over."

He elbowed me in the upper arm. "I knew you liked me."

I elbowed him back and fought a smile. We linked his laptop to the printer in my room, which was on the floor, canopied by a large unused poster board. He followed me across the room to get the printout.

"What the—"

He lifted his foot and found a jigsaw puzzle piece stuck to the bottom of it. Peter pulled it off and handed it to me.

"Thanks! I was looking for that one. There's nothing worse than finishing up a thousand-piece puzzle only to find nine hundred ninety-nine pieces." I examined it and then threw it on my desk.

He laughed.

"What? It's off the floor now. So be quiet."

"You know, that's how things go missing in the first place. They're put wherever convenient and easy in the long term, they're misplaced and miscategorized."

I crossed my arms. "Oh right, you have firsthand messiness experience, so I should do as you say, not as you do."

He puffed out his chest. "I think you and I have more in common than you think. And I think we're bantering again."

The old Chloe would have rolled her eyes. Instead, my gaze traveled from his warm, dark brown eyes down to his adorable quirk of a smile. He was so good looking I couldn't stand it. Elias and Soph would die if they knew Peter Li was in my room, just a few inches away from me. And that our bodies touched. Over and over again.

I snapped out of the Peter trance and stood up to grab the paper from the printer. "We have work to do." He walked over to me. The only thing worse than skimming a ten-page lease was doing it next to a really good-looking, charming family enemy who was reading over my shoulder. Just thinking about him, standing behind my right shoulder, gently breathing on me, made me shudder.

He reacted to my light shiver by squatting down, lifting my

Vanderbilt hoodie off the floor and handing it to me. He thought I was cold, but it was heat that rippled through my veins and arteries, even though my clammy hands would suggest otherwise. I couldn't concentrate with him so close.

I turned my head to tell him to give me some space but I caught him looking at me, not the document.

We both turned beet red, but he held his gaze and smiled.

And just then, I wanted to kiss him. But not here, with my sister just downstairs. And among my bedroom mess. It was like making out in a dumpster.

As these thoughts whipped through my mind, Peter kept staring at me. He said softly, "I know it's not the best time, but I really want to—"

"*Hey!* Come down, you two! I think I found something!" Hannah's stern voice echoed through the entire house.

Peter quickly shifted his focus to the floor and scooped up his backpack, stuffing his computer inside, like we were quickly packing up to make a run for it. I clutched the printout close to my chest with one hand and wiggled the bedroom doorknob with the other. He reached for it too, and momentarily Peter's fingers and mine overlapped, sending tingles of electricity flowing from his hand to mine.

I shivered again while turning the knob and was welcomed by a colder draft of air, providing some relief to my overly flushed face. Did Peter feel this change in chemistry between us too? Or was I just imagining it? I didn't dare turn my head to find out, though; I feared what I'd discover. That yes, he and I were recalibrating our banter-bicker status and were thinking about "what ifs" between us. Or maybe that nothing had changed and it was all in my head. Or even worse, not only was it all in my head, that it was one-sided and unrequited. Basically, most of these scenarios were terrible, and it was best to ignore everything because we had to focus on our main objective. To save the mall.

Hannah was waiting for us at the bottom of the stairs. "Well that took a while. Check this out!" She held up a page from an older lease in one hand and a yellow flyer in the other. "This was from when we were little."

The flyer read "Riverwood Mall Presents: The Hottest New Names in Country Music!" It was a holiday concert series at the main fountain where the Christmas mechanical bear was currently singing holiday tunes. The concerts coincided with the major holidays that were prime shopping days, like Memorial Day, Labor Day, and, of course, the winter holidays.

"I don't know when this stopped, but the restaurant coalition used to have special promotions for concertgoers. It was ticketed and roped off, and they had news and media there. The concerts used to be a big thing where they hired a local events company nearby to handle the promotion and some of the coalition dues went into the project manager and advertising. But then it just stopped when Rick Senior became less involved due to health reasons. According to some of the older meeting minutes, this used to bring in so much money."

I said, "And with social media now, it would be livestreamed and promoted like crazy. Maybe we come with a list of business ideas when we meet the landlord, in priority order, and include this. He can see some older ideas they had, and Peter, you and I can come up with some new ones."

For once, Hannah didn't argue. She looked at the stack of papers in my hands. "What's that?"

"Oh!" I handed them to her. "This is a tenant's lease and some of Peter's parents' papers. Wow, that's a tongue twister."

"And?" Hannah rolled her eyes and sighed.

No time for joking, I guess. "These first pages are the Lis' latest lease." Another tongue twister. This was starting to sound like I was doing this on purpose. "He found out that his lease doesn't have a demolition clause, and ours doesn't either. The other ones he looked at from three other businesses had them though. We were thinking about asking other businesses for their leases too?"

I always lost confidence around Hannah, even if my ideas were good. I looked over at Peter, who offered me a reassuring nod. My sister always gave her opinions in such a matter-of-fact sort of way. She'd definitely make a good lawyer one day, because she never stated things as questions or as something requiring a back-and-forth of any kind. Hannah Kwon thinks, therefore it is.

She paused a few seconds before answering. "Okay, I have other stuff that I'm working on, plus I have my full-time job. Can you look through the rest of the leases yourself and work on those new business ideas? Maybe get your little guy friend here to help?"

A few things about what she said that made me think she wasn't intentionally trying being a jerk. One, she really was working sixty hours a week as a paralegal and had no time for anything else, let alone this entire effort to save Riverwood. Two, she didn't use her "you're annoying me" tone, which meant... Three, this idea was good and she didn't want to admit it.

"We'll compare the contracts, fine. And we can also brainstorm some other ideas around saving the mall too. I'll add your concert one to our ongoing list."

Peter took his phone out of his pocket and checked the time. "I can help, but later. I hate to run, but I have to go. I'll look through a few more leases tonight. I feel bad about ditching early, so I can do that, at least."

Reading contracts was maybe the worst thing in the world, and if I didn't have to do it, that was okay by me. Let him feel guilty.

Of course, I couldn't let him just...go. Not without bicker-banter-intellectual discourse. "Thanks for giving us thirty minutes of your undivided attention." Maybe a week ago I would have said that with crossed arms and a barking tone. But I couldn't help it. I smirked.

Hannah did her typical Hannah thing. "Let Chloe know by nine tomorrow morning sharp if you discover anything else. Make sure you're using the latest leases in all cases, whether it's your parents contract, ours, or anyone else's at Riverwood. And please don't share the documents beyond the three of us here."

He threw his backpack over his shoulder and opened the front door. "Yes ma'am. Will report into duty tomorrow at nine a.m. sharp." Peter saluted her and shot me a wide-eyed WTF look as he shut the door behind him, causing me to bark out a loud laugh.

"What's so funny?" Hannah asked.

I thought back to Peter and me upstairs. Our fingers touching. Waves of electric pulses flowing from him to me. Me wanting to kiss him. And how something inside me changed, putting me in a buoyant mood. What was so funny? That I actually liked Peter Li. That's what.

"Honestly, I have no clue. I'll go work on those business ideas so we're prepared for the next coalition meeting and our landlord discussion," I answered, then headed back upstairs. There was so much going on. The mall closing and the National Art Council competition were the two most important. I needed to put my full attention on these pressing issues. Anything to keep my mind from playing back all those little moments together with him.

But then he texted me. I told you what I found was good. So you owe me a kiss.

TWENTY-THREE

PETER

CATCH. SHOOT. SCORE.

Block. Intercept. Pass. Shoot. Score.

We were winning, but barely. Cheremy had filled in for me and looked relieved when I showed up. Judging by his long wince and rubbing of his left shoulder, Sean had made him the interim punching bag.

A layup from Brach gave us two more points, and Kip called a time-out. I shouted, "Great deep penetration and use of your left hand, bro!" Brach and I looked at each other and burst into laughter. Dumb guy humor.

Both teams took water breaks, and I pulled some granola bars from my bag. "I owe you guys big. Multiple dinners at Empress Garden. Unlimited almond cookies."

Kip's eyes widened and I added, "For a week." He nodded. Kip loved our crunchy almond cookies. He was like a real-life Cookie Monster the way he devoured them, with crumbs spilling out the sides of his mouth—his eyes were more rolling back vs. googly, temporarily and blissfully happy.

Brach chugged an entire bottle of water and cracked open another one. "Did you watch some of the game? Any feedback, Coach Li?"

I looked at Kip and Cheremy to see if they'd be open to hearing my ideas. They both nodded, so I went ahead. "Cheremy, nice follow-through. And thanks again for filling in for me. Great catch and shoot, Kip. But I gotta ask—you're pretty far back on the three-point line sometimes...you're all about super quick releases. Maybe take your time?"

Brach snorted. "That's Kip, the quick-release guy."

Kip playfully splashed some water on Brach's head. "Shut up." He shrugged. "Yeah, I got really nervous every time Sean the Beast came my way. It was like hot potatoing the ball to avoid his full-speed ramming. But yeah, totally agree with you, I need to take a second more to land the shot."

I spent hundreds of hours in middle school with these guys studying classic NBA finals games. I was the most analytical and methodical out of all of us. The good and bad of it was that I always took enough time before shooting. I was good at drawing fouls and was able to hit the majority of my free throws, which always helped our overall score. But the pressure with everyone watching you at the free-throw line, trying to slow my breathing and wiping a ridiculous amount of sweat pouring off my forehead... It was intense.

Drawing fouls, according to our varsity coach, was an art form, but it didn't always work. Gigantic guys like Sean stuffed the ball or stole it if they had the opportunity, usually successfully. Luckily we were on the same team for school, so he only tried to mess me up in practice, in PE, or after school. In other words, often. Without a ref in pickup games, Sean slammed, elbowed, and wrestled the ball from people's hands, even if it meant tumbling to the ground. We suspected this was why he was always challenging us. Because he liked to punch down, and sizewise, we were way down from him. But we were wiry, quick, and nimble, so we held our own when it came to scoring.

By the looks of everyone's non-bloody and non-scraped arms and legs, he hadn't tried any of his usual brutish antics.

Not yet at least.

Cheremy sat on the bottom bleachers while Kip, Brach, and I went back on the court. The game resumed, and I used my speed and energy levels to our advantage, running the court and leading fast breaks. We scored twice, and I was getting excited, thinking faster was better, but then Sean decided it was time to unleash his Sean-nado on me.

Kip passed the ball to me, and I was just outside the

three-point line. Leaning side to side, I set up my shot as Sean's meaty hand swiped down on the ball. And my face. For a quick second I thought he might have broken my nose, but he had possession, and I couldn't let him score without a countermove. Standing around holding my nose would make our team look lost, overpowered, and stagnant. No way would I let that happen.

Brach was the tallest of all of us, and he was right in the path of Sean. But he'd seen what happened to me, and he did his best to block while Kip came around and tried to knock the ball out of Sean's hands. Somehow both of them teaming up together on Sean made him lose his opportunity. Sean wasn't a passer, or put more truthfully, *not* a team player, because he was an asshole and a ball hog. So rather than send the ball over to his teammates, who were wide open, he tried to shoot again. By that time I had recovered, confirmed my nose had not fallen off, and charged toward Sean. With a running start, I was able to knock the ball forward, out of Sean's hands, off the court.

"You little shit!" Sean growled when he whirled around. It wasn't any strategic move to get the ball back to my team. Nope. My only goal with that Air Jordan, old-school move was to have the ball *not* be in Sean's possession anymore.

The problem with this plan was Sean's fists were entirely in his possession, and they both came at me, swinging.

I ducked while bracing myself for impact. Kip and Brach held him back, one on each arm, and surprisingly, his two friends did too. It took four athletic guys to hold back this beast. I shook out my shoulders and said, "My nose is fine, thanks for asking."

Sean snarled, "You think sneaking up behind me is the way to play ball? You should quit. Go with your nerd friends and study and eat your disgusting Chinese food at your stupid mom and dad's restaurant. Or better yet, go back to China where you belong."

Ever since Sean's mom died in middle school, he'd turned into this angry whirlwind of hate. The bro code, especially among my friends, was that we would let him work out his shit his own way. If he broke out into a fight, we went a few rounds but never brought up his mom or his deadbeat dad. Never brought it to the principal, even though sometimes he got really physical. But him bringing my family into this, especially with their business in a state of crisis, was a low blow. Like, kick-me-in-the-balls-on-repeat-while-I'm-already-down blow.

Bro code also allowed retaliation if anyone dragged your mom. Moms were off-limits. My whole existence was grounded in the need to be agreeable, not rock the boat, and laugh stuff off to get ahead in life, thanks to Sam's guidance. I thought it was a strength, but maybe it wasn't. Putting my foot down was important so I wouldn't be a doormat to bullies like Sean.

I balled my fists. "First of all, fuck you. Second, don't make this personal, it's just a game. Someone wins, someone loses, or we tie. You should have passed the ball, so really this is about you being a lousy teammate more than anything else. No one likes a sore loser, you loser. Third, my parents were born here, you moronic asshole. We're just as American as you. And fourth, fuck you again."

Sean looked over to his right, then left, at his two friends' faces, who showed a flicker of "yep, should have passed the ball" in their fearful eyes as they loosened their grip on his arms, deferential to their leader. Back to bro code, they needed to get out of his way to let Sean escalate or stand down.

I didn't know what he'd do. He had a wild, homicidal look in his eyes before, but his pupils were dilated, his jaws had loosened. He could use his battering-ram arms to go in for another few quick swings or grab my shoulders and throw me down on the asphalt. I wouldn't put it past him to keep yelling racial shit either, because he was a level one thinker, if you could even call it thinking.

A handshake and a muttering of "good game" was probably out of the question at this point.

The school grounds attendant broke my train of thought. "You boys finishing up? I gotta lock up the fence in a minute. New security protocol. Pack up and move on out!"

There were a few ways this could go, but truthfully, I had other more important stuff to deal with.

As I took a swig of water, I thought of something I'd never tried before. "Good game, guys. I'm treating my buddies to dinner at my parents' restaurant in a few minutes, to fuel our studying tonight. If you three want to come, you're welcome to. But because you lost, you have to pay tip."

Brach and Kip both shot me a "WTF-YOU-DID-NOT-CONSULT-AND-WE-WANTED-TO-TALK-SHIT-ABOUT-THEM-AT-DINNER" look.

There's that saying that a way to a man's heart is through his stomach. I had no idea who said that or if it even applied to these guys who had limited cognitive capacity when it came to emotional intelligence or good sportsmanship. But I'd seen them at lunchtime, and boy, could these guys eat. I was trying to tug at the stomachstrings instead of heartstrings. Who didn't love free food?

Before Sean could speak for his posse, his clones both said, "Cool" at the same time.

Turns out, they loved free food.

We all knew that Sean's money situation was tight, and honestly, a free meal would be an impractical thing to pass up. But he was still thinking about it.

As we stuffed our water bottles and sweaty towels into our gym bags, I heard Sean grumble, "Okay."

I barely suppressed a smile as we passed the attendant on the way out the gate and waved goodbye. "See you guys at the food court."

Sean had said "okay."

I could work with "okay."

TWENTY-FOUR

CHLOE

WHILE WALKING UP THE STEPS OF LORRAINE'S PORCH to ring the doorbell, I jotted one more idea onto the notes app on my phone. My #savethemall list of ideas was too long. Hannah, Peter, and I would need to finalize, prioritize, and propose the final plan to our landlord, and it would just be us, since Mom and Dad made it clear they would never work with the Lis, even in dire circumstances. Hannah would handle my parents, because we all knew they were more likely to listen to the future lawyer daughter vs. the artsy one.

I tucked the phone away in my messenger bag and looked upward. As I stood in front of a white house with a heavy, nine-foot-tall oak door, it hit me that I had never seen a bona fide mansion before. The architecture was the kind you saw on the front cover of *Southern Living* or *Country Living*, what they would call "farmhouse flair." My money was on this entire inside being farmstead chic, with prominent white wood and dark brown or metallic modern accents. Maybe some kitschy country decor here and there, like gingham curtains or rooster paraphernalia. It might even smell like apple cinnamon potpourri or pine from a twelve foot, freshly cut Christmas tree. Lorraine seemed like the tree-hitting-the-ceiling type.

Clip-clopping heels echoed in the distance. It always threw me off when people wore shoes inside the house. My parents had never allowed that, not even in cases of extreme emergencies like carrying bags of heavy groceries or needing to rush to the bathroom after a long drive. My parents would yell "Shinbal beosuh!" and off came our shoes just past the front door.

The solid knock-knocking of her shoes against her expensive-sounding floor grew louder as she approached. The door swung open, and there was Lorraine's familiar smiling face.

With the entryway in full view, I could see I was wrong about the house being in pristine farmhouse-style condition. So very wrong.

"Don't mind the mess," Lorraine apologized, interrupting my exact thoughts.

I didn't mind it. I just couldn't believe it.

The house was full of art. But not in a fancy museum or curated hipster gallery sort of way. Oil canvases and wooden and metallic frames littered the foyer, along with opened boxes of various art supplies strewn on the floor. We passed a living room with blown-up photos mounted on the walls. I glanced in and could make out images of people posing in basically no clothing...not *nudes* exactly, but definitely like Victoria's Secret catalog level of scanty attire. My face blushed when I realized any of these images could possibly be of Lorraine in her younger days.

Reading my mind again, she said, "We don't need to go in there. It's my friend appreciation photo room and some of the pictures are a little avant-garde for even my tastes. They're not my photos, by the way, and none of them are of me. They're the works of my colleagues in Europe and Asia. Not my style, but I do find them inspirational, especially when I'm in a creative rut."

I asked, "You get in creative ruts? I don't believe that for one second."

Her shoulders shook with laughter as she led me down the hall to the left. "I get in creative ruts all the time. Having thirty years of experience gives me enough breadth of work to look like I know what I'm doing. But honestly, each new project starts with a blank page, or canvas, and with that comes a bit of anxiety. Imposter syndrome strikes all the time, even for people like me. I don't think there's any sort of magical way of making it go away. I've learned that talking about it with trusted colleagues, thinking about my accomplishments to date, and speaking with my therapist have helped tremendously."

I'd assumed that artists like Lorraine knew exactly what they wanted to create and were productive and prolific. Some of my peers at school were the same way, in that they'd chosen extracurriculars that they were now expert-level in and seemed to know what they wanted to do when they graduated. Like Kylie, my childhood BFF, who'd wanted to be a violinist since kindergarten. She was first chair in state orchestra last year. Her path to the top wasn't easy: she had lessons, rehearsals, and practice starting in preschool that took up so much of her time it was like a full-time job. She complained about it a lot, but maybe it was worth it if you never had to feel directionless.

Lorraine flicked the light on in her art studio, even though the room didn't need more brightness with all the skylights and the large French doors. The studio was the size of the entire bottom floor of my house, with its own kitchenette, bathroom, and large sink, and as I walked around the perimeter, I discovered a darkroom in the back. I peeked inside, curious because I had only seen these photo-developing rooms in movies or on TV. I'd never come across one myself.

She explained, "I haven't renovated this place in twenty years. Even then, digital was taking over. I'm still nostalgic sometimes and have all of my old cameras and always have film at the ready, although it's so expensive now because no one produces it anymore."

I marveled at the vintage cameras on the shelves. "I'd love to try one of them sometime."

She smiled. "Absolutely! I'd love to pass on this knowledge to you, but another time. We should get started with your official mentorship session and final presentation requirements before we jump ahead to film development lab tutorials."

Lorraine pulled two chairs up to her large Apple monitor and took me through some photo collections from around the world that inspired her. We chatted about line, shape, form, texture, pattern, color, and space and then discussed whether we preferred symmetry or could find beauty in asymmetry (not surprisingly, I was squarely in the symmetry camp).

"If you don't have questions about today's overview, I'd love to take you to your competition's updated entry page, where we'll upload your two-hundred-word essay. The topic is of your choosing, and it doesn't have to be connected to the photos you submitted, it just needs to be something you're passionate about and potentially wanting to explore as a future photojournalist."

Lorraine clicked around and smiled at the screen. "I can't wait to show you your artist page. Your profile photos and original submission materials are already uploaded and available for viewing worldwide! Watermarked, of course, so no one can claim your work. They unveiled the updated website yesterday, and we already have thousands of visitors."

She double-clicked my name. My photo, grinning face and all, took me by surprise, as it was not only huge on her monitor, but I hadn't thought to retouch or photoshop it before submitting. All

I could see was blemishes, ruddiness, and splotches. All things I would like to change and edit after seeing the beautiful site design. Why didn't I take the time to prep the profile image?

My eyes finally unlocked from my photo and scanned the rest of the page. There were seven comments at the bottom, and two immediately jumped off the page. ASIANS BELONG IN ASIA. And the classic slur going back many generations: CHING CHONG, CHING CHONG. My heart shrank and I pressed my hand to my chest. This was a well-respected organization for the art community, and these racists had left their mark on it.

Lorraine hand trembled as she clicked her mouse and closed out the page right away. "Oh, never mind, it's not ready yet, I—I have some questions for the staff, some updates...um, so no need to log in right now until we get that sorted."

I said softly, "I saw the comments."

"I am so sorry." Her chin quivered. "A few minutes before you arrived, I checked the site. There were a handful of comments and they were so lovely; ...I couldn't wait to show you. From judges, from other contestants, and new fans of your work, everyone was so excited about your submission. I wanted it to be a surprise." Lorraine's blue eyes brimmed with tears. "Obviously, it was meant to be a positive experience, and this...it's so horrendous and offensive and ignorant and...I'm so sorry we let you down. I'll ask the webmaster to delete these comments and monitor this closely. How awful that they ruined such a wonderful online experience."

She looked plenty distraught, fighting hard to keep tears at bay. The irony was she was showing so much emotion over this, but I was stuffing my feelings down as far as they'd go.

How many times had I heard "go back to your country" or "ching chong" in my lifetime, maybe twenty, thirty times? I used to come home crying about how mean, rude, and horrible people were with their overt staring and racist commentary. I was so used to it now. I had hardened on the outside and inside, over time trying to not let the comments get to me. I used to think that my toughness was a good thing, that these comments would roll off my back now, like I had a nonstick exterior.

But there was something about these racist declarations this time that bubbled up a new anger. It felt different. These racists and bigots had come into my safe space and tried to shake me up when I was pursuing my dreams.

Stupid ignorant assholes. How dare they do this to me?

They ignited a fire inside me that couldn't be ignored. "Ms. Finch, I know we still need to finish my mall video and go over my portfolio, but I know what I want my essay to be about. Could we work on that instead? I'm so sick of this. I want to fight back."

She patted my hand. With Lorraine's help, I composed my words.

To the racists (note the lowercase r) who trolled my profile page,

You know nothing about me. You think you do, but you don't. Let me educate you.

My parents escaped poverty in South Korea to move to the United States. They'd experienced a lifetime of financial devastation, loss, and suffering and had the grit and determination to start life over again and build a home here in America. The only thing they had was a dream and hope for a better life. Your pitiful, hateful words will not destroy their dedication and love for this country. How dare you sabotage the idea of the American Dream, the very foundation of this beloved land?

My parents' home is here. My home is here. Your words are powerless and futile. Your attempts to diminish my dreams did not work, let me be crystal clear. But you did do one thing. You gave me a purpose. I will use my voice to fight racists like you. Now, and in the future. You may think you're loud and proud with your unwelcome words, but know this...my success will be louder.

—Chloe Kwon, age 16

We double-checked the essay for grammar and uploaded the file in the portal. I had wanted to do well in the competition all along, but now I had to fight to win.

TWENTY-FIVE

CHLOE

"SHE WON'T STOP CRYING. BOOPIE...PLEASE STOP." THE toddler's mother dug around in her diaper bag, looking for something to offer her daughter. All she came up with were Kirkland baby wipes, diaper ointment, and hand sanitizer.

My squeaky dog toys weren't working either.

I had to go with my instincts and use my newest toddler weapon, one I'd purchased a few months ago but never had to use because I always had a way to stop the full throttle tantrums and crying.

I asked the harried mother, "Is her name really Boopie?"

She shrugged. "It's Vanessa, but we called her Boopie once and she laughed so much, it stuck with us. I promise, she does laugh. She's just really upset for some reason." She sighed deeply. "I wish I had baby ESP."

Vanessa's face was bright red from so much wailing. She took one look at Santa and was like, "Nuh-uh, nope" and then kicked and screamed when her parents put her within ten feet of Santa's orbit. Each time she shrieked, her mom took retreating steps back to me.

It made sense. Even at my age, if someone asked me to come over to a guy in a fake beard and hat and then tell him what I wanted for Christmas, I'd maybe do it, but fearfully, and I'd have pepper spray ready to go at a moment's notice.

Santa was trying his best. He was there to make kids happy and also earn a living wage, so it was in everyone's best interest to make the best of the situation. I personally knew Santa Dave was hoping to move out of his parents' basement soon.

So out came my weapon of choice.

The XL whoopee cushion.

I blew it up while Vanessa screamed loudly, "Go 'way Santa! NO NO NO!"

Without warning, I pressed the whoopee cushion so it blew into my face, making my bangs flap in the air expulsion.

Immediately, Vanessa stopped crying. In fact, everyone stopped doing what they were doing just to see what the deal was with the farting Elf photographer.

The toddler squirmed in her mom's arms and asked me, "Again?"

So I blew it up and while pressing down with a whole lot of

farting gusto, I tossed another whoopee cushion over to Santa. I'd gotten them at the "Buy One Get One Free" sale at Spencer's Gifts a few doors down. Dave caught it one-handed.

He knew what to do. This clearly wasn't his first toddler rodeo. "Vanessa, you can stand over there with Mommy and tell me what you'd like for Christmas while I try to figure out how to blow this up? Or would you like to come here with your Mommy and help show me how this works?"

Vanessa yelled, "Mommy, come!" and ran to Santa. Dave blew it up and let Vanessa expel the air into his face, which caused his beard and mustache to flap wildly. She laughed and requested "again!" like she did with me, giving me plenty of opportunity to take photos of the two of them together, hysterically laughing, with Mom giggling in some of the shots. There was a giant whoopee cushion in every photo too, but you know, a happy kiddo with a whoopee cushion in a Santa photo was better than crying one. Mom could always photoshop it or just leave it in there as a funny memory to reflect upon later.

I showed the mom some of the photos as Vanessa told Santa about the big-girl LEGO sets she wanted. She also requested a loud fart balloon, like the one Santa and Baby Yoda had.

A familiar snicker made my ears perk. "See, she thinks you have Yoda ears too. Those are *not* Santa's-elf ears." I turned to see Peter's quirked smile and sparkling eyes lighting up his handsome face. "And in case you're wondering, no, I didn't come here to *banter* with you. I was lured by the sound of your farting siren serenade. You have lots of people passing by very curious about your flatulent Santa and his gassy elves."

He somehow said all of that with a completely straight face. How? I burst into a fit of giggles, and he broke his stoic demeanor to laugh too. The sweaty, should we kiss tension wasn't there anymore, or at least not in that moment. All that was there was his fart commentary and me staring at his handsome face, tracing his angular features with my eyes.

Vanessa and her mom left Santa's side, finally. "Bye bye Santa! I miss you! Mwah!" Vanessa blew a slobbery kiss as her mom scooped up the toddler and carried her from the booth. Vanessa's mom whispered to me, "Thank you!" and dropped a ten-dollar bill into the tip jar.

I turned to Peter. "Are you working today?"

He leaned on the gingerbread house backdrop, and it began to roll. "I was at the gym for a bit. I have a coworker covering for me when we go to the coalition meeting."

For a brief moment, while I was in my photography zone, I'd forgotten about all the mall stuff. I took a deep breath. "Yeah, you'll get to see peak Hannah. In charge and loving every minute of the Hannah Show." Earlier that morning, on a video call, my sister showed me the stapled, color-printed packets she was bringing to the meeting for the coalition members. Twenty-five of them. Hannah was ready to herd cats and get the whole group on board to fight for the mall. She would share the legal strategy and the marketing plans with them in the meeting, and let them know everything we'd use to reason with Ricky Junior. I'd given her the complete rundown of the most lucrative promotions ideas and offered to answer questions if anyone had any. Hannah never asked if I wanted to join her to speak, maybe because we both knew Hannah loved it, and I didn't. Public speaking was bad enough, but getting people to listen to and follow was another skill set I didn't have. This kind of thing caused me nightmares. For her, this was a reward.

Peter stuffed his hands into his pockets. "It's almost time. I'm hoping they bring those Costco pastries platters. I'm starving." Normally I'd be annoyed that he was mainly going for the freebies, but I was all nerves, and having Peter there with me would probably make things a little better, even if he was infuriatingly Peter-like, giving me goose bumps and cheerfully cramming cream-cheese Danishes into his mouth.

I handed the camera over to the other elfin assistant on duty. She hung the SLR around her neck by the strap. "Cool. I've been watching you work for a few weeks. I can't do it as well as you, but I'd be honored to try. I love your photos and the way you handle tough customers. You're good at smoothing things over. And while I'm already fangirling, one more thing. That whoopie cushion was a genius move. I'll need to remember that when I babysit my three-year-old niece."

Peter laughed as we walked down the carpeted path to the meeting rooms.

"What's so funny?" I asked.

"I was just thinking about Farting Santa. That elf back there was right, that was a genius move."

Grinning, I said, "It was, wasn't it?"

Peter laughed. "As Yoda would say, 'Clever you have become.'" He tapped my head and I swatted his finger away.

We reached the community room and he pulled the door open. Half of the seats were filled, with a few people standing around the back table, examining at the Costco croissants. Peter walked straight to them, leaving me by myself. I searched the crowd for my mom or dad, but neither of them were there. Peter's parents were no-shows too.

The clock on the wall read 5:25 p.m. Five minutes before the meeting was supposed to start. Where was Hannah? Where were the collated handouts? As I was about to message her, I received an incoming call from the law office where she worked.

"Shit, shit, shit. Chloe, I need you to stall. Or to start without me. I got held up at work and I'm just now leaving." Her law office was downtown, and we were in the suburbs. This would be fifteen minutes, assuming there was no traffic. There was always traffic. Especially at 5:30, during rush hour on a weeknight.

"Wrishumpingwrawg?" Peter came up next to me with a mouthful of food. He had a pastry in each hand and offered me one.

I closed my eyes and took a deep breath in and out. "My sister. She's not going to be here on time. She wants me to stall or speak in her behalf."

He swallowed. "That shouldn't be a problem, right? You basically put the entire presentation together. You and I even found the biggest hole in their legal standing with the demolition clause. All the marketing and publicity stuff was yours, she was just the person to filter out bad ideas, not that you had any."

"You found the demo clause. And...I can't." My voice grew faint. A wave of nausea passed through me, making it hard to stand. "I'm the behind-the-scenes person. I hate public speaking. I'm not a strong speaker like Hannah, and I'm not likable like you."

He wiggled his eyebrows. "You think I'm likable?"

"Not now," I said flatly. *You know how I'm falling for you, Peter Li. But not now.*

He walked over to the trash can and threw his croissants away, then grabbed a bottle of water from an Igloo cooler on the floor. "I'll try to stall. Maybe you can mentally prepare yourself for what you need to say to these folks in the meantime." He thrust his hands forward, palms out, gesturing toward the seated crowd. "We need to get going or they'll get cranky and leave early. I'll, like, do a warm-up set."

Before I could protest, he ran to the front of the room and cleared his throat. "Hi everyone, we're going to get started soon. How's everyone doing tonight?"

Oh no. It was like he was doing a talk show monologue or a comedy routine. I needed to focus on what I had to say, but at the same time, I couldn't peel my eyes away from him.

The shoe repair guy asked, "Aren't you the Empress Garden kid? Hey, you're tall now! I remember you when you were yay high." He held his hand three feet off the ground.

A few of the older store owners asked him how school was going, and one nosy perfume boutique owner asked if he had a girlfriend.

He guffawed and said, "I wish." In that instant, he looked up and offered me a "can you believe these people" grimace. Half amusement, half embarrassment, but he was winning over this crowd. Of course he was. People relaxed their shoulders, sat back in their chairs, and laughed along.

Maybe it was his ease with speaking with this ornery group, or his sheepishness when barraged with questions about his relationships, or that adorable grin. Seeing him "on" like this gave me shivers. *He is so good at this. Hannah too.*

I had to hand it to him. Watching him do his Peter thing made me forget about the existential crisis I was dealing with right then and there.

And it all screeched to a halt when the gym equipment store manager asked, "So can we get this show on the road? Is there even a point to being here? We're tired of all the discussions about whether this place is going to stay or go. We're about to cut loose and sign another lease in Hickory Hills Mall if nothing gets settled soon. Not seeing the point of sticking around if getting tossed to the curb is inevitable."

One of the restaurant owners chimed in, "We received an eviction notice last week. I thought the landlord wasn't doing anything until after the holidays. Are we just swirling down the drain hoping for a miracle? I need to look for other lease availability then."

Others nodded, also commenting they'd received the same notice.

Neither of my parents mentioned getting an eviction warning. Why were they always trying to hide everything from us, especially now, when we were trying to save their business?

The door slammed closed. I turned my head, hoping it was Hannah. But it was Dad. Like Peter, he immediately went straight for the flaky day-old pastries, not seeming particularly pressed to find out more about the imminent closing of the mall. I walked to the back to join him while Peter talked to the crowd about the Ultimate Virtual Reality North Pole Experience, and how his exhibit was drawing in a younger crowd. Of course he'd be pitching his business. He was a natural at this.

"Dad, did you get an eviction notice last week?"

He furrowed his brow. "Me?"

Normally I would have laughed at this. Who else would I be talking to? But we were pressed for time, with every second mattering.

He pulled out his phone and tapped around. "I get two things from landlord. Your umma and I waiting until Hannah comes home this weekend to ask her. She coming?" Appa showed me his phone.

One email was the aforementioned notice of eviction, ninety days. The second was a city council meeting reminder forwarded by the coalition leader Justin Chambers, with no explanation. I skimmed the message—it was confirmed to be December 23rd, and it was the last opportunity to plea to the councilmembers to deny permits for demolition. Would we be able to provide a strong enough case in such a short period of time if the landlord meeting didn't go well?

Looking around at the business owners, it was clear that there was no coordinated effort within the coalition. No rallying. No protesting. Business owners like my parents didn't know what the full implications of these types of notices were, which ones were just nice-to-knows or which were time sensitive and required immediate attention. They were waiting for someone else to take action, and no one did. So that left Hannah and me to help them sort this out, with Peter's help. To do that we needed broader support from this eclectic group of small business owners.

Where was Hannah?

"And without further ado...Chloe will be coming up now to discuss some key initiatives and ideas for the coalition to consider, as well as some observations about...um...your legal... things. So Chloe Kwon, come on up please!"

Two people clapped as I walked to the front. One of them was Peter. Not even my dad put his hands together.

As I took steps toward the front, Peter's eyes widened and he pointed to his head, then mine. Lifting my hand, I reached for my head, only to find that I had never taken the elf ears off. Mortified, I yanked at the elastic and stuffed the Santa's Village ears into my apron pocket.

I couldn't do this. There were twenty-five pairs of eyeballs staring at me, their brains probably trying to make sense of this awkward high schooler wearing a Santa's Village smock, standing before them to urge unification and participation for upcoming promotional and marketing opportunities. A teenager, begging them to come to the city council meeting to show support.

"Hi everybody," I squeaked. Peter's mouth curved into an earnest smile as he put his index finger behind his right earlobe, signaling for me to speak up. Since there was no microphone, I had to project my voice. "Hello everyone!" I said with a boom, close to the level of shouting I used when communicating with Hannah across the house. *Dinner's ready! Did you drink all the juice and not add it to the grocery list?! Someone get the door...I'm in the bathroom!*

Even my dad in the back looked surprised that I commanded the attention of the entire room. "Hannah Kwon, my sister, will be joining us shortly to discuss some of the legal concerns of the demolition plan and talk about ways we can work together to save the mall."

Someone in the back called out, "Who are you? You're just a kid."

Yes, compared to everyone in the room I was, in comparison, a kid. And factually, I was sixteen, which also made me a kid. But for some reason that comment really bothered me. Like "kid" meant I had no place here. No voice. Nothing at stake.

Tears welled in my eyes, but I fought hard to suppress them. "My family has been at the mall for over fifteen years, running and operating Kwons' Café. I grew up here. This mall is my home. Although I don't know all of you, your faces are all familiar to me. And I consider you my community. My family. My people. I'm here today because I want Riverwood to stay."

I shot a look at Peter, who nodded along. He gave a me a thumbs-up and smiled. Maybe to face my fears, I needed to find a way to make it less frightening. And having Peter here, offering me rapt attention and encouragement, was just the thing. I stood up straight and pulled my shoulders back.

"Kwons' is the place that had the Styrofoam containers and cups right?" That was Mrs. Fry, the wife of the ornery restaurant owner of the Hamburger Palace.

"Yes, we were among the last to adopt eco-friendly packaging. But that's because it took a while to switch distributors. Plus the packaging was more expensive and required us to raise our prices. But this has nothing to do with the situation at hand."

Peter tried to help. "Let's hear her out, everyone."

But that put a target on his back. "Wait, you're Empress Garden right? The ones who did that happy hour promotion that went against the food court business rules?"

Damn, he got called out. His parents really made a lot of people angry with that one, not just my unforgiving parents.

I tried again. "Let's please focus on the main issue today, how we can stop the mall from closing. We did a sampling of twenty leases, thanks to Peter here, and two of them were different from the others. The leases for Empress Garden and Kwons' Café were older, and in these agreements, there is no demolition clause. For those who are unfamiliar with that term, let me tell you what that is." I pulled up my phone, since Hannah's handouts didn't include this detailed information, and read aloud. "A demolition clause states that if the office building is sold, the landlord has the right to serve the tenant with a notice that states he must vacate his office space within a given period of time." My voice warbled, but I continued. "Here's what is in your leases, but not the Li family's lease or ours: *Landlord shall have the right to terminate this Lease if Landlord proposes or is required, for any reason, to remodel, remove, or demolish the Building or any substantial portion thereof. Such cancellation shall be exercised by Landlord by the service of not less than ninety (90) days' written notice of such termination. Such notice shall set forth the date upon which the termination will be effective.*" I looked up to see everyone staring at me. "Hannah is a paralegal and says this is enough grounds to stop the demolition, at least temporarily, because two businesses can fight to stay, Empress Garden and Kwons' Cafe."

Hannah burst through the door. "I'm so sorry I'm late. Chloe, can you pass these out? And get me some water?"

My mood shifted instantly. Here I was, coming out of my shell, commanding an audience, and she immediately shut me down. I'd slowly crossed this new threshold, gaining more confidence over the last few minutes, and Hannah toppled everything I'd built up with one swift blow by commanding me to be her water gopher in front of all these people.

Without even asking me what she'd missed, she instructed everyone to flip to the first page of the packet past the table of contents. Shame and inadequacy quickly replaced my self-assurance. Hannah looked the part of a leader. A commander. A somebody.

I swallowed my pride and reminded myself that this was all for the greater good—to save the mall. It wasn't about her, or me. After passing out the packets to everyone, I moved to the back of the room with Peter. During all of this, my Dad had sneaked out undetected. "I guess your parents aren't coming?" I whispered to Peter.

He shrugged. "I'm annoyed, to be honest. They should be here, like everyone else who showed. They should want to be involved to stop the mall closure. I mean, even your dad came. Not that he did anything but take some Danishes and walk out, but he showed up at least. My parents need to be here. They need to care."

A sadness stirred inside me as I grabbed a bottle of water for myself. "I bet they do care. If they're anything like my parents, it's probably because they hate the idea of working with everyone. I mean, Mr. Jamison is here. He's a miserable human." He was notorious for scaring customers out of the Candy Shoppe when they entered in too big of a group, if they were too loud, or merely looked like the loitering type.

"Well, I need to ask them to step up more. At least one of them should have come. They'll probably expect me to relay tonight's events." He looked longingly at the mostly empty box of croissants. "So what's the plan now, boss? Looks like Hannah is handling the legal stuff, and from what she's saying now, there's officially a case to be made that if some tenants don't have the demolition thing in their lease, the landlord can't kick them out. And that might sway the council members to consider postponing or canceling any sale or demolition of the building."

I nodded. "I'll probably go ahead and finish the Riverwood heritage video. I have a bunch of other ideas too."

"Other ideas? Like what?" He cocked his head and crossed his arms.

"The easiest one to do is a holiday gingerbread house competition. Maybe on Christmas Eve, when the mall is full, we can do that to bring on the yuletide cheer. Then there are some country music stars who grew up in Riverwood. Maybe we could do an indoor or outdoor concert in the spring, like the ones Hannah saw in the flyers? The other big idea is banding together to offer local food deliveries. Hannah still wants to do that food festival. Also, now that it's dead of winter, I was thinking we could offer 'Mommy and Me' and 'Daddy and Me' indoor activities at the mall with exclusive caretaker lunch specials. That way parents, nannies, and guardians can socialize and get exercise by strollering. Is strollering even a word? And they can eat while their babies nap."

Peter ran his hand through his hair and grinned. "Wow. I had no idea you were a parent culture enthusiast. How do you know so much about this stuff?"

I shrugged. "Astute observation from the two seasons of Santa photography."

He laughed. "These ideas are all amazing. Happy to help if you need me for anything. I don't feel all that useful right now, to be honest, with you putting together the video and list of landlord ideas, and Hannah handling the legal stuff." His smile flattened and his rueful dark brown eyes filled with sadness. "Maybe it'll be best to step aside and let the pros handle it for now."

"Hey, you were key to the legal case." I reached out my hand and after hesitating for a moment, I thought, *screw it* and touched his arm, in front of whoever was around. I don't know what I was expecting, maybe inner fireworks? Angels singing in my head? But other than my nerves making my hand a little clammy and shaky, I didn't feel jolts and tingles like before. "You cracked this whole thing wide open by finding the demo clause. And you were the one who charmed everyone and helped warm up the crowd for my once-in-a-lifetime public speaking appearance."

"You think I'm charming?" The corner of his eyes crinkled and the moment his lips curled into a wry smile, the jolts and tingles I anticipated from before hit me all at once.

He added, "Mind if I take a video of you saying that again so I can keep it for posterity?"

I released his arm and with my hands on my hips, I playfully cocked my head. "How 'bout a video of me mouthing off cusswords instead?"

He laughed and put his hand on my shoulder, all natural-like, like it wasn't a big deal at all. And then the tingles came rolling in, along with a light shiver down my spine. The heat of his palm radiated through my sweater.

I joked, "You're never going to get that kiss if you keep this up." Peter knew I thought he was charming. And surely he knew how badly I wanted to give him that owed kiss.

Putting my feelings out there was mortifying, and something I thought I'd never do, but I was glad I did.

He smirked. "I don't think you understand what's going on here. This here? This thing we're doing? It's whimsical banter."

I swear, if he said banter one more time...

I held my tongue and didn't move, because I didn't want him to take his hand away, but I also knew we had a lot going on during the week and we couldn't stay here forever like this. We had tests to study for, and I had the mall video to edit and the landlord presentation to put together. And then there was Thanksgiving, which had completely slipped my mind.

It wasn't until he lifted his hand that I was aware of the effect he had on me. I craved his touch, his heat, his energy.

"Oh, one more thing."

"Yeah?" I asked.

He glanced over at Hannah, who was still taking questions from the audience. His pursed lips twisted into a lopsided grin. "I know you compare yourself to Hannah. I know, because I do the same with Sam. But just so you know...you're great. Like, you're pretty charming yourself, Chloe Kwon."

I beamed. "Shut up. And thanks for that, Peter Li."

TWENTY-SIX

CHLOE

"HAPPY FRIENDSGIVING, BITCHES!" ELIAS BURST through our front door while holding a two-tier chocolate cake in his hands. "I'm so sorry, Mrs. Kwon. I didn't know you'd be standing there. Oh God, I'm so embarrassed."

Umma wiped her hands on her apron. "Hi Elias. Come in! Hi Sophia. Come in!"

Sophia wiped her boots on the mat and handed me a warm pie. "I left the ice cream in the car, it's freezing outside so it won't melt. Oh my God, your house smells amazing."

It was a long-standing tradition to have my friends come over for Thanksgiving lunch. A nice thing about having parents who were restauranteurs was they really knew how to cook. This was the one meal where Mom and Dad went straight-up country:

butter-roasted turkey, cornbread stuffing, potatoes gratin, sweet potato casserole with marshmallow topping, southern style green beans, broccoli casserole, and buttery dinner rolls. Honestly, my parents' once-a-year American meal was my absolute favorite. I happily ate leftovers for days.

Elias and Sophia had come over for Friendsgiving lunch for six years straight, and they always brought homemade dessert. Then, when they finally went home, they had Thanksgiving dinner with their own families. But they always insisted that my mom's meal was the best, which of course made my proud Korean umma beam. The conversation always went the same way, every single year.

Sophia: "Mrs. Kwon, your turkey looks amazing. It's always so juicy and perfectly cooked."

Mom: "Nooo, I keep in oven too long. It's too dry probably. But you think it look good?"

Elias: "Your gratin dish is my favorite. I wish my mom could make it like you."

Mom: "It so easy. Just potato, cheese, milk, salt, butter, and other things. I give you some to take home!"

Me: "The stuffing smells so good. I can't wait to eat it."

Mom: "Chloe, you need to learn how to cook."

Every. Single. Year. To my defense, I had been helping her that whole morning, though she was so particular on how she prepared and organized the kitchen that "helping" meant me taking out trash and making sure the sink was always empty, instead of properly learning how to make my mom's signature dishes. Once the turkey was in the oven, Mom poured herself some wine and read the newspaper, while Dad watched pregame college football sports commentary and asked me to grab him a beer. This Thanksgiving, this special day of feasting, fellowship, and friendship, we pretended everything was okay. That our lives were not unraveling. Just for a day of reprieve.

Elias and Sophia knew the drill: they helped each other take off their coats and hung them in the front closet, took off their shoes, then brought the desserts to the kitchen where they could ooh and ahh over my mom's feast preparations. In previous years, she had a glazed ham and a few other sides, but she'd scaled back. We all knew why. Money was going to be tight if they lost Kwons' Cafe. We were preparing for the worst.

"Time to eat!" my mom bellowed as she placed the perfectly browned twenty-pound turkey at the center of the table. "Hannah is joining for dinner later tonight, so we can eat now."

Elias cheered, "Her loss. More for us then! Right Mrs. Kwon?" He held out his fist for my mom to bump. Which she did. Only Elias could get away with fist-bumping with my mom.

Hannah was the one who usually cut the turkey, so Dad and I had to rely on YouTube to guide us through the steps. He put on yellow rubber gloves my mom insisted he wear and held the carving knife like a light saber.

"Okay Appa, you first cut through the area that connects the breast and drumstick, then you'll separate the leg and thigh from the bird by pulling out and back." Using his chef's knife, he took apart the sections and on his own, removed a wing and transferred it to the platter.

My dad joked, "No one here like white meat, maybe we skip the rest of cutting." It was true, we were all dark meat people, but he still moved forward with removing sections of second-class white meat, which were still juicy and tender.

He pulled the wishbone from the front end of the breast. "Who wants to make wish?"

Sophia and Elias scrambled for it, but I was seated closest to my dad. "It's mine, bitches! Sorry, Mom."

Mom sighed. "Everybody is talking about bitches today. Just eat and be thankful."

Sophia and Elias both said in unison, "Amen." But then Elias sneak added a quiet, "Yeah, bitches," which made us all burst into a fit of laughter.

While Dad put slices of turkey on our plates, I told Sophia and Elias they could arm wrestle for whoever got to split the wishbone with me after dessert.

We passed the side dishes counterclockwise. I added a double scoop of fluffy, fragrant herb stuffing, my absolute favorite, and sent the bowl to Sophia on my right. The green beans with bacon bits and broccoli casserole were next, followed by the cheesy potato and sweet potato dishes. There was no room left on my plate for any rolls, so I took my bread from the basket, made a turkey stuffing sandwich, and scarfed it down. Problem solved.

Lifting a forkful of potato gratin, the steam plumed from the thin wedges as the cheese stretched. I took a slow bite and savored the creamy, salty goodness. "Mom, this is the best you've made." The flavor reminded me of the stone-ground grits with cheese at Loveless Café.

Mom said, "I get this recipe from *Southern Living* magazine this time. Add my own special touch." She took a bite and chewed. "You need to learn how to cook."

And there it was. Thanks, Mom.

We chattered on about school and teachers and how the new Pumpkin Spice and Peppermint Mocha backdrops at Santa's Village, Elias's and Sophia's joint creation, were the most popular set pieces and getting a lot of social media attention. Elias went for a second helping of all the sides while Sophia attacked a turkey leg. I had a third scoop of stuffing while I contemplated how much chocolate cake and pie I'd be able to eat before going comatose from food overload.

Dad cleared his throat. "Maybe before we eat dessert we share why we are thankful this year. We can start a new tradition."

Mom said, "Appa, nuh gah." Then she added, "I go second."

I shot looks at Elias across the table and turned my head to exchange a quick glance with Sophia. My parents were getting all sentimental, which wasn't like them at all. In fact, it was disturbing. And ominous. Like someone giving away all their possessions right before predicting their own death.

Dad said, "I am thankful for my good health and good food." He shoveled sweet potato casserole into his mouth, leaving marshmallow cream on the corner of his mouth. Wiping it off with a napkin, he said, "Who else? Umma? Chloe? Elias? Sophia?"

Mom took a sip of wine. "I am thankful Chloe is passing her classes."

Thanks, Mom.

Elias jumped in to de-escalate. "I'm thankful that you all let me crash your wonderful meal every year. And I'm excited I got the lead role in our school production of *Dear Evan Hansen*. And I dyed my own hair this week, and it came out great."

Sophia clapped and went next. "I'm thankful for being here, and that Chloe has been my friend for so many years. I'm also grateful that the pie I made is good. I made two pies and brought you the nicer one." She smiled and leaned back into her chair.

I finished chewing my last bite of turkey. "I'm thankful that my favorite people are here for Thanksgiving and Friendsgiving and—" A flash memory of Peter flicking my elf ear popped into my head. I squeezed my eyes shut, hoping it would help make the image of Peter smiling at me disappear. I wish I could have invited him, since he met the basic criteria of "friends" for Friendsgiving. Was Crush-giving even a thing?

I opened my eyes, and the entire table was waiting for me to say something. I looked over at my dad, and then my mom. "And I hope Sophia and Elias and I can stay friends forever, and not let anything ever come between us, even if we end up in a heated business dispute that is not each other's fault, and not blame each other if it's actually the fault of a swindler who should be in jail right now."

Dad threw his napkin on the table. "That's enough, Chloe."

Mom exhaled out her nose. "Don't start trouble today."

Sophia's and Elias's eyes both pleaded with me. *Leave it alone. Or we don't get cake and pie.*

They were right. I needed to drop it, not only because it was Thanksgiving, but also because it was impossible for her mom and dad to undo fifteen years of resentment and animosity. Their hearts were surrounded by iron fortresses, and they would go to their graves being bitter about the Lis. Peter and I could never truly be friends. He could never come over for Friendsgiving. We could never be more than friends. At least, not openly.

Elias changed the subject while we all had slices of cake and pie, asking questions to my mom about recipes and asking dad about his favorite college football teams. In between bites of dessert, Sophia grabbed my hand and squeezed. A simple gesture of "I get it, and I'm sorry."

My phone buzzed with a message. Mom went to the kitchen to get her third glass of wine and didn't notice my phone lighting up while my dad stood to change the channel.

It was Peter. I'm outside. Can I give you something?

I leapt from my chair and bolted out the door, barely putting on shoes and stepping into the brisk air without a coat.

My mouth quivered as I saw Peter on my porch. He wore a forest green knit cap pulled low, covering his ears and barely showing his eyes. His thick black and white striped scarf wrapped around his neck twice. He was smiling at me, holding up a brown paper sack.

"Happy Thanksgiving! I brought you dessert. My parents had extra." I opened the bag and peered inside.

Sesame balls.

I picked up a seed-covered mini-globe. It was warm to the touch. Without any hesitation I took a big bite. The chewy mochi dough pulled and separated, revealing a sweet red bean paste stuffing inside. It was one of my favorite Asian desserts. And he brought it just for me.

When I finished chewing, I said, "Thank you for bringing this...and not flinging them at my face. This was much better than the almond cookie experience."

He grinned and shoved his hands into his pockets. "I hope I've made up for that now. We still don't offer this on our menu, so it's a rare treat."

"You came all this way to deliver sesame balls?" I took a step down from the porch so we were on the same level. "I don't have any spicy pork to offer you. We just have a traditional Thanksgiving spread. Would you like something to go?

We have plenty. Elias and Sophia are here, and they brought pie and cake."

"Oh, your friends are here?"

His face fell a little, but we both knew why I couldn't invite him in to say hello.

"Nah, I'm good. I wanted to stop by and say Happy Thanksgiving." His lopsided smile tugged at my heart. "Let me know if I need to help you with anything else. I'm free this holiday break. I'm all yours."

He's all mine.

That sounded like an invitation. *Seize the day, Chloe!* I stood on my tiptoes and with my free hand, I tugged his scarf downward. He lowered his head, stooping to just above my height.

Just do it, Chloe Kwon!

Closing my eyes and taking a deep breath, I inhaled Peter Li's Tide-Ivory Soap-Sesame ball scent, then kissed him squarely, firmly, affectionately on the lips.

His eyes stayed shut as I slowly pulled away.

Did I really just do that?

He reached out and put his hands on my shoulders. "Can we do that again? One for each sesame ball? I have three in there."

The door flung open, and Sophia came out, bundled up head to toe, prepared for the inclement weather. "I forgot the ice cream in the ca—oh shit."

I giggled. "Nothing to see here. Move along."

She looked over her shoulder back inside. "Your mom's been looking for you. You better hide him."

Peter laughed. "Where, in your attic? Under your stairs? Nah, I'll head out before I start World War Three. But Happy Turkey day, Soph."

"Happy Friendsgiving, Peter. Or should I say Happy *Hands*giving?" She looked over at my shoulders, and Peter dropped his palms to his side and blushed.

I rolled my eyes at her and then turned back to Peter. "We might need your help actually. Maybe we'll make one last effort to meet with the coalition before we go to the landlord so we give everyone full transparency into what we're sharing with Rick Junior. I'll call you soon about that. Thanks for the dessert." I lifted the bag as a flurry of snow whooshed by us. "You better head home before the weather gets worse."

Hannah's car rumbled up the driveway. She hopped out and walked toward us, then sighed when she saw Peter. "You're here too? I thought you were banned for eternity. Does Mom know—"

I pleaded, "Please don't—"

She cut me off. "I won't rat you out to Mom and Dad." Grabbing the sack from my hand, she pulled out a sesame ball, handed the bag back to me, and walked inside.

I looked at Sophia and Peter and shrugged. "Well, that was surprising. Anyway, happy Thanksgiving, Peter."

"Happy Thanksgiving, Chloe. Sophia." He turned around and walked back to his car.

I clutched the bag to my chest and followed Sophia inside. Mom asked, "Where were you? I need help to clean up!" I grabbed some used plates and silverware, suppressing a smile as I brought them over to the sink. No one in my house liked the cleaning-up part of Thanksgiving dinner, so any display of pleasure as I cleared the table would be a sure sign that something was off. And that would lead to an interrogation. No thanks.

What I needed was to savor that blissful, perfect kiss.

Elias pried his eyes away from the TV. "Hey, where were you?" He smirked at me while my dad changed the programming from football to HBO's *Game of Thrones*. "I have my guesses, but I'll save my questions for later."

The theme song filled the room in stereo sound. Where was I? With Peter Li, The Second of His Name, the borderline annoyingly well-rounded Son of James and Pam Li, the King and Queen of the Empress Garden Dynasty.

Peter the Great, Breaker of Holiday Rules and Visitor of Mortal Enemies. Bearer of Rare Sweets.

And I kissed him.

TWENTY-SEVEN

PETER

CHLOE PUT ME IN CHARGE OF GETTING THE WORD OUT about the ad hoc emergency coalition meeting, the last get-together before the meeting with the landlord. I handed out flyers to all the owners and managers during my lunch break and late-afternoon rest break. I emailed everyone too, to cover all bases. For the most part, the response to my outreach was positive, and I got a lot of in-person feedback.

"See you there, kid."

"You're the Empress Garden boy, right? I'm a fan of your orange chicken."

"Hey, I'll be there. While I have you, can you tell your cooks to make the broccoli beef with less salt? Just some friendly advice."

And then there was the candy store guy, Mr. Jamison, who

was his usual testy self. "I won't be there unless there's food. That's my dinnertime."

I gritted a smile. "My parents offered some pot stickers, and Mr. Fry has donated a build-your-own burger station."

The ornery old man grumbled. "Leave it to ol' man Fry to show me up. I'll throw in some fudge for everyone. The regular kind and some with nuts."

"Thank you. See you there." I pulled my phone from my pocket and let Chloe know that the coalition meeting details had been distributed. She replied with a quick **Thank you!** I expected more instructions, more ways to help, but there were no more messages from her. I didn't want to bother her since this was such a busy time, but I wanted to be useful. I'd have loved to discuss what was going on between us at some point too. I mean, we kissed on Thanksgiving. That had to mean something, right?

Once I got back to work, I was bombarded with questions about the new "Santa's G-Force Blastoff" experience that had been downloaded to our menu that morning. I'd heard from customers earlier that day that it was smooth and that the chairs didn't jostle as much as other rides. Confession time though: I hated g force. It made me feel like my face and balls were left behind while my heart and stomach were thrust forward. Not the most pleasant feeling for a dude.

One of the ninth graders at my school who was a regular could tell I hadn't tried it out and was giving me a lot of shit for it. "C'mon Pete, how can you tell people they should try it if you haven't even done it yourself? You keep calling it zero-g, which is different from g force."

Yeah, both made me want to puke. Because of that, they were interchangeable.

This Blastoff ride had the top thrill rating, rated a point higher than "Rudolph's Rude Awakening" and "Ho-Ho-Hold Your Hats," both of which had a lot of drops, falls, and twists. The highest rating wasn't in terms of satisfaction, it was a measurement of adrenaline and heart-pounding moments. There were literally five out of five beating hearts listed next to the name. The highest I'd ever experienced was four-and-a-half.

"You scared?" he asked.

Yes. Yes I am.

"No. No I'm not."

"Well, it seems only right for you to try it out. C'mon, brah."

The line was only two people deep now, and before I could open my mouth to talk my way out of this, the guy who worked with me lifted his eyes from his phone screen and said, "You got back from break early. I have ten more minutes left here if you wanna do it. Knock yourself out."

Thanks for having my back, guy whose name I can't remember.

Was it really so wrong that I hadn't tried this ride? It was one minute long. That was like fifty-three seconds too many. I could last that long, right? Kids half my age could handle some of these high-thrill rides. Lifting my chin high, I said, "If you're okay with me skipping line, then cool. I'll just gear up then."

No one protested.

"Heyyy Petey!" It was Sean. My basketball foe. Although lately, or at least since I'd given him that free dinner, he was cool with me. And by that I mean he didn't challenge me to pickup games and slam into me on purpose at recess, during practice, or after school. His two clones flanked each side of him, as usual.

Sean slapped my back. "Can we go after you? Someone in the parking lot is puking now, saying that new game or whatever really messed them up. Sounds like something my guys and I would like."

The clones nodded.

Better to get this over with.

I should have taken Dramamine.

When was the last time I threw up? Maybe a few years ago, on the Wild Eagle ride at Dollywood.

I settled into a chair and programmed the ride to start after a ten second delay. Placing the helmet on, my ears and eyes were completely covered with noise-cancellation insulation. I could barely hear that horrible holiday song blasting throughout the mall, "Simply Having a Wonderful Christmas Time."

That song, the bane of my existence, was stuck in my head.

In some ways it was the perfect soundtrack to this vomit-y adventure.

The robotic female voice counted down in a British accent. *Five. Four. Three. Two. One. Good. Bye!*

At first, nothing happened. Pitch black and no sound. I prayed to the VR gods that this was a malfunction, but that lasted maybe only a few seconds before sleighs appeared all around me. We were at the starting line for a drag race.

A flag waved, and the quest began with a high-g-force start through the clouds, but instead of slowing down at the end of the long, straight path upward, I launched up again through a snowy wind tunnel where giant hail rained down. Santa and Rudolph used their super speed and dodging skills to zip back and forth, avoiding pummeling.

Normally, if this were an actual rollercoaster ride, this would be when I'd start screaming all sorts of NC-17 profanities, but I had no idea who was nearby. Santa's Village was next door and had all those little kids coming through to see Santa. I bit back my words and pressed my lips together, bottling in all my anxiety, fear, and stress while my heart rate doubled.

My stomach dropped, rolled, and lurched.

When I thought things couldn't get worse, they did. Virtual Santa turned to me and yelled, "Hold on tight!" and then our sleigh made one huge g-force blast forward and then looped upside down. Then again. And a third time.

I could hear someone faintly shout, "Peter, you okay? You're too quiet. And pale. You need me to ask the guy who works here to turn it off?"

Another snow tunnel. This time with pointy ice daggers. What the hell were those called? Icicles?

Yes. Icicles. Shooting at me. I rocked left and right to avoid them. When I did get hit, the seat vibrated hard.

After more high-speed turns in and around the clouds, we made our descent. And by that, I mean we plummeted, because of course the sleigh and reindeer separated, so Santa and I plunged to our deaths. This was all happening in a fast spiral, and I spun like a dreidel while shooting down, down, down to the ground.

Thankfully, Mrs. Claus came to the rescue. She zoomed upward in a high-tech snowmobile vehicle and hitched us to her electric sleigh. Mr. Claus calmly announced our safe return to the North Pole as we glided to the finish line. There, a gold trophy and a coupon code to ride again for 50 percent off awaited us.

I snatched off the helmet and handed it over to the guy whose name I still couldn't remember. Shaking my head when he tried to talk to me, I stumbled away. Behind me, I heard Sean say, "Epic. Did you see his face? Now I really want to ride this." He didn't ridicule me, which was the only good thing that came of this experience. To help with the nausea, I walked to the closest exit to get a blast of cold air. It was near the employee parking lot, so I headed directly to my car, where I had a full tank of gas, a nearly frozen bottle of water, and plenty of distance between me and the aroma of the mall, which I hadn't noticed until now smelled like buttery pretzels and popcorn, both of which made me want to retch. It was almost 5:00 p.m. Everything made me feel woozy, including breathing.

I opened the door and turned on the ignition. After reclining the driver's seat to a hundred-degree angle, I shut my eyes and breathed in deeply.

Then I fell asleep.

TWENTY-EIGHT

CHLOE

WHERE WAS HE?

The meeting was about to start, six o'clock on the dot. Everyone was here, including Peter's parents. Including mine. Everyone was accounted for; the only person missing was him. I hadn't asked Sophia or Eli to come, thinking Peter would be enough emotional support. How could he let me down like this?

Hannah shrugged. "Look, I know you want your boyfriend to be here, but we have to start. We're on a tight schedule, and some people have to leave early."

Boyfriend? Hardly. Especially after he ghosted me. I nodded and pressed my lips together in attempt to hold back tears. She was right. The meeting needed to begin.

She walked to the front and cleared her throat. "Good evening, ladies and gentlemen, and for all the people who didn't attend the last meeting, I'm Hannah Kwon, and this is my sister, Chloe. My parents, Yoon Hee and Sang Min, are in the back; they're the proprietors of Kwons' Café. Thank you all for coming on such short notice. For your troubles, feel free to help yourself to the food and drinks in the back, supplied by our parents, Hamburger Palace, the Candy Shoppe, and Empress Garden."

She nodded at Peter's parents, showing them friendliness and respect. I glanced over at Umma and Appa, who were across the aisle from Peter's parents. Their non-frowns and non-glares suggested a degree of civility. Progress.

"Some of us will be meeting with the landlord tomorrow. As part of what we're proposing, we have a few committees for upcoming events, and we'd like your participation. The sign-up sheets are in the back. There are descriptions of the events, and time slots are on the forms; feel free to sign up for more than one. We want to show the landlord that the entire mall community is committed to positive change, and to do that we would like to see one hundred percent involvement."

Glancing across the room, I could tell this was the first time some of them had even heard of committees and events. My voice cracked as I chimed in, "Maybe I can quickly go over the upcoming events, for those who are joining us the first time."

All eyes were on me.

This would have been the perfect time for Peter to offer me

a reassuring smile. But he still wasn't here. What a complete letdown.

My hands turned clammy and shook as I stumbled and stammered through the initiatives to support the mall. I went over the ideas for local office deliveries, Annual Food Fair, and the "Baby and Me" indoor playground with rotating lunch specials. Although the audience looked fully engaged, it was such a relief when I finished. I added, "We have stickers and T-shirts with the slogan 'save the mall,' if you'd like one." I took off my jacket and modeled my black shirt with #WeAreRiverwood on the front and #SaveTheMall on the back. After my brief and awkward fashion show, I received a smattering of applause. One person in the back yelled, "Riverwood! Hell yeah," and everyone laughed. Surprisingly, Hannah laughed the loudest.

"I'm done," I said and took a seat. Introverts like me drained to zero when having to do things like that, and what I wanted most was to recharge in private, away from all these people. While I took a breather, Hannah continued to explain to the crowd that after a lengthy legal audit, the strongest case we had legally was with the leases of Empress Garden and Kwons' Café, the only two businesses without demolition clauses in the contracts.

"We would also love all of you to come to the city council meeting on December 23rd to share your love for Riverwood, even if our meeting with the landlord goes well. That's not that far away. The more voices from the community, the better.

I know it's not the best time, being holiday season. But this is our last shot at taking a stand to stop the sale of the mall. Bring whomever you like, the more the merrier."

My voice warbled as I added, "One last thing. You're not obligated to stay and watch, but while you sign up for committees I'll play a video I worked on that I'll be sharing with Mr. Jones. It's the history of Riverwood Mall."

While members of the mall coalition signed up in the back of the room, I dimmed the overhead lights and pressed play on the media player on my laptop. The video image projected on the whiteboard in the front, and the sound played over the room's Bluetooth speakers.

Peter's pleasant voice filled the room with his narration. "Riverwood Mall, founded in nineteen ninety-one, was the largest one-story, enclosed mall built in Middle Tennessee. Doctor Edward Rich, Dean of the School of Architecture at the University of Tennessee, Knoxville, who grew up here in Riverwood and spent a lot of time at the mall as a teenager, is amazed that over the many years, the design of the mall hasn't changed or updated much from the building plans, and much of the original building remains."

The scene cut to an interview with the dean at the mall, in front of JCPenney. "For any teen, Riverwood was the place to be in the 90s and 2000s. You could eat there, hang out with friends, go see a movie, go shopping, and it was open till nine or ten at night."

He added, "Riverwood Mall also houses a large indoor local art collection. It's home to more than one hundred paintings, ceiling installations, and sculptures from local artists in the region."

The faces of the people in the room softened, and the audience grew quiet as they listened to the dean's interview. The narration switched back to Peter. "Riverwood Mall isn't just about commerce, it's about social interactions. Experiences. Community. And livelihood for many local families since the doors first opened so many decades ago."

I had made a conscious decision to not make the video too old-timey, with 50s-era fonts, nor did I want it to be a homage to 90s cheesiness or grunge. My goal was to show the then and now of restaurants and stores that had been there for many years. To show how this mall was a home away from home for many people, like me.

A montage of older photos appeared, many of which were contributed by the local business owners here, as well as the archivist at the *Tennessean*. Photos of young restauranteurs and store owners in front of their grand opening signs, coupled with present-day images of their now-expanded, multigenerational families. I included images of my parents, who were maybe only a little older than Hannah at the time, chatting with Silver Sneaker customers while Dad held baby me in his arms. Some of these same Silver Sneaker veterans were still alive and moving around the mall in their upper nineties, and many of them agreed to be interviewed and have their photos included.

Peter's narration came to a close. "Riverwood has become a lifestyle center that offers a multidimensional experience for people of all ages. Adding non-retail experiences over the years—like gyms and communal café-like meeting spaces—shows we've evolved and can continue to change if we work together to keep Riverwood in our hearts and minds."

The video concluded with a fade to black and a simple "We Love Riverwood Mall" message on the end frame, with a "Preserve Our Community" plea underneath it.

The room filled with applause as I flicked the lights back on. A few of the oldest audience members dabbed their eyes with tissues. Finally, this was sinking in. What we needed to fight for. What we would be losing if we didn't.

Hannah added her final words. "Wish us luck with the Jones family. And see you all at the city council meeting on the twenty-third. If you're having trouble with business coverage or childcare, please see me or Chloe. We have some Silver Sneakers who have volunteered to help with that. Oh! One last thing. The city council just voted to change their name to 'City of Riverwood Planning Commission' a few weeks ago. So, as they transition to their new name, you might hear them referred to as both city council or planning commission, just wanted to clarify to avoid confusion if the meeting information is listed somewhere under the new name. Thank you, everyone, for coming."

She stepped away from the front and took a swig of water from the thermos in her leather bag.

I looked over my shoulder. "I'm going to make sure people are actually signing up. And talk to Mom and Dad about contributing their time too."

Hannah bobbed her head up and down while she chugged more water.

We had put Peter in charge of the food fair, but that duty would have to fall on someone else more trustworthy, probably back on Hannah or me, or Elias and Sophia if they were willing.

Where the hell was he? I texted him a fourth time. His parents were still here and didn't seem too worried about him, especially by the way they were taking advantage of the popular burger bar setup in the back and not checking their messages nonstop like I was.

To encourage more sign-ups, I joined the burger eaters and smiled at everyone.

All eyes were on Mr. Fry, the center of attention. He lamented, "And when did the restaurant customer service script change? Now everyone says, 'How's everything tasting?' I personally think it's odd to center only on the tasting experience. Usually waitstaff are tipped for service, and that's separate from the actual food prep. Do people answer truthfully about what they tasted? 'I detect a hint of garlic and thyme on my taste buds, but the chicken was a little stringy. But the saltiness levels were spot on!'"

The restaurant folks really liked that one. There were lots of hoots and guffaws.

The Candy Shoppe guy said, "And what does it mean when they say, 'If you need anything, my name is John.' Is their name something else when they don't need something?"

Another big round of sniggers and laughter.

It was great seeing everyone come together like this. A true community. Hopefully it wouldn't be the last time.

My smile quickly faded when I spotted Umma and Appa bickering with Peter's parents by the community sign-up table.

Oh God, what now?

"We want Monday, this cheap pen on table not working, and I go get a new one. We here first," my mom growled. "You can see fading ink spot where we try to sign our name."

Mr. Li shrugged. "The time slot was empty, so we took it. It's as simple as that. And I always carry a working pen with me." Peter's dad crossed his arms and harrumphed.

They were arguing over which day they would have their special lunch promotion for new parents. It wasn't supposed to be a big deal. But of course it was for these two families.

I asked my parents why Monday was so important to them. "Meat and seafood come two time every week. Monday has freshest food. Good for mom and baby."

Okay, it was good to hear it was for an unselfish reason, instead of "just to spite the Li family."

Peter's dad said, "We wanted Monday because it's our slowest day. We can give the moms and dads more attention."

Also a valid reason.

As they were talking, the other lunch special slots filled up. All the other days were accounted for.

This made my dad angry. "Now look, Monday is only day left. We supposed to have this day. If you look under your name, you can see she try to write KWONS' CAFÉ first but no ink come out." He lifted the paper to show me. I mean, there was definitely a pen indention, but you couldn't make out the name because EMPRESS GARDEN was written on top of it in all caps. But I was no handwriting expert at the FBI.

I sighed. "Mom and Dad, just let them have it. It only runs through January as a pilot, just to prove to the landlord it's bringing in new customers. Then we can evaluate the whole effort and do something more formalized once the landlord and city council meetings happen."

Mom shook her head. "This is about respect. We were here first. *They* know. *They* don't care about respect now, and never did before. Never change!"

Peter's dad snorted. "There are rules, and we followed them. They always get angry and things blow out of proportion, like always because of their tempers."

Heat prickled the back of my neck as I sought out Hannah to help me with this disagreement. I tried to make eye contact with her, but she was on the phone. Peter was obviously no help since he was nowhere to be found. My shoulders sagged with the weight of my growing disappointment. How dare he not be here to help me with this parent confrontation? How dare he not be here at all to support me, even as just a friend?

My parents had asked me a while ago if I could trust him. I had not only trusted him, but I had fallen for him too. Fallen in a big way. But now it was time to pick my ass back up.

"M-m-maybe we can skip Monday for now," I said. "Let's just get through the city council meeting and decide on who gets Monday later."

My dad, the calmer of my parents, barked, "They never apologize. We don't want to be involve with Li family with anything. If they come to city council, then we not going."

Peter's family dished it right back. "We're supposed to work together, but we don't want to do this anymore." He swirled his finger while pointing to my dad. "Peter can go in our place, but we don't want to go to the city council meeting either."

Mom and Dad stormed out of the room. Peter's parents followed suit after a few seconds. The hamburger gathering had quieted down to just whispers and murmurs—the Lis and Kwons really brought the energy level down to subterranean levels.

These two families needed to be supportive for the greater cause. They were our only hope at swaying the city council, with their lease discovery. But with them arguing so much, we'd give off a bad look if they came and bickered in front of the committee.

A gentle tap on my shoulder stole my attention. For a brief second I thought it might be Peter. "Oh, hi there. I just wanted to introduce myself. I'm Stan, the owner of the VR Santa booth. I've seen you around at Santa's Village and wanted to say hello since you're our neighbor. I've seen the cool photoshoot backgrounds you've added over there. So many of my friends' families have gone to your place for their holiday photos."

I smiled. "My friends Elias and Sophia are the masterminds who came up with those. They really helped the business grow and succeed this holiday. Did you see the latest one, the Elvis-themed Blue Christmas? That might be my favorite."

"I'll have to check that out." He nodded his head toward the front of the room. "That video was great! It reminded me of all the years I spent here at the arcade with my high school buddies. Was that Peter doing the narrating? I told him that leading this save the mall effort would be a good idea."

I crossed my arms. "You did?"

"Yeah, it'll be great and all for the whole community, but it would make him a shoo-in for any college he wanted, leading a grassroots effort from the ground up. Looks like he listened to me. No one ever listens to me, even though I'm full of great ideas. Where is he, by the way? I wanted to ask him to do some voice-over work for our business too."

My phone vibrated.

Oh shit, I fell asleep. Long and dumb story. I'm coming now.

I narrowed my eyes at the screen. Peter. The guy taking all the credit.

My stomach tensed. How could he be this opportunistic? Ugh. "Well, Stan, it was great meeting you, but I have to run and prepare for the landlord meeting. If you could please show up for the city council meeting though, we'd appreciate it so much."

He nodded. "Sure thing. Anything for Peter."

I tried to keep my composure as I turned and walked away.

Peter texted again. **Oh shit, is the meeting over? I see people leaving.**

"Oh shit" was not an apology. It was an excuse. How could I forgive him, especially after knowing he was planning to take credit for everything Hannah and I did? AND he was napping during such a critical meeting.

NAPPING.

I replied. **Don't bother coming.**

I shot through the door and ran to the parking structure as hot tears streamed down my cheeks. Peter kept messaging, but I ignored him. Just like he had ignored me.

TWENTY-NINE

PETER

IN HINDSIGHT, MAYBE SENDING CHLOE 13 TEXTS IN A row filled with only emojis was a little much.

But then I had to send #14 just to apologize for all those texts.

Then I sent #15 to say Can I come over later tonight? It's probably easier to apologize in person.

My heart sank when she responded I'm mad and busy. Our parents fought at the coalition meeting, and it was bad. And you were nowhere to be found.

She followed up with another text. We still need your parents to be at the city council session, it's important. Can you make sure they come?

Could I? After waking from my motion-sickness-induced

nap, I was still in a fog when I got an angry voicemail from my parents, letting me know that 1) they were fed up with the Kwon family and how they were letting their kids run the entire plan to save the mall and 2) I was never allowed to speak to Chloe ever again, because her family was "no good." Then after a few seconds of delay they added 3) That they'd only come to the city council meeting if the Kwon parents weren't there. From their tone, they were mad. Like "red-faced, v-brow emoji with bleep-out curse words" level pissed off. With their stubbornness, it might be something they could never get over.

But still, I had to deliver my parents to City Hall. I owed it to Chloe.

I replied, Sure. No problem. What about the landlord meeting? Can I help? Or come?

It was rescheduled. Hannah and I can handle it.

Brach messaged me as soon as I hit send. Are you still alive? Y/N? Can the corpse of Pete come over for Overwatch?

I gotta study, I'm way behind.

Study here and we can take Overwatch breaks.

Brach was a good student, and I knew he'd be a good study

partner. I used to think him saying "let's go study" was a euphemism for *let's play games in my basement/sneak into bars/go play bball at the Y*, but no, when I came over to his house the first time to do homework, Brach sat me at his desk and then he put on these giant noise-canceling headphones when he sat on his bed and ignored me. I was like, *ok I guess that's what's up* and we studied for two hours straight. And both got As. Kip was more of the slacker in our group, but he was also a killer athlete in multiple sports, so he wasn't as excited for our study sessions and always opted out. We never bothered to invite him anymore, except for the gaming after party.

Due to sheer laziness, and because it was cold AF outside, I invited Brach over to my place instead. He didn't get back to me right away, which was fine because I needed time to think of ways to convince Mom and Dad to show up at the council meeting, or Chloe would hate me forever. She might even possibly murder me in my sleep. She knew where I lived.

My list was sparse.

→ Try to reason with them using logic hahahaha
nope
→ Ask them to be empathetic/not petty AF also
nope
→ Promise them straight As on finals nah
→ Beg Santa at mall for Christmas miracle????

→   Lie (say the Kwons aren't coming?)

→   Bribery???

I wasn't a fan of begging, lying, or bribery, but I also wasn't a fan of losing our family's business because of a fifteen-year-old grudge. Maybe there was another way to get them to the city council meeting without needing to resort to deceit.

Loud banging ripped through my thoughts, and Brach plowed into my home as soon as I opened the door. "It's fr-fr-freezing out there!" He crossed his arms and ran his gloved hands up and down his upper arms. "Ready to study?"

I led him over to the kitchen table. While I got us sodas from the fridge, he asked, "What're you working on?" I brought him a Coke and caught him staring at my list of ideas on my laptop screen.

I sighed. "It's nothing."

Raising an eyebrow, he replied, "It's not nothing. Whatever's got you so stressed out you're behind in studying, so it has to be something. Spill it."

For fifteen minutes, I went through everything. The eviction notice. The history of East West Wok. The city council meeting. My car sleeping incident. Everything. Well, except that I left out the part about Chloe and me becoming closer and that I really liked her. And that we'd kissed a few times.

When I finished, he pressed his lips together and exhaled

from his nose. I waited to see if he had any ideas for how to deliver my parents to City Hall for the final demolition meeting.

"Well...that all sucks. I got nothing."

"Thanks, Brach." I plopped down into my gaming chair.

"But now I understand why you're hanging out with Chloe so much. She's helping you keep your parents' restaurants. For a while I thought you might really like her or something."

Squirming in my seat, I tilted my head so my ear nearly touched my shoulder. My face did this weird contortion while shrugging, like I was trying to fight a full-body Hulk transformation.

"Oh shit, so you *do* like her! I can see it, though. She's cute, but she seemed so different from you... I dunno, maybe opposites attract and all that?"

Chloe and I had different personalities, but she was maybe the most relatable person at school in lots of other ways. Did "opposites attract" really apply?

"Do your parents know you're into her? You think they have this sixth sense and...know?"

"Maybe? But what's more important now is getting my parents to agree to show up at the city council meeting soon, and we don't have much time to come up with a plan."

He nodded. "And if you get them there, you can try to save the mall. And you and Chloe."

My face heated up, but I didn't say anything sarcastic in

return. I didn't need to. He slapped me on the back and said, "I got you, bud. Your parents love me, I can't think of anyone better than me to help you convince them to go to the meeting. And I don't need weeks, I can get them to agree tonight. When do they get home?"

"Wow, Peter, did you buy all of this for us?"

Brach had helped me clear the kitchen table. He'd folded cloth napkins into little tents. Polished the silverware. Brought out crystal candlesticks from the dining room china cabinet that I didn't even know we had. Then he helped me order some food from a few restaurants in town and offered to drive and get it with me. There was a reason he was my best friend. I owed him big for this.

It was a spread of all their favorite dishes. Southern fried chicken, Japanese udon, and Italian lasagna. I made steamed broccoli and cut up slices of apples and pears because they liked those too.

Brach pulled out chairs for my parents. "Mrs. Li, Mr. Li, thanks for having me over. Peter and I got a lot of studying done. I think we're going to do great on our finals."

My mom sighed. "Brach is such a good boy. So polite. Such a good influence."

Dad sat down and examined a fried gyoza on the tip of his

chopsticks. These deep-fried delights had endured a twenty-minute car ride, so some sogginess was expected. But when he bit into one of the ends, the initial resounding crunch and the subsequent smaller ones made me want to add all the remaining crispy dumplings to my plate, but they were for Mom and Dad, not me. After he finished chewing and swallowing, he said, "Woweee, this is the best gyoza in town. I could eat these all day! Should we sit down? You cleaned up and brought us such amazing food. Let's all eat and you can confess to us what you want from your mom and me."

"Am I that obvious?" I gestured for them to eat. "Help yourselves. Brach and I bought these from the best restaurants in the area." I showed them the places listed on Yelp. "They all have high ratings and maybe just as important, they have over a thousand reviews, many of them recent. Brach and I went to the owners and told them about your restaurant. How you're doing well but you could use some new business. All of them suggested we do a cross-promotion. They do fundraiser nights with little league teams and local elementary and middle schools. They want to include you in the marketing materials."

Dad clapped with excitement. "We've never known how to do that, get more business from the local area with schools. We just have our mall regulars."

Mom smiled. "This is the news? When can we start?"

"Well, they have their next fundraiser for the school district late January, so in a month. But they want to make sure your business will still be around."

Mom's smile dissipated. "I see. You mean—"

"You need to fight for the mall, Mom. So you can still be in business next year."

Dad cleared his throat and picked up a fork to sample a piece of lasagna. "Wow, this is good." He picked up a serving spoon to scoop a large rectangle of lasagna on his plate. "We can think about it. Let's have dinner first."

They didn't say no, which was usually their immediate first response.

And a non-no was better than nothing.

THIRTY

CHLOE

THE TWICE-RESCHEDULED MEETING WITH THE landlord didn't go as expected.

And that was because he was a no-show. Hannah and I sat outside his office, per his admin assistant's request, for over an hour. We even showed up thirty minutes early which Hannah insisted we do even though she needed to be at work and would be staying at the law firm past midnight to make up the billable hours.

There were no signs Rick Junior had even shown up that day: the office mini-blinds were mostly closed, there was no light of any kind coming from under his door, and it was eerily quiet. All I could hear was the admin assistant clacking away at her keyboard and my stomach making "pew pew pewww" noises from eating nothing all day.

The original plan was to have Peter with us, but I was still so mad that the thought of being around him made me nauseated. Hannah agreed it was best to not have him come to the meeting and be a distraction.

She adjusted her silk blouse/wool skirt/pearl necklace paralegal uniform and stood from her seat. "It doesn't look like Mr. Jones is going to make our meeting today, is that right?"

The admin removed her hands from her keyboard. "It appears that way. He would be in the office by now if he was planning to be here."

I wanted to yell, "Couldn't he let us know? The disrespect! Doesn't he know everything at stake here?"

Hannah kept her cool. "When was the last time he was in the office? And is there a way we could maybe call him on video? We wanted to discuss a time-sensitive matter, and we'd be happy to chat with him virtually. I love your earrings, by the way."

The formality melted away, and suddenly Hannah had made a new best friend. "Okay, so he was here earlier, it's odd he's out because his day is packed with meetings." She paused. "Do you really like my earrings? I got them at Kate Spade for my birthday." She lifted her earlobes with her two index fingers so we could get a better look. "I never buy statement jewelry, but I loved these crystal flowers. I'm Casey, by the way."

Hannah nodded. "Well, Casey, I do love them. They definitely suit your face. I can't wear dangling or hooped jewelry because of my giraffe neck." She looked over at me. "Chloe probably could. Her neck is reasonably proportioned."

This was the weirdest, nicest thing Hannah had ever said to me. I needed to put this in my baby book next to "Chloe's first step," "Chloe's first word," and "Chloe's first A+." Chloe's first semi-compliment from Hannah.

My sister pointed at the computer screen. "Any chance you could tell me when we could squeeze into his schedule soon? We have an urgent matter to discuss with Ricky."

Casey took a sip of coffee. "I guess he snuck past me somehow. When his lights are out, it means he's left for the day. Maybe he's going to work from home." She pulled herself up from her swivel chair using her desk for stability. After knocking three times and jiggling the locked doorknob, she put her ear against the door and listened. "He's definitely not there, and I'm afraid he's on vacation for most of the holidays. I don't supposed you'd want to leave materials here for him to review later? I'll make sure he gets them."

I noticed a shadow move across the bottom of Rick's office door. Was someone inside? Or were my eyes playing tricks on me?

Hannah smiled. "We can leave some materials with you, and if you see any openings in his schedule could you let me know?" She pulled out a bound copy of the presentation we had planned to share with him and handed it to Casey.

"Do you have two envelopes by any chance?" I asked.

Casey walked back to her desk and opened her middle drawer. It was full of stationery, office supplies, and fun-size Halloween candy. She handed me two blank envelopes and a small pack of Sour Patch Kids. "Don't tell the boss," she joked.

Dropping a USB stick holding heritage video into each envelope, I used the Sharpie from the nearby cup of pens to write "For Ricky Junior" on one and "For Rick Senior" on the other.

Hannah whispered, "Why two?"

I shrugged. "If I was Rick Senior, I'd want to watch this video of Riverwood's history. It's his history too."

Casey took the envelopes from my hands. "I'll make sure they both get it."

"Thank you," Hannah and I said in unison.

We grabbed our belongings and walked in silence until we were out of earshot. Hannah asked, "Did you see that there was someone inside his office? He was avoiding us!"

Hannah's car was parked just outside Ricky Junior's exterior window. We thought that by getting a good spot it was an omen.

She complained, "Well, that was a bust, and I doubt he'll read anything we left with him. So I guess our last shot to save this place is the city council meeting. I have to go to work, but I can drop you off at home." She unlocked her car and plopped down in the driver's seat.

I looked up because something caught my eye. It was Ricky's office. The light flicked on.

Hannah looked over to the building. "That prick! He played us."

"What an asshole!" I balled my fists and tried to steady my breath. Wasn't it the season of love, peace, and generosity? Hard to believe there was someone I was angrier at than Peter at that moment, but lo and behold, Ricky Junior was the world's shadiest human and took first place. This was the opposite of a Christmas miracle, and something no one had wished for.

THIRTY-ONE

PETER

I FLICKED CHLOE'S YODA EAR FROM BEHIND. "MY parents will be at the city council meeting. I promise."

She looked over her shoulder. "Okay." She went back to cleaning her camera lens.

"Look, I'm sorry about last week. Sorry I didn't show up for you. It won't happen again." She wasn't exactly given me the silent treatment, but something between us had changed. And each day that went by, I could feel the distance between us widening. Besides groveling over texts, I didn't know what else to do, other than show up to her work, flick her plush ear, and beg for forgiveness.

"I need time. And I'm busy." She shoved her long lens into one of the padded slots in her SLR camera bag. "My shift ended and I need to head home and study for finals. I gotta go."

I couldn't let her leave. Not without clearing the air. "Can I walk you to your car? I'll talk fast."

Chloe put the camera bag strap on her shoulder. "Suit yourself."

I walked with her in lockstep. "I'm sorry I disappeared that night. I'm too embarrassed to tell you what happened, but you're so mad at me I figured I might as well spill it all."

She halted. "You can't charm your way out of this one, Peter. I was counting on you that night. A lot of people were. I needed you. And you let me down."

My heart ached inside my chest. Chloe was known for her bluntness, but this really hit me hard. "I know, and I'm sorry. I should have set an alarm or something."

Her walking resumed and I trotted after her.

She grumbled, "Yeah, maybe you needed a reminder to skip your gym workout for once and prioritize someone else over yourself for a change?"

I stopped. "What? You think I was at the gym? I was passed out in my car from motion sickness." My insides lurched, like I was back on the ride that made me nauseated that night. "And you really think I'd choose the gym over you? Do you even know why I go to the gym in the first place?"

She turned around. "The same reason most guys who look like you do."

"No, I don't think you get it. I—" My voice went faint. "I

was always scrawny, ever since I was born. Kids made fun of me, calling me 'Bones,' even Sam did. My parents teased me too. It was just one more way Sam was better than me. But it was the one thing I figured out how to change. In junior high, I went to the gym on my own and joined a bunch of sports. I grew muscle. I ate more. I finally could be something Sam couldn't. It was a way to show mom and dad I was different and special."

That was the thing with my parents...they never saw me as a separate person from my brother Sam. He was successful, so in their minds they had the model kid template: make good grades (check!), take test prep classes (check!) ace admissions tests (check!), and voilà, they had a winner. I thought sports might help me stand out, but the more I strayed from their ace proto-type, the harder my life was. Following in Sam's footsteps seemed to be the only thing that made them care about me.

Her eyes widened. "I...don't know what to say. I'm sorry I misjudged you. I can relate. Hannah, she's the perfect Korean daughter specimen. So I know a lot about what you're going through."

I sighed. Maybe Chloe would forgive me after all. And we could let bygones be just that.

"But the napping part isn't the only thing that made me so angry."

Ouch.

She continued. "I had a little chat with your boss Stan after the coalition meeting. He said he'd advised you to help save the mall so it would look good on your résumé." Chloe shook her head. "So in the end, it *was* all about you. It was always all about you. Never about anyone else."

"That's not true!"

Chloe turned her head away, like she couldn't bear to look at me. "Then why did he say that? Did he make all of that up?"

I took a deep breath. "He did say those things, but that doesn't mean I listened to him. You gotta believe me, I helped out because I wanted to, it wasn't about college. Okay, maybe when he said it I thought about my personal gain...but...I can't believe I'm saying this but I can't think of any other way to say it. I listened to my heart instead. I did it for the mall. For my parents. But especially for you."

She turned toward me. Her lips trembled. "Really?"

"I don't comb through dozens of boring leases for just anyone."

She reached out her hand and cracked a smile. "No one has ever said anything as romantic as that my entire life."

I intertwined my fingers in hers and followed her outside into the parking lot.

She didn't hate me anymore!

"Oh shoot, I forgot to grab my share of the cash tips!" She looked back at the door. "I need to head back."

"I can come with you!" Now that we reconciled, I wanted to

spend more time with her, even if it meant walking to and from the parking lot to Santa's Village. "And I forgot to ask, how did the landlord meeting go?"

She stopped abruptly at a notice posted on the automatic doors. "Oh no."

The sign read:

PERMANENT CLOSURE

LAST DAY OF MALL OPERATIONS January 15

Dear Mall Patrons,

We are sad to announce the closure of Riverwood Mall, effective starting next month, with limited hours of operations. Thank you for shopping here and allowing us to be a part of your community for all these years.

Sincerely,

Jones Realty LLC

I collapsed against the brick wall and tried to compose myself. Chloe stood like a statue on the large welcome mat in front of the automatic doors, causing them to go haywire by opening and closing over and over again.

Chloe needs you right now.

And you need Chloe.

I pulled myself upright and put my arms around her, then

folded her inside my down jacket. We stayed that way, doors opening and closing on us, silently shivering and breathing in the frigid air as her warm tears formed a multitude of dark circles on my puffy sleeve.

THIRTY-TWO

CHLOE

"EARTH TO CHLOE, COME IN, CHLOE!"

Lorraine grinned as I refocused on her face. My mind had wandered again. Not leaving the best impression in our last mentor session.

"I'm so sorry." I considered giving her a list of excuses, but she already knew what was going on in my life.

She stood up. "Would you like a refill?" She shook her glass and the ice clinked. "More sweet tea?"

"No thanks." With the caffeine and sugar already coursing in my veins, I would be up all night. Which wasn't a bad thing, I still had a million things to do to prepare for both the National Art Council Gala and the city council meeting, both happening within the next twenty-four hours. Luckily the city council was in the early afternoon and National Art Council was in the evening. I would have to leave the planning commission session and hightail it over to the National Art Council regional banquet thirty minutes away. I was one of two local high schoolers selected as finalists, and the State Arts Foundation funded a mocktail/cocktail hour pre-event with fancy food and invited well-to-do patrons. It was the first time in history more than one student from the same metropolitan area had placed in the finals. They were livestreaming the reception to other locations across the country, and they had previously recorded contestants who lived outside of the United States that they would broadcast too.

Mom and Dad had shut down the restaurant for the evening. For people who only closed their restaurant twice a year, on Thanksgiving and Christmas Day, this was a big deal. They agreed to go to the event with me. I didn't exactly tell them that we would be stopping by the city council meeting though. I had something planned that would hopefully make them less hateful toward the Lis as long as they didn't figure out our detour plans.

It had to work. So much depended on it.

Lorraine asked, "Did you have any new material you wanted to add to your portfolio? It's not required, but some participants add in last minute photos or pieces that reflect what they'd learned during their mentorship, or they share a new skill expressed in art concepts. Happy to help you with that, since we have a little bit of time left today. I thought your historical video of the mall's history showed so much of your growth as an artist, but I there's still time to push you to even greater heights."

"I do have some new photos I wanted to share with you." I scrambled off her industrial bar stool and grabbed my camera out of my bag, along with my laptop. "I haven't uploaded these to my computer but I will now. It will be quick. Wanted to get your thoughts on adding these."

I inserted the memory card into the USB port and various photos popped up on my screen. Santa photos galore! My body burned a million degrees as random children and families with Mr. Claus populated on my computer. "I'm so sorry, how embarrassing, my work camera wasn't working one day so I had to use my own. This isn't what I wanted to share."

She tapped the right arrow as I cringed. "Getting paid for your work is nothing to be ashamed of. I'm proud of you. And honestly, this Santa isn't the most photogenic, so you're really using flattering angles and lighting to their utmost extreme."

I laughed and she did too. I would miss working with Lorraine.

"Here," I said, pointing at the newer photos flowing down the screen. "These are people I've interviewed for a personal project of mine. I wanted to make sure someone seeing these for the first time would engage on an emotional, human level." I showed her some news articles I'd found and explained why I'd tracked them down. I also typed out soundbites from my interviews, quotes that were particularly meaningful to me, and took photos of the printouts placed inside antique bronze frames that Sophia let me borrow from the school's theater department.

"These aren't just meaningful and pleasant images, Chloe, you're crossing the threshold into something much more elevated, something that is new and challenging by not just simply capturing the beauty of what you see in front of you, but also by stirring deep, raw emotion. You're putting yourself out there by showing the world your point of view and letting everyone see your kind heart through the process."

Yes, I was telling a story, reflecting my own voice and passion. I wasn't just hiding behind a camera anymore. No more hiding. No more being invisible. It was a breakthrough moment.

"Do you think I should share these?" I scrolled through my final few images.

"Bravo, Chloe." She wiped away a tear. "Without a doubt, you must."

Elias and Soph were dying to catch up with me, but I had no time. They also knew me so well that when I didn't respond to Instagram, Twitter, Discord, Slack, WhatsApp, or group text messages, they knew to quit bothering me. Just before leaving for the city council and National Art Council events, they messaged, "Will be there tonight to support you. Lorraine also snagged us tickets to your fancy gala. Free dinner and dress up! WOOOOO!"

I truly had the best friends.

With some of my savings, I bought myself a velvety black dress, imitation pearl earrings, and chunky black Mary Janes. Stepping back from my mirrored closet, I was able to see my Chloe transformation from Santa elf to Dignified Awards Recipient.

I fidgeted with the backing of my earring as I made my way down the hall to my parents room. They had the door wide open, which could have been bad if they were roaming around half dressed, but luckily they were fully clothed. Both of them looked like they were going to a memorial service, but I couldn't say anything in my all-black, slightly less funeral-y outfit. To my surprise, my mom handed me a tube of red lipstick. "This look bad on me. But make you look pretty."

I pulled off the top and swiped the stick across both lips. Pursing my lips and then tapping them together, I checked out my reflection in their vanity. It was red all right, and it added a punch to my look. A festive one at that.

Mom wore a black polka-dot dress with cap sleeves. She asked, "Where you get that earring?"

"It was on sale."

She tut-tutted her tongue and disappeared to the closet. I could hear the slide of the lockbox from the top shelf and the clasp creak open. Umma reappeared, holding out her right palm.

"This is mine, from wedding day. It's real. You can have. Not the cheap thing, so it won't cause skin infection." Umma had gone into her box of most treasured possessions and found the perfect gift for the perfect time.

For me.

Not Hannah.

Me.

I plucked out my fake pearl earrings and put them on the vanity. With slow and cautious movements, I lifted each earring from my mom's palm and put them on with the utmost care. They were a little larger than the other ones, with an off-white shimmer. They were beautiful.

"Thank you, Umma." I looked over at Dad, who came out of the bathroom fully dressed in a black pinstripe suit, light gray shirt, and dark red tie. "Thanks, Appa."

He furrowed his brow. "What I do? Beside looking good?"

I lifted my earlobes so he could see. "Umma said I could have them."

Dad bobbed his head and smiled. "Yes. You should wear. It was wedding gift from Halmoni."

To avoid letting them see me tear up, I scampered out of the room and yelled, "The train leaves in five minutes!" over my shoulder.

The only monochrome bag I owned was a black, ratty cross-body messenger I'd gotten from a poorly thought-through

Amazon Prime Day purchase. Sadly, no other bag or purse I owned would fit my laptop and printed speech papers. I messaged Hannah to let her know we were heading out early, then texted Peter, telling him to meet me in the City Hall atrium with his parents in fifteen minutes. I grabbed the keys and my black puffy parka from the wall hook and ran out the back door.

As busy as I had been, I still wasn't able to push Peter fully out of my mind. My thoughts would wander throughout the day and I'd see something random that reminded me of him.

A Santa snuggie in an ad on YouTube? I thought of Peter Li paying for a Santa's Village deluxe photo package so he could talk to me.

Pastries in the local bakery window? Images of Peter double-fisting Costco Danishes in the coalition meetings flashed before me.

Grilling Kwons' Café spicy pork under the industrial restaurant hood? How could I not think of Peter?

My parents loaded into our Corolla and we drove to City Hall, only a few minutes away. They were too busy listening to a Korean news satellite radio show to notice where we were at first, but as soon as I turned off the ignition, they definitely put two and two together.

"City Hall? Chloe nooo, we tell you if Li family here, we not going. We only agree to award ceremony."

"Umma and I stay in car. Leave the key."

We were twenty minutes early, and what I'd planned needed to happen immediately. "Mom, Dad, I never ask you for much. I show up to the restaurant and help when I can. I'm asking you for fifteen minutes of your time. That's it. Then you can go back to the car. I promise it'll be worthwhile." *Please let it be worthwhile.* "And it's almost Christmas. It's the season you should be doing nice things for others, a time you should reflect that you're here for others, not just yourselves."

Dad looked at Mom. "Only ten minute."

"Okay, ten minutes. I promise."

Umma sighed but then said, "Okay."

With the rapid drop in temperature, we could see our white puffs of exhaled breaths while walking to the front doors of the building. Opening the doors to City Hall released a gust of welcome warmth. My teeth chattered as I said to my parents, "F-f-follow me, please."

The others had arrived before me, just as I planned.

I greeted my guests. "Hi, Mr. and Mrs. Kang. Mr. Davidson. Mrs. Jackson. Reverend Davis." The five of them shook my hand.

Mom asked, "Are you city council people? Such an honor!"

Dad nodded and whispered to me, "They look like good people."

"I'll let them introduce themselves," I said. And perfect timing, the Li parents arrived with Peter.

My mom's and dad's eyes widened as a confused Li family inched over to where we were all standing.

Before either set of parents could complain about being there, Mr. Kang and the rest of them gave quick introductions. They represented a wide range in business ownership: restaurants, billiards, body shops, and churches.

Reverend Davis added, "There's one thing we have in common. Do you know, Mr. and Mrs. Kwon? Mr. Li? Mrs. Li?"

Our parents shook their heads in silence.

"Uncle Joe scammed all of us. And by all of us, I'm even including God Almighty."

Peter and I chuckled. Our eyes met briefly, and I walked over to him to squeeze his hand. He got his parents there, as promised. I offered him a slight smile and diverted my attention back to the Reverend.

"Uncle Joe scammed more than just us folks here. There are so many in the community, and he'd been doing it for years. Thank you, Chloe, for getting us together. This was so cathartic."

I turned to my parents. "Joe Brewer swindled a lot of people. I saw it mentioned in some news articles and met with a few business owner victims. They're all angry they were fooled by someone they trusted."

Mr. Kang said in Korean, "So much shame."

My parents nodded.

I said, "I asked them to be part of my final National Art Council photojournalism project. I interviewed everyone and took photos of their everyday hardships. One day when they find Uncle Joe, and one day they will, I'll be ready with our story." I choked up with those last words. Hearing how this man had taken money from so many kindhearted people broke my heart.

Peter's mom spoke. "I'm still so angry. It's been fifteen years."

My dad said, "Actually sixteen. But nobody counting except me."

With that, both families laughed. Peter and me included.

My dad said to me, "I'm sorry we hide everything about the mall landlord. We were ashamed."

"Why?" I asked.

His voice grew faint. "We didn't want to bother our kid. And then when things look bad, we are ashamed we lose our business again. Like last time."

The Li parents nodded. "Same for us."

Dad added, "The anger in our heart, so heavy. Weigh so much."

I swallowed hard and fought back tears. "If you both could stay to show support, we can try to make sure you won't lose it this time." I turned to my five new friends. "I'll mail you all prints from the photo project. Come by the mall and we'll get you a free dinner. Thank you so much for sharing what happened to you. We have to go now, to fight for what's ours."

Mr. Jackson, who barely spoke the entire time, grunted, "Give 'em holy hell in there!"

Reverend Davis laughed. "I think God would be okay with that."

I nodded firmly. "Yes, sir!"

The agenda was posted by the door. This demolition appeal was slated last, much later than we'd been told in the email, which meant that I wouldn't be able to go to the National Art Council event. Or if I went to the National Art Council, I'd need to skip the city council meeting. Sweat trickled down my temples as I considered my two options. Both events were so important to me, but I couldn't attend both. Why did life have to be so utterly unfair?

My interim decision was to wait a few minutes. There was a slight chance the council would move through the agenda quickly. Maybe I wouldn't even have to choose.

The meeting was already in session by the time we entered the room from the back. I looked around and saw so many familiar faces.

Mr. Fry from Hamburger Palace.

Mr. Jamison, the grumpy Candy Shoppe owner.

The Silver Sneakers Walking Club, in their tracksuits!

Elias and Sophia were in the front row. They looked back

at me and smiled. Sophia pointed in between them. It was Cheremy!

Where was Hannah?

My phone's reception in the City Hall building was spotty. Every once in a while I'd end up with one or two bars of signal, but it was rare. After a minute, the two-bar fairy granted me temporary access. Two messages appeared.

Peter. **Good luck, Baby Yoda!**

Hannah. **Stuck at work in client deposition. I'm so sorry.**

Stuck at work, but I'm still coming? Or stuck at work, sorry Chloe, you're screwed?

My breath grew labored as I fumbled with my reply. **Let me know when you're on your way.**

I waited thirty minutes for Hannah to write back, turning my head every few seconds to see if she was here. *Please walk through the door. Please walk through the door.*

The council took a brief recess. Upon resuming, they would discuss the final item on the docket. It was time to make the game-time decision. City council or National Art Council? A large number of people were here waiting to get their two minutes of speaking time, as Hannah and I had instructed them to do. With Hannah not here to lead, I knew what needed to be done.

I fought back tears and texted Lorraine. **I am so sorry. I'm still at City Hall. I won't be able to come tonight.**

How had everything come down to this critical, pivotal moment? Where I had to choose between my parents' livelihood and my own future? I knew as you got older it came with making bigger life decisions. I never thought that by choosing a direction I knew was right I'd be saddled with immediate regret.

I pulled a tissue from the front pocket of my bag and dabbed my eyes. Not only was I giving up the National Art Council Competition, I also had to do something I was not ready to do. I took deep breaths in and out, then pulled out the papers from my bag, trying to cram during the eight minutes left of recess.

Peter, Eli, and Soph came over. All I said was "Hannah's not coming" and they scattered away. They knew me well enough to know it wasn't the right time for any chitchat or condolences. There wasn't any time.

Hannah's notes were organized, but she knew what legal-y stuff to say. Should I just read her memorandums verbatim? I only had two minutes up there to speak. Skimming her notes, she had two main arguments. The first one was the one that Peter and I found...the demolition clause, and the second was that the mall was just shy of thirty years old, which could qualify as a historic preservation site. The last one felt like a long shot, given that the nineties feel of the mall didn't really feel aesthetically inspired, unless you considered Orange Julius or Sbarro to be long-standing cultural icons. But it was worth trying.

One of the councilmembers tapped his mic and began

speaking. "The last item on the agenda is for Riverwood Mall, Case number RIV-3386-HCM-CC1. Today we will discuss the sale of the mall, and the subsequent approval of the proposed demolition permits for Riverwood Mall in favor of rebuilding for a mixed-use space. The councilmembers have reviewed the proposal of land use and base plan. The developers have pointed out that the zoning district allows for commercial use, however it's currently not been approved for mixed residential. Mr. Rick Jones Jr. is here to represent the building owner, but the developer is unable to be here today. They have both provided written statements prior to the meeting. Highest and best use construction plans were submitted last week."

He adjusted his reading glasses and continued. "We also received paperwork from a Ms. Hannah Kwon, stating that in addition to zoning issues, there are two tenants of the mall who do not have a demolition clause in their lease, Kwons' Café and Empress Garden. And finally, that this demolition would require a separate permit request by the Historic Landmarks Commission. Is Ms. Hannah Kwon in the audience to confirm and verify all of those statements before we begin?"

Everyone glanced around the room, and I prayed a Hail Mary that she'd come running through that back door like people did in the movies. When it was clear she wasn't, I rose from my chair and squeaked, "I'm Ms. Kwon's proxy this evening. She isn't able to come."

"And you are?"

I gulped. "I'm Ms. Kwon."

The audience tittered.

"Chloe Kwon, sir." I sat back down fast, like it was a musical chairs game and the song had abruptly stopped. *It's okay to fear stepping out of your comfort zone, Chloe. It means you're about to do something courageous.*

I stuffed my phone into my bag. There would be no use for it while the meeting was in session. The one person who I needed to communicate with wasn't going to save me.

Perching in my seat, I waited for him to invite members of the public to speak. Mr. Fry went first, talking about how many burgers he'd flipped since the restaurant opened close to twenty years ago. I don't know if he made that number up, but the number 700,000 came up several times. After he finished, the Silver Sneakers came to the podium. A few of them offered two minutes of heartwarming stories of deep friendships, loyalty, and community. One of them ended with, "Where would we do our daily walks? At Costco? Around the condo complex? Hell no!" She snorted as everyone in the room cheered.

The Candy Shoppe guy rambled a bit about how the mall had deteriorated over time, and for a while I wondered whose side he was on, but he ended with, "Riverwood Mall is my home, and I'll chain my body to my store before I let you demolish it!" He received enthusiastic applause from a few people in the back row.

"Ms. Kwon? Would you like to speak?"

Before I opened my mouth, my mom called out from her chair, "No, I not speaking today. But I just want to say that I work so hard at Kwons' Café. I love my restaurant. I love my customer. My husband and me, we work hard for our American dream. We too old to start over again. Li family here too. We both want to stay. Our lease say we can stay." Her voice, unwavering, persuasive, and clear, startled me. So this was where Hannah got it from.

The councilman chuckled. "Thank you Ms. Kwon. We were asking about final words from the other Ms. Kwon, but your points are all valid and duly noted. I also want to say how much I love your spicy pork combo."

Peter cheered, "Yesss! I love that too!"

His mom slapped his arm. *Thanks, Mrs. Li.*

With my papers in hand, I walked to the front. My hands trembled as I grabbed both sides of the podium. I looked to my left, where Peter offered me a reassuring smile.

"What if I screw this up," I mouthed.

"You won't," he whispered. "And I won't let you."

Trying not to cry, I looked to my right, where Elias and Sophie sat. They also cheered me on with upturned thumbs from each of them.

Four thumbs up total.

And a gorgeous smile from Cheremy.

I nodded to them and began reading the main summary of Hannah's memo, a repeat of points about the demolition clause and historic landmark. Then I realized the council had all of this information and going over it all wasn't going to be the best use of time. What they didn't have was the full picture behind the bright and shiny condo money veil.

I looked up from the podium and addressed the mostly male, all white council. "Today I was supposed to be at an awards ceremony, hosted by the prestigious National Art Council Junior Arts Foundation. That's why I'm dressed up today. But I had to make an unbearable decision, to choose between two things I love the most, my parents and my art. Both are built on the foundational belief that dreams in America can come true. That despite financial hardship, and criminal activities and racism targeting my parents, someone who looks like them can have the same opportunities as anyone else.

"But it turns out I'm here to not only support my parents, but to also fight for the broader community as well. We have great ideas on how to revitalize the mall, and it's all feasible with little investment and nominal resources. We shared them with Mr. Jones and I know we can do this: I'm literally betting my future on it.

"Earlier today, my parents and the Li family came face-to-face with other business owners just like them who had all faced devastating adversity and overcame it." I turned and smiled at my Umma and Appa, then made eye contact with each member of the council. "My parents are all dolled up and looking fancy in their nice clothes, because we thought we'd be at an awards banquet. They took their first vacation day in fifteen years. That's how dedicated they are to their restaurant. I know you have a lot to consider, and my sister Hannah isn't here, but she spent a lot of time researching everything, and—" I gestured behind me, "I hope that you remember that there are a lot of people who depend on and love Riverwood Mall." Finding Rick Jones Jr. in the audience, wearing an untucked chambray shirt and black overcoat, I said directly to him, "We have so many great ideas for the mall. Some are easier to implement than others, but the community is willing to work together to make things happen. Please give us a chance to save Riverwood."

He sat upright, pursed his lips tight, then offered me a single nod. Pretty much the most confusing feedback ever. I turned back to face the council and said in a firm voice, "Thank you, council members, for your time."

Peter and his family rose to their feet and clapped. Others soon followed.

"Chloe, look over here and wave!" Elias was filming me and I did as I was told. I grinned and also wiped away a few tears that had tumbled down my cheeks.

As I made my way back to my seat, my parents grabbed my hands and squeezed hard. Their Kwon way of saying *good job*.

The crowd chattered quietly while the councilmembers turned off their microphones to deliberate. The room noise rose and died down as one of the councilpeople, the only woman, cleared her throat and said into her microphone, "Thank you everyone. There's a lot to consider here, and given that we're so close to the holidays, we will put forward the following decision...We are objecting to the issuance of the Riverwood demolition permits for a 180-day period. While this is a delay rather than a yes-or-no decision, it will give you all time to meet with the landlord to see if you can implement some of the ideas you have."

She pulled out a page from an accordion folder and smiled. "I'm compelled by these business proposals personally, particularly outdoor spring concert and the Pooch Pride Parade. If at 180 days the owner is still looking to sell, we will reconvene and review the demo clauses and permitting requirements again. Empress Garden and Kwons' Café leases end in approximately a year, so there wouldn't be any eviction prior to that, as I understand they are paying rent in full and on time. I have full faith though that the initiatives will not only generate new business, but will also breathe new life into our community. I have high hopes in you all. Especially you, Ms. Kwon."

She winked at me, but my mom cried out, "Thank you Mrs. Council Man! It is true honor."

The entire audience burst into laughter.

Over the noise, a booming voice spoke up. "Excuse me, I'd like to speak."

Next to the landlord, a man in his sixties, with a full head of white hair and metal framed glasses, raised his hand. If he had a goatee, he would be the spitting image of Colonel Sanders.

"Of course, Mr. Jones. We would be privileged to hear words from you today."

Mr. Jones?

"I'd like to speak from here, if that's all right. Bad case of rheumatism. Hello everyone, I'm Rick Senior. It might not be well known information, but I am still a co-owner of Riverwood Mall, as I am still a member of Jones Realty LLC, although most of my other real estate properties have been placed into a new LLC in Ricky's name. I haven't signed the mall over yet. I received a lovely video from Chloe about Riverwood Mall's history that I viewed this past weekend and enjoyed very much. So much in fact that it had me going through old mall photos myself, remembering all those good years. Separately, I was thrilled the Silver Sneakers reached out last week with a formal invitation to join them. What an honor!" He turned to the gaggle of elderly women in the corner. "Were you roped in by my doctor? He told me he wanted me to exercise more, and in what better company could I do this than with you lovely ladies?"

The Silver Sneakers section whooped and cheered.

"I don't want to take up too much time, but I wanted to

express my gratitude to everyone here. And we'd be happy to listen to your ideas, come January, after the holidays."

The main city council member spoke into the mic. "And with that, meeting adjourned. Have a happy and safe holiday everyone!"

The crowd quickly dispersed, and my parents went to the back of the room to chat with the other Riverwood Mall business owners, including the Lis. While Sophia chatted with Peter, Elias rushed over to me. "Don't be mad."

"Why would I be mad at you?"

"Because-I-filmed-your-speech-and-uploaded-it-to-Google-Drive-using-WiFi-and-Lorraine-broadcasted-it-to-the-National Art Council-awards-ceremony-when-it-was-your-turn-to-give-your-presentation?" He shrugged his shoulders and offered a half-wince-half-smile.

My mind clouded with confusion. "You wh-what? And there was Wi-Fi?"

Sophia came over. "Hey! Did he tell you he sent your speech to Lorraine, and they're broadcasting it right now at the ceremony? How cool is that? I love technology."

Stunned by the news, it took me a few seconds to speak. "I... guess?"

Elias and Sophia group hugged me. Soph said, "We love you. And we are so proud. We just wanted you to have your shot at that grant."

Elias added, "And don't worry, I took it from your good side and then cropped it and added a soft light filter so you look stunning. The fluorescent lights in here are atrocious."

I laughed. "Thank you both. I guess we'll hear from Lorraine who the winner is."

Hannah entered the room through the back entrance. "Oh my God. I missed it, I'm *so* sorry. We almost lost our client today, and I was asked to stay late. I was really torn on what to do, but work came first." She looked over at Mom and Dad. "I guess it went well if they're talking to the Lis?"

I nodded. "It went well." I explained the whole 180-day delay, and that we had a ton of work to do to show the mall owners this place could be turned around, but we had Rick Senior on our side. While I talked, I couldn't help but wonder why she had made the decision to skip out on this important meeting for work, while I gave up the National Art Council Gala to be here. She had sent all those memos beforehand and yes, she had me as her backup, but wow... We really were so different in so many ways.

Hannah wandered away to talk to a lone remaining council member. Elias pretended to lick his finger and then touched me, then made a sizzle "Sssst" sound. "I'm sorry, I'm just so proud of you, and you killed it. And those National Art Councilors will be fools if you don't win. By the way, Soph and I are going out to Hamburger Palace now, apparently there's some ad hoc after party and we're invited. There will be unlimited milkshakes." He whispered in my ear. "Cheremy is coming. and he offered to drive us. And I even said more than two words to him today, can you believe it? He's pulling his car around."

Before I could answer, Lorraine texted me. **Phenomenal!**

I was unsure of the context at first, but then a shaky video appeared of the audience at the banquet. My portfolio projected on one screen. My City Hall speech projected on another. A standing ovation.

They were standing...for me.

I stared at the video, then pinched and widened, examining every face.

Peter was one of the few people left inside the City Hall building. He asked, "Can we talk now? Actually, I set it up so you kind of have to, because I told my parents and yours I would take you home. Elias and Soph left with Cheremy already. Hannah went back to work. There's no way for you to leave other than riding with me."

"Okay," I said, grabbing my coat from the back of my chair. He picked up my messenger bag and put it on my shoulder after I zipped up.

Like the warm air had blasted us upon entry, the cold, brisk air hit us like an icy punch to the face.

Peter yelped, "Oh shit! Damn, it's cold." He pulled his coat collar upward and pulled his hunting cap further down over his ears.

Once we reached his car, he turned on the ignition and turned the heat to maximum blast.

"Hold on." He got out and closed his driver's side door. The trunk popped open, and I turned to see Peter completely enveloped in a balloon bouquet.

He opened my door. "These are for you. Since you hate flowers."

I laughed. "I don't *hate* flowers, I just...never mind. Thank you." He went through all this trouble for me, getting his parents here wasn't easy, and getting those balloons required a lot of planning.

A mix of Mylar and latex globes bobbed and swirled in the wind with Congratulations! You did it! You're #1! messages.

"Hold on, let me put these back in the trunk. They're really overwhelming and stressing me out." My heart melted as I watched him fight the balloon rebel resistance in the rearview mirror. He finally stuffed them in and slammed the trunk. A "pop!" echoed, making me jump.

"Sorry, one tried to escape," he said, reentering the car. He smiled apologetically. "Congratulations for being a finalist tonight. And at the city council meeting you were great...congrats for being so...Chloe!"

"You mean being woozy and terrified and awkward?" I dipped my head down, remembering all the worry and anxiety just before taking the podium.

"Are you kidding me?" He looked right into my eyes, his stare making my entire body below my chin go wobbly like Jell-O. "You were amazing. And you were so passionate and spoke from your heart. I can't see anyone else doing what you did."

I didn't want to ask this, but I couldn't help myself. "Don't you think Hannah would have done better?"

"Hey," he said, taking his index finger and brushing my long bangs out of my eyes. "It couldn't have gone any better. I'm serious."

I took his hand and pressed it to my cheek. "Thank you for keeping your promise. How did you get your parents here?"

"Best not to reveal my secrets." Peter grinned. "Want me to take you home? So you can celebrate with your parents and Hannah when she gets home? Did they announce the winner?"

"Lorraine said she'd message me, and the award ceremony should be over in a few minutes." I bit my lip. "In the meantime though, we finally have some time to ourselves." I let go of his hand and let my index finger travel down the front of his coat, moving southward along the vertical line of his zipper.

He cupped my face with his hands and his mouth swooped down for a kiss. My mind flashed to us in the back of the restaurant. The flowers. Our bodies pressed together in an embrace. A smile spread across my face when he leaned back, leaving my lips tingling with heat.

"What's so funny?" he asked with a slight pout.

"I was just thinking about us. And how I didn't really know

you just two months ago, and now I can't picture life without you. It's truly a Christmas miracle." Considering how unlikely it was that we were pushed together by the universe to save Riverwood, it really was a miracle that I would be in Peter's car, kissing him, with a balloon bouquet in the trunk.

He took his cap off and tossed it in the back. Leaning toward me, he unzipped the top of my coat and caressed his lips along my neck. Tiny jolts of electricity rippled down my chest as his right hand continued to work on the rest of the zipper.

"I like you a lot, Chloe Kwon," he whispered. I pulled off my coat while he removed his.

"As much as you like spicy pork?"

He used the motorized lever to push back his seat and recline. "Way more than I love spicy pork."

I scrambled over the center console, my lips descending to meet his. "Now *that* is the true miracle."

EPILOGUE

Hannah tied her hoodie around her waist, revealing her new Georgetown Law T-shirt as she chatted with the moms on the recently built indoor playground. It was her top law school choice and she'd gotten in, so she basically wore that shirt nearly every day, including bedtime, ever since it arrived in the mail. I bought her an identical one for her birthday, which would be delivered later in the week. At least then she'd have two in rotation.

I also bought one for Umma, Appa, and me. Because we were so proud of her.

Hannah surprised us all by deferring a year. She wanted to make sure the mall initiatives were rolled out correctly. It wasn't a trust issue; I think she felt so guilty about that city council appeal meeting that she would do all this for a whole year to make up for it. It was better for me anyway, with her handling more than her original share of tasks, and dealing with the landlord, which she did masterfully. The first annual food fair had just ended and was the hardest to implement, but she did it all on her own. It not only made a profit for all the vendors, but it got lots of foot traffic and local press coverage too. Peter and I led the local office food delivery initiative, which also turned a profit after four months. It took a while for businesses to know about us, and for us to recruit drivers primarily from the local high school, community colleges, and universities, but thanks to aggressive flyering and postcard outreach, we received a steady stream of business and our third-party partner delivery service was happy. They even developed an app for it.

But the "Riverwood Rascals" program was our winner. Thanks to the new parent community getting the word out, the mall not only repopulated with new clientele, but new stores opened and flourished, catering to families. The Silver Sneakers offered babysitting services too, so the parents could hang out in the mall, giving newborn dads and moms chances to take nap breaks in their minivans. For strength training, some grannies wore the babies in carriers around Riverwood. Babies loved that. And come lunchtime, the famished parents took the food court by storm.

Hannah and I left the indoor playground and walked back to the restaurant together. "Did you see that Mom and Dad had your Georgetown acceptance letter framed? It's hanging by their business license and maximum occupancy sign."

She elbowed me. "Whatever. It's still hung below your National Art Council award."

It was so mind-blowing to think that six months ago I had thought I'd given up on my dream. I couldn't have been more wrong. That night, after Peter snuck me home past dinnertime, the official email arrived. "*CONGRATULATIONS CHLOE, NATIONAL ART COUNCIL PRIZE RECIPIENT!*" Lorraine had accepted the award on my behalf.

While my parents hung the actual plaque on their restaurant wall, I printed out this email and taped it up next to my desk in my bedroom, as a reminder of how far I'd come, and how much farther I would go to use my voice to share my stories, help the underrepresented, the vulnerable, and to help stamp out racism. Following my dreams would be my act of resistance. I was determined to make them a reality.

Lorraine messaged me, snapping me out of my zoning-out session. **5 p.m.! Don't forget!**

How could I forget? We'd been planning this for months. I arrived at five o'clock on the dot and there she was, looking as stylish as ever in a floral dress and Burberry beige trench.

Lorraine greeted me on the marble steps with a warm hug. "I'm excited. You ready?"

Peter sprinted up the stairs two at a time, not even huffing one bit because he was in such good shape. Ugh, why was he so genetically blessed?

"Hey!" He pecked me on the lips and greeted Lorraine with a quick hug. "Sorry I'm late. You wouldn't believe the—I hope you're not mad at me?"

I laughed. "You're fine. Right on time, in fact." I reached out my hand and grabbed his. Together, with Lorraine, we flashed our VIP badges and entered the Frist Art Museum.

The docent greeted us and gave us an exclusive tour. "As a non-collecting museum, the Frist does not have a permanent collection. Instead, is renowned center for the arts focusing on creating unique exhibitions as well as securing traveling ones from around the country and the world." Lorraine's wooden heels clicked and echoed on the granite floors. We entered the latest temporary exhibit. "Are you three familiar with the National Art Council?"

I couldn't help but grin. As we proceeded toward the junior photography exhibit, she added, "We're lucky to get this one here. It was just in Atlanta a week ago and it's moving up the coast. It'll be leaving us in two weeks."

Peter elbowed me in the ribs, right in my ticklish spot. "That's your giant face!" he said laughing.

And it was. On the wall was a giant photo of me and my multimedia collection "Voices of Riverwood."

Peter asked, "Can I take a photo of your face in front of your giant one?"

The docent raised both eyebrows. "That's you? I thought you looked familiar!"

Peter took a photo of me first, then one of Lorraine and me. Then Lorraine took one of Peter and me.

"Do you want one of all of you together?" The museum tour guide asked.

"Yes, please!" we all chirped in unison. With Lorraine on one side, and Peter on the other, I took a moment to appreciate these two important, life-changing people.

The docent took a few photos from different angles. "I didn't know which one was best. I'll be honest, it's a little intimidating to be taking a picture of an award-winning photographer."

Peter added, "Especially taking one in front of her giant face photo."

The docent laughed. "Yes, especially because of that."

As I walked through the exhibit and stared at my images in disbelief, Peter wrapped his arms around me from behind, hugging my waist. "You did this. You're pretty amazing, Chloe Kwon."

I snuggled in close. "Thanks. You're pretty amazing too, Peter Li."

ACKNOWLEDGMENTS

I conducted an Instagram poll to ask if people read the acknowledgements section and found out that a lot of readers do (!!!) especially if they enjoyed the book, so I feel lots of pressure now to make this part really good and not too long-winded. Here goes nothing.

I was overjoyed when Sourcebooks asked if I'd be interested in writing a holiday themed romcom. As I brainstormed I thought back to my most fond holiday memories, and I couldn't stop thinking about the one place that was such an important part of my childhood: my neighborhood mall. When I came up with the pitch for this book, I had heard that RiverGate Mall (which apparently has a capital G in the name, which I didn't know until today years old), the place that was practically my second home, was up for sale. I didn't think it would survive through during the pandemic, but RiverGate Mall was bought by a regional property developer and still exists, though it's barely hanging in there. Like many malls of its kind, the anchor stores have left and it's in danger of becoming extinct.

As I do with all my books, I jumped helmet first into a research deep dive, trying to understand why some malls succeed while others fail. I studied the rise and decline of dozens of famous malls and included some of the more interesting commercial real estate business strategies and pitfalls in this book. This story is an homage to suburban mall culture, hopefully one that any boomer, Gen X, Millennial, or Gen Z person will recognize and appreciate. And in case you were wondering, that Bear Animatron mishap actually happened at RiverGate, and my brother was there to witness it all go down.

I started this book shortly after the AAPI shootings in Atlanta. As I write these acknowledgments almost a year later, it feels like the racism and violence against the Asian community is getting worse. While this a comedic story, I've included scenes of racism and harassment, hoping to address and shed light on a very real problem for my community in a way I hope can make a difference.

Thank you to my editors Eliza Swift and Wendy McClure, who understood what I was trying to do with this mall business rivalry idea. Your input helped shape it into a much more streamlined, cohesive story. It's so much better because of you!

The Sourcebooks Fire marketing, sales, and editorial teams have always been so responsive and helpful. Thank you Madison, Ashlyn, Cana, Cassie, and the rest of the SBF fam for your magical book wizardry! And thanks so much to Jin Kim and Liz Dresner for the lovely, festive cover.

To Brent Taylor, who always shows so much enthusiasm for my wacky ideas, thank you so much for helping me get this project off the ground. And thank you again for your sensitivity read!

Kathleen Carter, you are a master at what you do, and I appreciate you so much for making the last two years so much better.

Helen Hoang: I did the math. We've known each other for six years! How many messages and DMs is that??? I love that we became fast friends and have stuck with each other through so much. I heart you. Roselle Lim, thank you so much for the daily food digests, pep talks, and real talks. I'm still so honored to be your friend and accountability buddy.

Each of my books showcase Asian American protagonists with families from different walks of life, and I do this to showcase the breadth of the diaspora and to show the multidimensionality of he Asian experience.. To my writing group (Ken Choy, Michael Hornbuckle, and Katrina Lee), thank you for your encouragement and helpful advice with the Chinese family and food scenes!

To my pandemic DM and texting friends Alexa, Kellye, Liz,

Dante, Jeff, Stephan, Alison, Kathleen, Chelsea, and Kristin: Thank you for keeping my head on straight when I have my "wtf" and "halp" moments. There are many. Huge thanks to Whitney Schneider for sticking by me for so many years. I appreciate you so much. To my OG Pitch Wars buddies Annette, Judy and Jenny, thank you for being there for me, always. I know you're just a DM away.

OG cheerleader pals April, Katrina, Tracy, Lee Ann, Julie K, Mahshid, Corinne, Sherry, Simu, Claire, and Kristina: Thanks for being there for me all these years. You are true friends.

To the OC Brunch bookstagrammers, thank you for letting me crash your events and being so supportive with every new book release. To the bookstagram, librarian, and bookseller community, I am so grateful for the energy and love you bring to shouting about new books from diverse creators. You are wonderful and amazing. Nurse Bookie, I am so grateful for your friendship. Let's go to Din Tai Fung to celebrate this release!

To Mark Downton Esquire, thank you for all of your Tennessee commercial lease advice. You're a great legal mind and a true friend.

To my family, thank you for putting up with me, especially around deadline season. Hopefully I don't annoy you TOO much? Wait, maybe you shouldn't answer that.

Some bibliophiles have read and enjoyed one of my novels and then picked up other books from my backlist—this means so much to me. I am honored to be a repeat author who you trust with your valuable time.

And last but not least, thank you, dear reader, for getting to the last physical page and/or 100% on the progress bar of your ebook or audiobook. You get a five star reader rating from me! Thank you from the bottom of my heart for taking the time to read *The Christmas Clash*, I hope it brought you the same amount of joy I got from writing it.

ABOUT THE AUTHOR

Suzanne Park is a Korean American author who was born and raised in Tennessee. In her former life as a stand-up comedian, she appeared on BET's Coming to the Stage, was the winner of the Sierra Mist Comedy Competition in Seattle, and was a semifinalist in NBC's Stand Up for Diversity showcase in San Francisco. Suzanne graduated from Columbia University and received an MBA from UCLA. She currently resides in Los Angeles with her husband, offspring, and a sneaky rat that creeps around on her back patio. In her spare time, she procrastinates. She is also the author of the young adult novels The Perfect Escape and Sunny Song Will Never Be Famous.

FIREreads

⑤ #getbooklit

Your hub for the hottest young adult books!

Visit us online and sign up for our
newsletter at FIREreads.com

 @sourcebooksfire

 sourcebooksfire

t firereads.tumblr.com